GREATER GAINS

GREATER GAINS

K M Peyton

David Fickling Books

OXFORD ✶ NEW YORK

GREATER GAINS
A DAVID FICKLING BOOK : 0 385 60811 X

Published in Great Britain by David Fickling Books,
an imprint of Random House Children's Books

This edition published 2005

1 3 5 7 9 10 8 6 4 2

Text copyright © 2005 by K M Peyton
Illustrations copyright © 2005 by Jeff Fisher

Set in New Baskerville

DAVID FICKLING BOOKS
31 Beaumont Street, Oxford, OX1 2NP, UK
a division of RANDOM HOUSE CHILDREN'S BOOKS

RANDOM HOUSE AUSTRALIA (PTY) LTD
20 Alfred Street, Milsons Point, Sydney,
New South Wales 2061, Australia

RANDOM HOUSE NEW ZEALAND LTD
18 Poland Road, Glenfield, Auckland 10, New Zealand

RANDOM HOUSE (PTY) LTD
Endulini, 5A Jubilee Road, Parktown 2193, South Africa

THE RANDOM HOUSE GROUP Limited Reg. No. 954009
www.**kids**at**random**house.co.uk

A CIP catalogue record for this book is available from the British Library.

Printed and bound in Great Britain by
Clays Ltd, St Ives plc

To Joan

PART ONE

1

My name is Ellen Garland. I am the youngest of four. The eldest, Margaret, died of the wasting disease when she was sixteen. My brother Jack, a year younger, had to flee from home to escape hanging after he fired Mr Grover's hayricks, and my other sister Clara, now fifteen, is pregnant and still at home at Small Gains. I don't know who by, but I can guess. To give the baby a decent name she married the vicar's son, Nicholas Bywater, just before he too died of the wasting disease. To give Clara her due, she loved Nicholas dearly, as did we all. But the baby isn't Nicholas's.

You can see this is a strange kettle of fish for a very ordinary farming family to be in, and our father is very depressed. He misses Jack terribly. Jack and his friend Martin were so strong and did all the hard work on the farm, and now there is only my father's rheumaticky self and old Soldier Bob, our lodger, and even older Sim, taken in for pity. Good hired men are hard to come by, and round here they are mostly collared by Grover's farm across the way. Grover is so powerful: it does not do to cross him in this village. If he says come, you come. Go, and you go. Jack and Martin can never come back while he is here. We hate him like poison, along with his arrogant son, Nat. Unfortunately hating Nat is hard, for he is incredibly handsome and desirable and under our noses most of the time, the Grover farm drive coming out on to the road opposite our own. I think, in spite of how beastly he is, Clara is susceptible to him. Certainly she is in love with his horse, Crocus, for horses is all Clara thinks about. She has her own, Rattler, and I doubt she'll love the baby when it comes better than she loves Rattler.

I skived off school today to go bird-nesting with Barney and when I got home, my stepmother Anne was angry with me.

I said, 'At school I'm just an unpaid teacher! I don't learn any more, I only have to teach the little ones.'

Anne shook her head. 'I don't think you're cut out to be a teacher. You've no patience.' She had been a teacher at the village school before she married our father. Our own mother had died several years before. I don't remember her.

'It's time you buckled down to something or you'll get into trouble. That Barney is no good, and you know it. He can't even keep a job on a farm, he's so unreliable. What sort of a friend is that for you?'

'He's fun.'

'Ellen, my dear, you're not a child any longer. If you don't want to be a teacher you'll have to go into service, or get yourself apprenticed to a seamstress in town, or work for your father on a regular basis. You can't go on playing.'

'I don't want to work on the farm!'

'You don't want to go into service either,' Clara said. 'So what else is there?'

My sister Clara has a work ethic: she never stops. She works on the farm as horsemaster, a job always done by a man anywhere else, and her great passion is breeding the Norfolk trotting horses that are so famous around our parts. Both Father and Jack are into this game and, given you are successful, it is a lucrative trade. Good horses are matched against each other in long-distance races, and a lot of money can be made through prizes and betting. I suppose it is the only way our family will ever get rich.

Being pregnant hasn't stopped Clara working. In fact she is one of those suited by pregnancy, having grown markedly prettier and more blooming than before. The baby doesn't make much of a bump and she makes light of the condition, riding out on her star Rattler still, to keep him fit for competition. She always has straw on her skirts and mud on her boots, a brave, tough, impetuous girl with whom I have little in common. I am wild and silly they say, and Clara is wild too but very clever, not silly. Not clever enough to avoid getting pregnant though. I think it was Martin who made her pregnant, her old childhood friend now banished along with Jack, but there is some secrecy about this pregnancy that I don't understand. I know it isn't her so-called husband Nicholas for he never had the strength to make it as a father, so close to dying all the last year. But for some reason she doesn't admit to the father being Martin. She makes no bones about saying she doesn't want the baby but Anne and Father seem to have taken to the idea. I daresay when it's born Anne will look after it and Clara will be back in the stables all day or else out riding. Myself, I hate babies. Maybe I should leave home!

'Mrs Grover'll give you a job,' Clara said, grinning.

The Grovers can never keep indoor staff, what with old Eb Grover's violent temper, Mrs Grover's whining and Nat's arrogance. And the pittance they paid.

'Thank *you*! I'd rather muck out Rattler.'

'Well, that's a good idea.'

'Only joking.'

'Yes, well, it's no joke, Ellen. You decide on something soon, or I'll find a job in service for you and you'll go, no argument.' Anne rarely got heavy, and I realized my good times were coming to an end. Work! Going into service, you were lucky if you got to bed before eleven, and up again at five. Seamstresses went blind and teachers got crabby. A nice rich farmer . . . but it was a bit early for that. I needed another year or two. I didn't want to get married. I wanted a bit of excitement first.

Well, I got it. A lot more than I bargained for. A terrible lot more.

Barney hung around the Queen's Head, our village inn, hoping to pick up tips for holding horses or running errands, and it was he who told me the chambermaid had just been sacked. Why didn't I apply?

'You'll meet nice rich travellers. They'll tip you well, you're so pretty.' He laughed.

'If that's what rules tipping, I wonder you get any!'

'Mrs Binder's bound to take you on, if you ask. She gets on well with your stepmother.'

But Anne was doubtful. 'That's a rough place to work. A gentleman's house would be far more suitable.'

'But I can live at home. I needn't go away.'

'I thought you *wanted* to leave!'

'Pooh! Emptying chamber-pots and changing smelly sheets – you must be mad,' Clara said.

'That's what you do around the horses all day – what's the difference?'

'They smell nicer than humans.'

'*Please*, Mother!'

'I'll speak to Mrs Binder. Maybe until something more suitable turns up . . . or you see the sense of going on with your teaching. You've made a good start there—'

'I don't want to be a teacher!'

I was excited by the thought of working in the Queen's Head. The people who stayed the night were often gentry passing through, or gay young blades making a long journey on their own horses. It was fairly rough in the taproom but smart enough in the dining room where the travellers usually rested over their meals. Mrs Binder was a good cook and the inn had a fair enough name. And the lure of journeying: to travel away, to see other places, London, even! The road through the village led to the London turnpike and the stage coach came through once a day, always a bit of excitement, being in such a hurry, horn blaring, everyone jumping out of the way. I longed to go to London. No one in our family had ever been. Yet it was only a day's ride away, seventy miles. Rattler could do it, no trouble. Clara showed no interest, never had, but I often dreamed of making the journey. If only we had relations there! Charlotte, the squire's daughter, went every autumn to her aunt, to go to balls and appear in society but she hated it. Amazing!

'You are so restless!' Anne said. 'Perhaps some hard work will settle you.'

I got a harsh lecture before I started. Anne said being so attractive could be my downfall and on no account was I to flirt with the customers. But this thought pleased me a good deal. She took me herself to see Mrs Binder. Mrs Binder said she would prefer an older, settled woman but she and Anne were quite friendly and I think Anne persuaded her that I would suit – probably against her better judgement. Hence the lecture. I wasn't to let her down.

I don't know why I ever got excited about the job for, after a few days, I knew I couldn't stand it for very long. I had to clean all the rooms and change the sheets if anyone stayed, and empty slops and make fires and wash dishes and go on errands, clean the brass and silver, mend the linen, clean the windows and, if a lot of travellers came in, wait on them in the dining room. I quite liked that bit, especially if a private carriage came and the people were gentry, dressed in high fashion, or if a dashing curricle pulled in with a couple of young blades wanting to warm themselves and drink brandy by the fire. I was allowed to take their driving capes and put them to dry in the kitchen, but Mrs Binder was wary of my getting close. She served the brandy herself. But it was a link with a wider world than I knew of, and it fuelled my desire to get away from Gridstone. Yarmouth would do, where the ships came in, or even Lowestoft where the fishermen were. But Norwich . . . London! How I dreamed! Quite often, Norwich people stayed, ones with their own horses, and when they were dining downstairs and I lit the fire in their room, I looked over the luggage and stroked the pretty dresses and tried on a hat or two. There was a bit of smoky old mirror on the wall in the best room, and once I put up my hair and put on a hat made of feathers, with one long plume hanging down the side, and I looked so lovely, as good as Miss Charlotte any day. Anne was right, that I was pretty. I hadn't noticed much before, not being of an age to bother. But now I could see that I could pass for a lady any day if I just had the clothes. I know from hearsay that my own mother, who died when I was young, was very beautiful. The women in the village still spoke of her beauty, and Margaret, my sister who died at sixteen, had certainly been very beautiful. Clara wasn't bad, but not a patch on me and Margaret. I was wasted in Gridstone, with only village oafs to court me.

Maybe I was a bit too outspoken at home, for Anne upbraided me and told me not to fill my head with silly ideas.

She said, 'You are too intelligent to be wasting yourself the way you are. If you stayed with your books you could become a governess, and then you could mix with the gentry you are so fond of.'

It was all Anne spoke of, using our brains, I suppose because she had been a teacher herself. Now she had become the heavy mother, I didn't dote on her as I once had when she was my teacher. She didn't understand how I felt! Clara did but wasn't very optimistic.

'You are just like Margaret, dreaming, wanting all the time. Nobody gets what they want round here, you've only to look. Father grieving for Jack, Jack losing his future here, Nat having to jump to his father's tune, me in my trouble. If I didn't have my horses . . .'

'You must be happy with the baby!'

'Not with whose it is!'

We were in the kitchen at home, just the two of us, which was rare. Anne had gone to see some sick person and the men were all at work. I had come home to fetch a special recipe from Anne that Mrs Binder wanted in a hurry (I couldn't find it but I hadn't looked very hard) and I found Clara cleaning tack at the kitchen table. She was buffing up the brasswork, no easy task. She looked tired and dispirited for once, and her sudden shout of despair shocked me. No sooner had she spoken than she pushed her work away from her and burst into tears. It was more a wail of anguish than an ordinary sob. I was amazed. Clara never cried!

'Whose? Tell me! Not Martin's?'

I had always assumed Martin, because he was banished for ever along with Jack and he had always been her childhood sweetheart, the one she was going to marry.

'How ever many men have you lain with, Clara? I thought you were such a goody-goody! Whose else can it be?'

She just sobbed harder. There was grief there I knew nothing about, had never suspected. Clara did not show her emotions easily. But now, with no one around except her silly little sister, she was opening up her proud heart for – I suspected – the first time ever.

'If it were Prosper's, I would be the happiest person in the world,' she sobbed. 'I love him so. Oh, how I love him! And he's gone away for ever and I'll never see him again. And this beastly baby – if only it was his, I would still have him, wouldn't I? Prosper's baby—'

She was so bad, I actually got up and put my arms round her. We weren't very huggy people in our family. She was hard and muscular and smelled of horses.

'Prosper? You mean Prosper Mayes?'

This was news to me, that she was in love with Prosper Mayes. I know he had brought her his mare to look after while he went to India, but I thought he was just a young man she had met when she had travelled her stallion Rattler in the spring. Prosper lived – or had lived, before he went to India – some twenty miles away. He was the youngest son, of seven, of a very well-off and successful farmer, and I understood that

Clara had stayed at the farm for a week or so. So there was more to her journeying than selling Rattler's services!

'Yes, Prosper. Darling Prosper!' she whispered.

Her outburst was now under control. She sat with her arms on the table and her head buried in them from my gaze, her shoulders shaking with now silent sobs.

As far as I knew, people who went to India usually died, or got so rich they never came back. Prosper was only a boy, perhaps seventeen, no more.

'Does Prosper love you back?'

'Oh, yes! Yes!'

Funny he went off to India then, I thought. But didn't say. Maybe he had to, no choice. Seven at home – some of them had to go, it was obvious. I seem to remember seeing him at one of the matches on his white mare, Cobweb – the same one now out in our fields – and I remember that he was gorgeously handsome. Anyone would fall for him.

'Oh, Clara, if he loves you he'll come back and marry you when he's made his fortune.'

I gave her another hug. She was quite human after all.

'No, he'll forget me. It's too long. And me with this child, all tangled up, and no Jack here any more to ride Rattler.'

In Rattler's last match, with Jack on the run, she had ridden Rattler herself, astounding the neighbourhood. And won, beating Nat Grover. That had been a day to remember and no mistake.

Now that she was in this rare, confiding state, I

remembered how the conversation had started and my curiosity over the baby's father. Why had she said, 'Not with whose it is'? Martin, of all people, had always been her sweetheart. To be carrying his baby seemed quite normal, the way things went in our village. But if she now loved Prosper . . .

She then said, 'You might as well know the story, as our mother and father know. Nat Grover blackmailed me into lying with him. He knew where Jack and Martin were making for, and he said if I lay with him, just the once, he wouldn't tell his father where they were. His father would have got them met and hanged if I hadn't lain with Nat. He kept his promise. I lay with him and he has never told his father where they are. But I lay with Martin too, before he went, so now I don't know whose the baby will be. I just dread that it will be Nat's.'

No wonder she cried! What a predicament for strait-laced Clara who, I'm sure, had never lain with anyone before the fateful affair of the rick-burning. She had lain with Nat to save Jack's life. I was awed. (Or was it so dreadful? another, naughty, part of me wondered.)

'What was he like? Nat?'

She didn't answer, but a strange expression passed over her face. It certainly wasn't of dread, the last word she had uttered. But she didn't answer my question.

'Now you know the story. The baby will be the spitting image of Nat and everyone will know. They will despise me and hate me, as I despise and hate myself.'

'Jack wouldn't despise and hate you! Besides it might be a little Martin. With red hair!'

'And no brains.'

'Oh, Clara, it won't be so terrible. The baby will be loved, whatever, and Prosper will come back and marry you!'

'If only!'

But the outburst seemed to have done her good, and she straightened up and wiped her face on her apron.

'I'm sorry. I'm stupid. I will soon forget Prosper, and he me, I daresay.'

I went off with my head reeling, seeing Clara in a new light. At fifteen she seemed to know love. I only wished I could see someone on the horizon who would inspire me to the same passion. I was being wasted in Gridstone, with my attractions closeted in the linen-cupboard with the slop buckets or down in the kitchen clearing ashes or out in the yard fetching coal.

A rough girl called Rebekah worked in the kitchen, cutting vegetables, and we got quite friendly, as we had no one else and were of an age. She was one of the nefarious Ramsey tribe who mostly worked for the Grovers, and were not known for reliability or honesty. (There were exceptions: Martin was a Ramsey and so was wonderful little one-armed Billy who worked for Clara in the stables.) Rebekah would rather have been a chambermaid, as she thought access to the bedrooms and the gentry's belongings – trying on the hats – was a great perk.

'If you snitched summat for yourself, they'd never know. They got so much, these people.'

I laughed, imagining myself going home with a 'snitched' bonnet and showing it to Anne. But seeing the pretty things made me more discontented with my lot. The year was getting on and the work was heavier with mud everywhere and more fires to do, boots to clean – 'chambermaid' covered a wide range of duties under Mrs Binder – and more people coming in out of the cold. Travel in the winter was always cold, especially for the travellers 'outside' and the coachman and guard. Journeys were shorter and more people stayed the night.

A week or so before Christmas a smart young couple came in with their own carriage, journeying across country. A sharp flurry of snow decided them to take a room for the night and I was sent to light the fire for them and put a warm pan of coals down the bed. (This was because they looked rich enough to leave a good tip – Mrs Binder was very sharp. Not everyone got such treatment.) The lady brought in a small trunk and scattered her things about in a very untidy fashion. Rebekah was sent up with a bucket of coals, and we tried on a fur pelisse between us and a lovely jet necklace this careless lady had left on the dresser.

'You could snitch this easy,' Rebekah said.

'She'd see it was gone.'

We put on her hat and admired ourselves in the mirror; then Mrs Binder bellowed for Rebekah and we scurried to our work. But when the couple left the next morning, I found a pair of earrings dropped on the floor half under the bed. If I hadn't been scooping for the chamber-pot I would never have seen them.

They were gold, set with pearls, which dangled from a gold bow where the wires went through the ears. Of course I tried them on against my ears (I had no piercings to put them on properly) and they looked so pretty against my cold pink cheeks I couldn't take my eyes away. The stupid woman, to lose these under the bed! Would she ever know where she had lost them?

I thought about it. If I gave them to Mrs Binder and the woman never came back, Mrs Binder would keep them. Why should Mrs Binder have them rather than myself? It was unlikely the woman would come back, as they were on their way to Cambridge, a fair way. I was so tempted! For the time being I put them in my pocket, to think about during the day. If the woman came back at once, I could produce them. If not, they might be mine. I didn't really know what to do. I showed them to Rebekah and she said, shocked that I should even doubt, 'Keep them! With what you get paid in this dump you got a get a few extras, gal!'

Well, it was true I only got my food and a pittance I gave to Anne. Anne gave me back a few coppers, that's all. Sometimes I got some joint ends to take home and Anne might pay me sixpence. With Rebekah's prompting I convinced myself I deserved the earrings. Honesty was ingrained in me, but longing for more in my life overcame my upbringing. If the woman came back, I could always own up and

16

give them back, say in all truth I found them under the bed. I might get a reward.

But I took them home and hid them in my private drawer, under my prettiest best blouse (once Margaret's). I knew they were safe there – Clara wouldn't dream of prying, just as I would never look in her drawer. We are so honest! And I knew then that I would not admit to taking them, even if the woman came back. Putting the earrings in my drawer instead of keeping them in the pocket of my apron meant I had stolen them. I knew this. But I loved them so much. I used to take them out and look at them often and often. They were so beautiful, so delicate, like nothing else in my life. They told me there was something else out there, something besides fields and mud and kitchens and stinking animals. I so longed to get away, just as Margaret had longed. We were two of a kind, my eldest sister and I, while Jack and Clara were devoted to the farm. The earrings seemed to speak to me when I held them up against my face, the little pearls dancing in the candlelight, telling me of balls and silk dresses and theatres and shops full of beautiful things, porcelain and silver and kid gloves and painted fans. I had read about these things and Miss Charlotte, the squire's daughter, knew all about them. Life was like that up at Friar's Hall, but it was out of our reach at Gridstone. We were supposed to accept our station and curtsey to Miss Charlotte and her sisters when we met them in the village, but I wouldn't. Clara did. Clara said Miss Charlotte was really nice, although her sisters were horrid. Their father came into the Queen's Head sometimes and I must admit he was very civil and not at all stuck-up. Clara said Miss Charlotte had to go to balls in London and Bath and hated them! I found this unbelievable. Holding up my darling earrings, I pictured myself in silks and satin at a ball on the arm of a gorgeous young man in tight breeches and stockings . . . oh, my dreams! I was the same as Clara for her Prosper, the unattainable.

Clara was now too fat to ride. Her baby was due soon after Christmas and she was in deep gloom, longing to be free again. Life was very busy at the Queen's Head at this time, so many people travelling to visit distant families over the festive season, and I was run off my feet. But just the week before Christmas I got a great shock when the couple whose earrings I now owned returned to the inn. They were travelling back to Norwich. The short day decided them to break the journey at the place they remembered – 'So comfortable,' the lady murmured. Not a word about the earrings.

I waited on them in trepidation. I knew I only had to deny all knowledge of the jewellery should she ask, I was in no danger. But I could not help being scared. I waited on at dinner, and heard them talking of Eb Grover.

'We ought to call, we're so close. A matter of courtesy.'

'Can't stand the man!' the husband proclaimed.

'We'll send a boy to see if they can receive us in the morning, say we've a day's journey ahead of us. It's only polite.'

'With luck they'll be away.'

The knowledge that they knew the Grovers made me uneasy. I told Rebekah.

'The sooner I see the back of them the better I'll feel.'

Rebekah said, 'She asked Mrs Binder if she'd found any earrings. I heard her. So she did notice.'

'Mrs Binder didn't ask me!'

'No. She trusts you,' Rebekah said with a snigger.

That made me feel worse than I did already. I had half a mind to go home and fetch the earrings back. But that would have been an admission of dishonesty and would no doubt get me into trouble.

The Grovers sent message that they would receive the couple, so in the morning they made a detour up to the farm and stayed half an hour, not long. I could just see the sycophantic Mrs Grover simpering over such smart visitors. She was always trying to join the gentry where she thought they now belonged, owing to their newfound wealth, but the local gentry wisely shunned them. My poor father was on better terms with the squire and funny old Lord Fairhall than Ebenezer Grover.

I was very relieved to see their carriage pass a short while later, on their last leg to Norwich. A day's journey, they'd said – Clara's Rattler could have done it twice in just a morning! Whatever else we didn't have, we had Rattler and old Tilly, two of the fastest horses in the land.

And I still had my earrings.

2

Clara was alone in the kitchen, putting out the men's dinner. They came to eat around midday, after ditching and carting wood all morning – her father, Soldier Bob and old Sim. Little Billy ate his own bait in the stables with his beloved Good Fortune, the runty horse that was Rattler's first produce. Clara had given him to Billy in disgust. Rattler had now served his first crop of mares and in the spring his produce would be born. Clara longed to see how they all turned out. All her hopes for the future were centred on her horse, for there was nothing else: no Prosper, no Jack, no Martin.

Oh, she was sick of being fat, of not being able to ride, of the wretched winter, of not having Jack in the house. How they missed Jack and Martin! There had always been the boys' laughing and horseplay and high spirits around the place, whatever calamities had befallen them. Even hoity-toity, discontented Ellen had given life to the place, but she was now only home to sleep, and full of grumbles. The house was full of old men. Soldier Bob and Sim were happy enough, having been given a home and job when they were on the scrap-heap, but her father, Sam Garland, had never been the same since Jack left. Jack's going had been a blow too much, after losing his first wife and his darling Margaret. His marriage to Anne had saved him from drinking himself to death, and he loved her dearly and could not have done without her, but the cloud of Jack's banishment hung stubbornly over him. Jack was the farm's future. Jack lived for the land and its wellbeing just like his father. He had begun to take over, easing the burden from his father. Then that stupid escapade, firing Grover's hayricks, and he was a wanted man, marked for hanging. The laughing stopped.

Clara missed Jack as much as her father did. He had been her collaborator with the horses; he had ridden old Tilly and young Rattler in their matches. They had no rider now and that was a looming problem, with Rattler needing to win a few matches soon to advertise his suitability as a stallion.

There was no chance of Jack coming out of hiding, not with old Grover just across the road to see him and make sure the hanging issue had not been forgotten.

What a Christmas! Clara had another month to go with her child but the burden was as much in her mind as in her body. She still had no maternal feelings; she hated the impediment to her work, not being able to ride any more; she hated the little brat for spoiling her life. Anne and her father seemed to be looking forward to it. That it might cheer her father was a consolation, but surely if it was the image of Nat Grover he would not be able to love it. Poor little stupid child. No wonder newborn babies were left to die all over the place, in ditches, on rubbish tips, unseen in woods . . . If only she might have the chance to dispose of hers . . .

Her thoughts were wicked, so low she felt. She crouched by the range, watching the flames. She remembered Prosper's mother saying if only she had never had her first child at sixteen – how she might have had more of a life. She had had twelve children, with seven still living. Clara remembered a successful, very hard-working, calm and patient woman, but not a happy one, she sensed. What was happy, anyway? Happy were her days with Prosper in the spring, riding over the rolling hills, lying by the trout stream talking, laughing and planning. It made her cry now just to think about it, now Prosper was gone. Prosper and Nicholas and Jack and Martin . . . her dearest people, all scattered away. And only Prosper with any future at all.

At that moment Clara could not see any future for herself, but when Anne came in and found her crying she hugged her and kissed her and said, 'Of course you are so low with the baby so heavy inside you! But it will soon be over and spring will come round and you will be with your horses again and we shall have a baby to cheer us. Don't get down, Clara. It's not as bad as you think now.'

And when the men came in Clara realized, noticing the satisfaction of Soldier Bob and Sim, that she did have a loving family, a good roof over her head and enough to eat – why could she not be satisfied with that? Many in the village had far less, in their rags and tatters under their leaking thatch, living on bread and dripping. But if she and Prosper had nothing, and were together, she knew she would be happy.

Anne ladled out soup and dumplings and Clara cut the bread and they all sat down to eat. Sam Garland sat at the head of the table, not saying much as usual. His blond hair was fading now into grey and the stubble on his chin was grey, his face heavily lined. Glancing at him, Clara felt a surge of love for him, remembering her sister, his beloved Margaret, and the faded mind-pictures of her mother, all laughing, laughing. Nobody laughed much now. Maybe that was the only good thing about her baby – babies made you laugh. Perhaps the baby would cheer her father up. What was the good of looking back? One day Prosper would come back to fetch the mare he had left for her to look after, and she would see him again. Think on that.

It was a wretched day outside and they were all glad to see the bright fire and the steaming stewpot. The kitchen was too small but that made it cosier. There was a smell of wet woollen clothes softly steaming and of bread not long from the oven and, even if there was no laughter, there was contentment. Clara sensed it. It soothed her. The low-ceilinged room was warm and with Anne's commitment the dresser was polished, the copper pans shone, the rag rugs were new and bright over scrubbed flags.

They finished eating and Sam lit up his pipe as

usual. Clara fetched another ale for Bob and Sim and collected up the plates. A knock came on the outside door, loud and peremptory.

'Come in!' Anne shouted.

To their astonishment – and horror – the caller was Eb Grover and his son Nat.

Sam pushed back his chair angrily and got to his feet. 'What do you be wanting from us, Mr Grover?'

It was a long time since Eb Grover had been seen by any of them at close quarters and he had not improved with time. A very big man, his habitual expression was one of contempt and ill-humour, his cheeks and nose red and heavily veined, heavy black eyebrows pulled down close over his evil little eyes. Although only in middle age he was stooped, his hands gnarled, gripped over the heavy stick he used for encouraging his workers.

Nat hovered behind him, looking acutely anxious, Clara observed, as if he longed to be out of this confrontation. She exchanged glances with him and could not help the colour flooding into her cheeks at the memory of their coupling and the delight he had coaxed in her body. If only Nat's nature was as lovely as his appearance! For now, in his prime (he was twenty to her fifteen), his gypsy-dark looks conveyed a pride and arrogance that would quite likely mature into his father's over-bearing, vicious mastery over everyone who came his way. Clara had little hope of his improving, having experienced his cruelty. Yet she knew he had a vulnerable, deeply repressed, soft, sad inner core which his vile family had shriven. His mother, with her shrill snobbery and discontent, was as awful in her way as Eb, but weak and without power, and the Grover family, for good reason, was reviled in Gridstone. Then why, exchanging a glance with Nat, did she feel a pull of sympathy, a whisper of longing? For what? She dared not look again.

'I have come about your daughter, Ellen,' Grover barked. 'I have knowledge that she is a common thief.'

This statement made everyone in the room blink in astonishment.

'You're out of your mind!'

'I am reliably informed that she stole a valuable pair of earrings from a friend of mine who lodged for a night in the Queen's Head, where I understand your daughter is a chambermaid.'

'Reliably informed? By whom?'

'That's none of your business.'

'Why so? I would have thought it was very much my business. This person is a paragon of truth and virtue, no doubt?'

'A knowledgeable person, no more. You can prove your daughter's innocence if you wish. I am told she keeps the earrings in a drawer in her bedroom. I would like to look in that drawer.'

Clara said indignantly, 'We share that room. I've never seen earrings there, nor seen her with any jewellery. She would surely have shown me?'

As she spoke, Clara knew this last appeal was false. She knew Ellen longed for pretty things, as Margaret had, and was often dreaming of pretty dresses and jewels and high living. She suspected that heedless

Ellen could well help herself to jewellery carelessly strewn in the guest room of the Queen's Head.

Anne was more trusting. She said coldly, 'You may look, if you wish. You will need proof for your accusation.'

Eb jerked his head at Nat. 'Go and look.'

Sam stood up. 'What a bloody liberty! You come here—'

Anne took his arm. 'Let him go. Clara will go with him.'

Sam shook Anne off but Eb stepped forward, a menacing figure. Clara thought, if he had been a small man he would never have had the opportunity to be so powerful. He was a brute, and small people buckled under. Her bile rose and she had to bite back her fury. She jerked her head at Nat and led him to the staircase door. She went ahead, Nat following.

Out of earshot, Nat said, 'This embarrasses me. I would rather not do it.'

'I wish your father was dead.'

'So do I.'

'You have that much sense? You surprise me.'

Clara was terrified of being alone with Nat. She went across the bleak little room and gestured to Ellen's drawer. If he had to riffle amongst her intimate pieces of underwear, so much the better. The rain beat against the window under the deep thatch and mice rustled under the eaves. Grover's farm had been recently rebuilt and she knew Nat slept in a bedroom with a ceiling adorned by Mr Adam and a fire flickering beneath a marble mantel. No wonder he looked round their pathetic little room in surprise. But he made no comment on it.

He opened Ellen's drawer. 'I hate doing this.'

'You'll hate it worse if you find anything. Your family has done enough damage to ours, I would have thought.'

'And you to ours.'

'You cannot compare it.'

'You bring it on yourselves. Do you think Margaret didn't tempt me?'

'Don't speak of Margaret!'

'No. It's better not, God rest her.'

He rummaged in the drawer, turning over Ellen's pathetic fripperies. He ran his hands round underneath and Clara heard him exclaim: 'What's this?'

He pulled out a small parcel of green silk and shook it out on the chest top. The earrings danced on the polished wood, the gold gleaming in the grey light.

'Oh, my God!' Clara moaned.

Nat cursed. 'Do you think I wanted to find them? I believed Ellen was honest.'

'Who told you she stole them?'

'That slut in the kitchen, Rebekah. And the woman who owns them. She is a friend of our parents. She told us she thought she had lost them, she thought in the Queen's Head, and Father went enquiring.'

'Bullying. He loves to get people into trouble.'

'I don't want to get Ellen into trouble.'

'Put them away then.'

But at that moment there was a crashing on the stair and Eb shouted up, 'We haven't all day! Come on, you imbecile! Have you found them?'

'Yes, Father!'

'Nat!' Clara was shocked to see how Nat jumped to his father's voice. He could have put them back. Surely Eb was not going to come looking?

'You didn't have to say!' she hissed.

Nat gave her an anguished look. 'I'm sorry!'

What a hold the old man had over him, Clara realized. He was weak, like putty, frightened.

They went downstairs and Nat held out the earrings. Clara did not dare look at her father and Anne. They were speechless.

'There. I was right in my thinking. My friend will press charges.'

'Why should she?' Anne recovered her senses quickly. 'Give them back to her, and Ellen will write a letter of apology. She will lose her job. Is that not sufficient? She's just a silly child, and could not resist temptation.'

'She will do it again if she is not taught. I will advise my friend to pursue the matter. I doubt if she will ignore my advice.'

'Having the earrings back will surely please her. Why should she want to be bothered with court business?'

'Because she, like me, would wish the world rid of scum like your daughter.'

'Get out!' Sam shouted. 'Get out of my house!'

Old Sim and Soldier Bob had to hold him back

and it took all their strength. Anne flung open the door. 'Get out!' she reiterated.

Eb laughed, tossing the earrings in his hand. Nat scampered after him, eyes down, shame flaming in his cheeks. Anne slammed the door after them, then ran back to Sam, taking him in her arms.

'Don't take on so! The man is so vile – despise him, don't let him make you ill! A little thing like that will never come to justice. The woman will surely have more sense. It is she who has to press charges, after all, and how many people can be bothered? The squire never even chased up that gypsy who stole his hunter, if you remember. Everyone gets away with it round here, you know they do.'

'Jack didn't.'

'No, well, that was more than a pair of earrings. That was politics. That's different.'

'Eb would have him hanged.'

'Yes, we know that.'

'I'll give our Ellen a beating when she comes home. The stupid little child, to get us wrong with the likes of Eb Grover – I thought she had more sense.'

'It was a terrible thing to do. I'm very surprised.'

But Clara wasn't surprised. She, who was only a glorified stable girl at heart, she too had hankered after pretty things sometimes. When she saw Miss Charlotte in her lovely fur cape and her soft kid boots with buttons up the side, and even the miller's daughter in the fine wool shawl her mother had brought her from Scotland, these things made her envious and she, boring frumpy Clara, was not a fraction as fond of pretty things as her sister was. She had the best horse, hadn't she? What more could one ask?

She did her chores in the house as quickly as possible and escaped to the stables. She could not bear to see her father so helplessly angry, in despair at Eb Grover's hold over him. She dreaded Ellen's coming home later. She would have no idea her theft had been discovered and would come in grumpy, cocky as usual, to a terrible reception. Sam would beat her and Ellen was never one to accept punishment without interminable arguments and justifications of her behaviour. There would be such a shouting and screaming.

Clara shuddered, pulling her jacket over her shoulders as she hurried across the yard. The stables were immediately opposite the back of the house, along with the feed sheds and cow byre. On one side were the open barns for the carts and plough and implements and behind them the big threshing barn, sagging with age. Its roof was forever being patched, but the great crucks of timber which held it up were still sound and glorious in their cathedral-like arches. On the other side of the road, Grover's big newly rebuilt farmhouse fronted a landscaped garden and behind it were new yards: one for the domestic horses, one for the cart-horses, one for the carts and machinery, then the rickyard and the beginnings of the grand new threshing barn that was to replace the one Jack and Martin had fired. It was all as new and spick and span as the Garlands' was patched and old.

But their horses were no better! Nat had one horse, Crocus, who could win matches, but he did not touch Clara's beloved Rattler who she had acquired as a foal in exchange for her mother's gold brooch. Yes, she had been beaten by her father for that deal, just as hard, no doubt, as Ellen was due to be today, but at least he had later grudgingly conceded her good judgement. His own trotting horse, Tilly, who had won so much in the past, was now too old to match, and all their hopes were founded on Rattler.

'Oh Rattler, lift us out of this rut, make Father happy, win us some money!'

She went into his stall and laid her cold cheek against his fine crested neck. She knew why Ellen had stolen the earrings, why Margaret had loved Nat, why Jack had fired Grover's yard – all were kicks against their fate, the desire to make things better for themselves . . . how well she understood! They cursed and hated Grover but they so badly wanted to emulate him in his success. Not by the ruthless way he had won it, but by fair means – to make enough money to buy nice things, and not to be forever slaving just to get by, not to slide back into debt and despair.

Rattler turned his big bony head and gave her a nudge with his lips as if to say, Stop being so stupid. Clara had to laugh then.

'Yes,' she said to him. 'I've got what I want, haven't I? You, you great oaf, my lovely boy, my darling. I haven't a lot to grumble about, eh, Rattler? There must be a lot worse off than me. We'll teach this brat to be a good groom and a good rider. When you're a great stallion and your produce are all winners, he can ride them in their matches and we'll be rich and famous!'

If only! And Clara laughed at herself then and said to her stomach, 'Are you listening, boy? Get a move on. There's work for you to do out here.'

They all called the baby 'he'. Clara knew it was going to be a boy.

She put the horses out, Rattler, Good Fortune and Cobweb – in spite of the mud and the rain. Tilly was too old and preferred her stable, and Hoppy was needed for work. The men scoffed at Clara for putting horses out in the bad weather, but Clara knew the freedom and grass were good for them. They might scoff but they all admitted that Clara was a good horsemaster, the best. 'She should've bin a lad,' as they said, all the time.

'Yes,' she thought, as the baby gave her another kick. 'So I should. And then I wouldn't be so miserable.'

3

'He dusted me that hard I've still got the marks after five days.'

'Show me,' said Barney.

Ellen pushed him in the ditch. 'You cheeky beggar!'

'What you going to do?'

'I'm going to kill Rebekah, for sneaking. That's one. Then I'm going to kill Eb Grover. He's reported me to the magistrate.'

Ellen gave a great whoop of defiance, of joy, to be free, out in the cold winter sunshine and running through the fields with Barney instead of scrubbing the flags in the Queen's Head. There was a lot to be said for getting sacked. Make the most of her freedom! She had left home to go back to school, but truancy was now a part of her nature and, in spite of Anne's pleas on her behalf, she wasn't sure of her welcome there. The whole village (of course) knew of her trouble. None of them held it much against her – more against Grover for reporting the deed to the authorities. But, as Anne pointed out, she now had a stain on her character and it would not easily be forgotten. Not when it came to finding employment.

But Barney was laughing too.

'The magistrate's only the squire and his punishments are nothing, unless you're a poacher. He can't abide poachers.'

'No. Father never touches game on our own land – he says it's the squire's. I say he's potty. The squire don't want all those rabbits, surely?'

'Better safe than sorry, I daresay. Your dad keeps his nose clean. I get rabbits – I'd starve otherwise – but no one's caught me yet.'

Ellen had met Barney on her way to the village, off to try out his new catapult, and they had now messed about for so long in Gridswood, pelting at rooks, that it wasn't worth going to school any more.

'Let's go down to the shop,' Barney said. 'I've got a halfpenny. I'll treat you.'

'Oh, what? Some silk stockings? A fur muff?'

'A liquorice string.'

'How delicious! What a gent you are!'

'I don't know why I bother with you.'

'Give me a go with your catapult.'

'Girls are no good at catapults.'

'Who said so? I'll bet you. Tell me what to hit.'

'Let's go up to the road then, to a stone pile. You can kill things, you know, with a good stone.'

'Maybe Rebekah'll come by!'

'Yeah, if you're lucky.'

They crossed the fields towards the road. It was a cold grey day just after Christmas, which neither of their households had had much cause to celebrate. Clara was in the dumps with her pregnancy and Anne and Sam were more worried about Ellen's mis-demeanour than she was herself. The squire had not moved on the information supplied by Eb Grover and Ellen optimistically believed he wouldn't. He was friendly towards their family and, like everybody else, hated Grover. But a cloud of uncertainty hung over the place and Ellen was glad to get away, playing truant again, hanging out with those friends who had no work or who were waiting to go into service. She knew Anne had sent off several letters to try and get her a place in service, answering all the advertisements she saw in the paper, extolling her virtues.

'All lies,' Ellen said, reading them.

'Not if you decide to do right. You've so much intelligence, Ellen, I can't understand you playing about in this silly way, shirking your responsibilities. You're not a child any more! You owe it to your father – he has suffered so—'

As Anne's voice choked with irritation, Ellen found herself wondering what had happened during the last year that had made her so impatient with her life. She had been happy enough up to now. But this business of no longer being a child, taking on responsibility – what did they want of her? To be a maidservant in a big house . . . was that so worthy, to earn ten pounds a year? Teaching the little children at school drove her mad. The farm bored her to tears. What did she want? Just to go away!

She snatched up a stone, slipped it in the catapult and fired in the direction of a distant sheep without even taking aim. The sheep gave a startled bleat and shot off down the field, sending all the others into a stampede.

Barney stared in admiration.

'Hey, that was good. Was that the one you were aiming at?'

'Of course it was!'

'You must have a natural eye.'

'Even for a girl?'

'Well—' Barney had the grace to blush. 'Maybe it was a fluke. Try it here, across the road. There's no one coming. That elm tree.'

The elm tree stood alone on the far side, some twenty yards off. Ellen thought she would be lucky to hit it, and aimed carefully.

'Yes! Great! You're really good.'

Now she had to prove it. Barney collected her some good stones, and she hit a tin kettle in the ditch, a rook's nest which shed bare twigs across the road and the backboard of a tinker's cart passing. The donkey pulling it broke into a surprised trot and the pedlar nearly fell off his seat. As Ellen and Barney were hidden behind the thick roadside hedge he had no idea what had happened.

'All we want now is Rebekah walking out on an errand,' Ellen said longingly.

'You haven't got Rebekah but – hey, Ellen, look! Mr Grover's coming.'

'Where?'

Ellen thought he was joking. The road was not empty: there was a dung cart passing, old Mrs Harris from the rectory with a basket on her arm and two yokels with pitchforks going towards the village. In the distance a post-chaise was in view. And Eb Grover on a big hunter, just emerging from his drive . . . Barney wasn't joking.

'You could get his horse on its backside as it goes by,' he said. 'Make it bolt.'

Ellen laughed.

'I dare you!' Barney said.

They were hard under a thick hedge of quick-thorn and nobody could see them from the road. Ellen had stood up to take aim. But once ducked down she knew she was well hidden.

'I can't!'

'He'll never know, daftie. Give it a try – get your own back!'

Ellen laughed nervously. She had to make up her mind quickly, for Grover had put his horse into a trot and was coming quickly towards them. A surge of excitement flooded through her at the glorious thought – maybe he would fall off! It was only a little thing after all, to sting his horse on its ample rump. She picked a vicious little flint with sharp edges. She was trembling.

'I don't dare!'

'Don't be chicken! I dare you!'

'Shall I?'

'Of course, idiot. He shopped you, didn't he?'

Ellen peered through the top of the hedge as the big hunter's hooves clacked steadily towards them. Mrs Harris was well out of the way and the two yokels farther ahead, their backs to her. The post-chaise was approaching but was still distant enough. No one would see.

'I will!'

She crouched trembling, with the catapult primed in her hands. She took her aim as the horse approached, and as it went by its big round quarters offered a perfect target. She drew back the stone. Grover was looking straight ahead, a dewdrop hanging off his big grizzled nose. Ellen stood up.

She let fly.

To her amazement the horse trotted on but Grover let out a blood-curdling cry. His great bulk collapsed suddenly and slumped heavily over the horse's withers. The horse, surprised, pulled up and threw back his head to shift the weight but the big man slipped down over the horse's shoulder and fell in a heap at its feet. The horse paused, looking down, then stepped carefully over him, moved to the side of the road and started to graze, reins trailing.

'Oh my God!' Ellen stood rooted, horror-stricken.

Barney was speechless.

The two yokels, having heard the cry, turned back and stared, eyes out on stalks, and at the same time the post-chaise arrived on the scene and pulled up. Two men on board jumped down with exclamations of alarm and ran towards the still pile of Grover's body, and the driver pulled up. He stood up on the driving board, holding his keen horses still, and looked around curiously. He saw Ellen and Barney rooted behind the hedge, but made no sign.

The post-chaise men, standing over Grover, shouted at the two village men.

'Hey, you! Who is this man? D'you know him?'

'It's Mr Grover, sir.'

'Run and fetch some help then – quick sharp! A doctor! His wife! Hurry!'

Between the two of them they turned the body over on to its back. Ellen, still petrified, unmoving, saw a great bloody hole where his eye should be. Blood poured down the side of his head. The sight was so awful she felt her senses leaving her. Spots danced before her eyes.

'*Barney!*'

'Hey up, Ellen, hold on! We ought to get out of here,' he hissed. He clutched her arm and shook her vigorously. 'Get moving!'

Ellen stumbled out of the ditch, shoved by Barney, and heard a shout from the road. Who it was she had no idea. Barney tried to make her run but the field was ploughed and she was so shocked and weak she stumbled and fell. Barney pulled her up.

'Run, Ellen! For God's sake—'

He could have left her but it didn't seem to occur to him. And when a man came running across the plough towards them, far faster than he could make with Ellen, he turned and faced him helplessly.

'Not so fast, you young 'uns! Let's have you!'

It was amazing how already a small crowd was gathering from the village, collecting in a squawking press round Grover's inert form. Dragged back by their iron-fisted captor to join them, Ellen and Barney stood trembling on the edge of the mob. Their names were eagerly given to the post-chaise man who seemed to have taken charge. Ellen was still clutching the catapult but nobody supposed she could be the culprit.

'Cor, good on yer, Barney!' someone shouted.

'Yeah! Yeah!'

'Fetch the doctor, for goodness' sake, you jackasses,' the post-chaise man shouted.

To Ellen the scene was terrible; she could not believe what damage she had caused. It was just a lark with Barney, and now it seemed like death. She sobbed, and Barney put his arm round her and whispered, 'Shut up, Ellen. It's my catapult. You won't get into trouble.' She did not believe him. She shuddered as a bitter wind skirled the dead leaves along the road. Nat was coming towards them on his horse Crocus and the villagers fell silent. From the other direction, poor old Dr Roberts was puffing along as fast as he could. The little crowd parted to let him through. Behind him now the women of the village were turning out, hurrying along towards the scene of all the excitement. Eager whispers hissed amongst the spectators, awed now at the arrival of Nat. He jumped from his horse and bent over the spread-eagled figure of his father.

'Oh my God! What happened?'

Barney and Ellen were hustled forward.

'This lad here, and the girl – a catapult—'

Nat glanced up, recognized Ellen and muttered, 'Oh God, not you, Ellen!'

40

He turned back, white-faced, to his father's body and stood staring. Horror passed on to a strange excitement, a gleam of exultation which nobody noticed, then a stony shut-down of emotion. Dr Roberts dropped with difficulty onto his knees to examine the patient, listening first for a heart-beat, then opening his bag of tricks to find materials to staunch the great flow of blood.

'He lives still. We must get him home.'

'Go for a flat cart,' Nat ordered. 'Hurry, take my horse.'

One of his men swung up onto Crocus and went galloping back to the farm. The crowd started to chatter again, huddled in the cold but warmed by the excitement of seeing their tyrant brought down. The atmosphere was not of sorrow: awe, fascination and grim pleasure were mixed. A burst of laughter, quickly suppressed, made Nat's face flash with anger. He snapped his riding crop sharply into the face of the nearest bystander and shouted, 'Get away, go back to your homes, you apes! Have you no respect?'

'Nor the likes of Grover we haven't,' someone muttered.

Eb's wound was soon obscured by a great mass of bandaging. The flat cart was approaching from the farm and, from the other direction, Sir James the squire was trotting towards them on his horse. For him the crowd drew back with the respect that was wanting for Grover and fell into silence again. The squire pulled up and took in the scene.

'So, how did this come about?'

Barney and Ellen were pushed forward.

'We saw it happen,' the post-chaise man said. 'The children let fly with a catapult and hit the gentleman in the eye.'

'We only meant to hit the horse,' Barney said.

The squire was the local justice and had to decide what action to take. He did not seem to relish the job. He watched as Grover was lifted into the flat cart and enquired of the doctor, 'What is the injury?'

'It's serious, sir. Very serious. He's like to die of it.'

'If he dies it will be a charge of murder,' Nat said.

'Go with your father. I will decide what the charge will be.'

The squire slid down from his horse and came over to Barney and Ellen.

'This is a bad business. It can't be overlooked. And you, Ellen, with the thieving upon you – what are you thinking of, to act so wild? Your parents are so good to you. Barney here, we know he's a bad boy, but why do you go with him?'

'It was his catapult,' Ellen said. She did not want the blame. The squire calling Barney a bad boy encouraged her – that was his reputation. 'We didn't mean it.' Yet was that true? If Grover died, how happy they would all be!

'I think I had better come home with you, Ellen. And you can come along too, Barney. There will be no getting out of this, I'm afraid, for the two of you.'

With the body borne away, the crowd was dispersing back to the village, still muttering with excitement. This was really something to talk about. Sir James spoke with the post-chaise men for some time and took their particulars, and Ellen heard the driver say to him, 'I saw it happen, sir. It was them two all right.'

They walked back to Gridswood behind the squire's horse. Ellen had returned to her senses but could not stop her body shaking with the horror of Eb's face. This was far more than nicking a pair of silly earrings, she could see that, and, if Eb died, it was no less than murder. It was hard to take in, what had been such a lark half an hour ago. Barney trudged silently at her side. He could have cut and run. The squire would never have caught him, the way Barney knew the country, the ditches and drains and deep woods. Barney was half a gypsy with no known parents. He lived in a broken hovel by the mill and worked for a few coppers to live on, or stole – so people said. No one trusted him, yet he had never been caught at any wrong-doing. He was twelve, and should have been holding down a decent job at that age, but he was too wild to settle and had no father to beat him into sub-mission. 'A good beating is what he needs,' the old villagers all said, but he was accepted in the way of village practice, and sometimes given a bit of cake by an old lady, or a pair of worn-out shoes. 'It takes all sorts,' they said philosophically. But he was branded 'the bad boy' in spite of lack of evidence.

Ellen's parents were at the driveway, having heard what had happened from one of their men. They were both pale as ghosts and Anne was crying.

'I think we must talk this over,' the squire said, getting down from his horse.

'Yes, come in, sir. Come along.'

'You too,' Barney was told.

Clara silently took the squire's horse at the kitchen door. She gave Ellen a look of such malevolence that Ellen burst into fresh sobs. Anne put her arm round her and gave her a little hug.

'Come, it must have been an accident.'

They went into the warm homely kitchen and Clara brought ale for the squire. They sat at the table, the squire at the head, and Ellen and Barney had to explain exactly what had happened.

'It was Ellen's stone that hit him, not yours?' Sir James asked Barney.

'Yes, sir. But I can say it was mine if it helps.'

The squire gave a sad smile. 'Maybe. You are very generous. But I think you are both in this together. There is no way we can shelve this one, as I was hoping to do with the theft, Ellen. If Grover dies it will be a murder charge and if he doesn't we can be sure he will press for the most serious punishment. I'm afraid it will have to go to the assizes and we can only pray that your youth and a plea of accident will lessen your sentence. It will depend on the judge, but of course he has rules to abide by.'

No one dared mention what the sentence was likely to be: hanging. The word could not be spoken. Children hanged for less, they all knew.

Ellen was silent now, trembling and stunned. Barney merely looked miserable, as if hanging had been an option for him all his life.

'You will have to come with me, Barney,' the squire

44

said. 'We can't leave you loose, can we, else you will surely disappear?'

'I would stand by Ellen, sir.'

'Well, we'll see.' He was unbelieving. 'Come all the same. As for Ellen, I trust you, Mr Garland, to keep her secure in the house until they come for her. You have a reputation for saving your children from punishment, but this time you will obey me, sir.'

Anne said softly, 'Our troubles all stem from the one family, sir, as you know, and if Eb Grover dies may we all hang for it. The world will be a better place.'

'I have to agree with you. But we cannot take the law into our own hands.'

'I dared her, sir, to hit the horse. We didn't mean—'

'That's enough, Barney. I know the story. Save it for the jury. Come along with me. You've wasted enough of my day.'

The squire departed with Barney tagging at his horse's heels and the Garland family was left sitting round the kitchen table, ghost pale, stricken. Ellen saw a tear trickle down her father's cheek. Her heart seemed to swell inside her as if it would choke her.

'Father!' She put out her hand to him and to her relief he put his own calloused hand over hers and said, 'My poor darling.'

'Poor darling!' Clara snorted. 'She—'

'No, Clara, be quiet.' Anne's voice was sharp. 'This is not a time for recrimination. It was a prank. That's all.'

Clara could not bear to see her father laid low yet

again, broken by his stupid children. She was the only one who had never harmed him, who had made him proud and happy. Margaret had broken his heart, Jack had deserted him and now Ellen . . . what had he done to deserve such blows? She went and put her arms round him and laid her cheek against his, willing him to bear up. She thought he could so easily go under in his grief, turn back to drinking, to oblivion, as he had before. She felt his tears on her face and hugged him fiercely.

'Oh, Clara,' he whispered.

Clara wanted to kill Ellen. She hated her, for bringing them all down.

'What did he mean, "until they come for me"?' she was asking.

'To take you to the lock-up,' Clara snapped.

At this Ellen burst into loud sobs, laying her head on the table, her whole body heaving. Anne got up and went to her, shaking her head at Clara.

Sam groaned, gave Clara a quick grasp with his hand and then stood up, finding strength.

'We've all played pranks in our time. Luck wasn't with you, that's all. And the whole village will love you for what you've done, if that's any comfort.'

Clara fought down her anger and went along with trying to make Ellen calm down. Strangely – they thought – old Dr Roberts called shortly afterwards and brought a dose of something for Ellen.

'Put the lass to sleep, it's best,' he said.

'How's Grover?' Sam growled.

'I think he'll die. An extraordinary injury, so deep

into the only vulnerable part of him. Extraordinary. I shall call again this afternoon. I will let you know what happens immediately.'

He looked Clara up and down.

'And you – maybe the excitement will bring your babe on. Call me, unless you prefer Mrs Hampton to attend you.'

'I would prefer you, please.'

'It will be a solace for you all, a babe. Take heart.'

Such a growly old man, he had never shown such sympathy before. They were grateful for his words, and found very quickly that the whole village was ready to show the same sympathy, in spite of a crime being committed. The old farmers came to call and brought bottles of brandy, the mothers of the children whom Anne had once taught, the miller, even Lord Fairhall of few words – a gruff consolation and another bottle of brandy. The house became like a fair, the brandy was passed round and the evening even found laughter and a joke or two.

'Best thing that ever happened,' was the general feeling. 'Great little lass.'

They none of them mentioned the likely outcome.

Clara, confused and shaken, went upstairs to her bedroom and looked at Ellen, unconscious under the old blankets. At thirteen, she looked ten in her innocence, breathing softly, even smiling in her sleep. She was pretty and going to be beautiful, just like Margaret. Not like me, Clara thought, good and hard-working and ugly and useful. But like Margaret, heedless and brainless and beautiful. A criminal. It was hard to take in. If Grover died . . . she did not dare think about Nat. He had wanted his father to die, he had said so in this very room a short while ago. Was he going to grow into another Eb if he became the boss, or would he mellow with being his own master?

Maybe Eb would live. He was as strong as an ox and pigheaded enough to spite them all.

'I don't know how such a child's toy could do such damage,' Anne said.

'Barney's good at catapults,' Clara said. 'He hangs around the knacker's and begs paddiwhack and tendons and things to experiment with.'

'What on earth's paddiwhack?'

'It's the gristle along a bullock's spine. It's got a stretch in it. Barney lives on rabbits and that's what he gets them with, his catapult.'

'It's tragic it was Ellen who shot it. If it had been Barney—'

Clara didn't say anything but remembered Barney saying he would claim he shot it 'if it helped'. That was akin to saying he would give his life for Ellen's. That hardly put him in the category of 'bad boy'. Hero, more like. Poor Barney. Perhaps he was so stupid he didn't know how the words would incriminate him.

But in the meantime the whole village waited with bated breath to hear if Eb Grover died. They all wished it. They prayed. There was no other topic of conversation.

4

Dr Roberts called the next morning as promised. It was raining hard and he huddled under the leaky roof of his gig as his cob splattered and floundered through the potholes.

'Your drive needs attention, Garland, if I'm called out for Clara's babe in the middle of the night.'

'Aye, Sim's bringing a cartload of stones to it today. But it's heavy work for an old man.'

'You want your Jack back. Maybe you'll get your chance now. Old Grover's gone, passed away early this morning.'

'Come in, man. We'll drink to it.'

Sam had recovered himself enough to realize it meant little difference to Ellen's fate if the man lived or died. For if he lived, he would get her hanged just as well for the loss of his eye. But without him in court to goad judge and jury, mercy might be shown to a girl so young.

They drank, but soberly, in the kitchen with the women standing silently by. Ellen sat shivering by the fire, wrapped in Margaret's old pretty shawl. Clara now felt desperately sorry for her, her anger run out. She knew there was no kicking against fate, only stoic endurance was required. Their family were well practised. Her father was calm now.

'The farm will pass to Nat. That will be a heavy responsibility on young shoulders.'

'Maybe Philip will turn up, if he hears the news.'

'How can he hear the news, if no one knows where to send it?'

Philip was Grover's eldest son, who had had the wit to leave home at the age of fifteen after a beating that nearly killed him. The farm now by law belonged to him. It was said that he had since become the commander of a ship in the navy but he never communicated with his family.

'I doubt he'll ever come back. His mother doted on him, but I doubt if it was reciprocal. He was five years old when Nat was born. She bore two still-born daughters between.'

'All she ever does is complain and nag,' Clara said. 'She's a dreadful woman.'

'Poor soul, she's not had an easily life, married to Eb,' Anne pointed out.

'At least they won't all have to live in terror any more. Eb beat them all, even the wife.'

'It's not often someone dies and no one can say one good thing about them,' Sam said.

Clara said softly, 'Ellen did the world a good turn.'

'Aye. All but us, my little lass.'

The events were hard to live with. Ellen, they knew, was to be taken away but when and by whom nobody seemed to know. It was said that Barney was locked in the squire's own cellar, awaiting his fate. Eb's funeral plans were put in hand, and it was said that the bishop was coming for the funeral and that Edmund from the Hall had pleaded a prior engagement when asked to play the organ.

'Yes, a prior engagement made on the spur of the moment,' everyone agreed. 'Good old Edmund.'

The Garland family kept out of the village, staying at home, receiving only friends as visitors, and none of them saw Nat before the funeral. They were in as much a state of mourning as the family at Grover's, but for Ellen, not Eb. Two days before the funeral a plain and not very smart closed carriage came lurching down the drive, pulled by an ill-bred horse. Clara, glancing out of the window, felt as if a cold cloud suddenly enveloped her, believing it was the moment they had all been dreading.

'Mother, look,' she whispered to Anne.

The horse pulled up outside the rarely-used front door and two men in black uniforms climbed out.

'Go to Ellen,' Anne said. 'I will receive them.'

Ellen was sewing a gaudy little shirt for Clara's baby, cut down from an old dress.

'Why are you so sure it's a boy?' she said to Clara. 'I think it will be a girl. I like the name Susannah. Will you call it Susannah if it's a girl? Or Caroline. That's nice.'

'I think you have to put your sewing away, Ellen. Some men have come.' It was hard to keep her voice steady.

Ellen looked up, alarm springing into her face. 'No! Oh no, Clara! No!'

If Clara thought she had had some bad times in her life, nothing compared to Ellen's departure. Ellen fought and screamed. Anne wept. Sam came running, shouting. The farm workers came to gawp. Clara crammed Ellen's few sad effects into a potato sack and fetched her old worn coat and tried to make her put it on, but she only flailed her arms and cracked Clara across the face. The two black-garbed men stood by, stony-faced.

'Ellen! Ellen! Calm youself! It doesn't help—' Anne wept. 'Please! For our sakes, don't make it so hard.'

'We haven't all day,' one of the men said.

'Where are you taking her?' Sam asked.

'To Norwich.'

'No! No!' Ellen screamed.

The men stepped forward. One of them held out a pair of handcuffs.

'Do we have to use these then?'

Ellen straightened herself up suddenly and spat straight into the man's face. The man jerked back, then brought his hand up and clouted her so violently across the head that she would have fallen if Anne hadn't caught her. In the moment she fell limp the other man stepped quickly forward and fastened the handcuffs on her wrists.

'It won't pay you, madam, to behave like this.'

Ellen moaned and the two men caught her one on each side and dragged her towards the door. Sam tried to stop them but they thrust him aside.

'Don't hurt her!'

'It's up to her, mate – if she don't fight, nor will we.'

Ellen moaned and wept and was bundled without ceremony into the carriage where she fell on the floor. The men climbed in over her and slammed the door. The driver turned the horse round, whipped it up and the carriage went lurching away.

'They'll knock her senseless as soon as they're out of our sight,' Sam said.

He seemed to accept the men's behaviour, saying, 'The silly little girl, to make it so hard! Let's pray she will learn sense. Oh my God, to think we have to bear all this!'

And then he sat at the table, laying his head in his arms, and wept.

Clara wondered afterwards if such a violent departure was in fact better than an affecting, embracing farewell would have been. To see the carriage disappear out of sight towards the village carrying its wild burden was a great relief, the way she felt. No more pussy-footing around spoilt Ellen; to have the house rid of her was almost a burden lifted. She was dismayed at her feelings and did not show them. All their feelings were so flayed that it was impossible to speak of them. Maybe the others were glad to see the back of Ellen too, Clara thought. The uncertain waiting time had been so fraught. Now the house was silent. A soft rain ran down the windows as if weeping for their thoughts and the fields stood brown and bare in the gathering gloom, the cold pheasants calling from the wood. The authority's coach would have its lamps lit, swaying along the road towards the bright city, the city Ellen had always longed to go to. Her wish was answered, but there would be no bright lights for Ellen.

With spirits so low, Clara took a lantern and went out to the stables. Sim fed the horses now and they were all contentedly snuffling around the remains in their mangers and snatching at hay. As usual, Clara went to Rattler's stall and wept for a little into his mane, then she laid her head on his broad back and told herself not to be so pathetic.

She was just turning sixteen, not sixty.

Eb Grover was dead, which would lift a huge pall from everyone in the village and hugely from her own family.

She was due to drop this baby at last and would be riding again in another month, planning a match for Rattler.

Rattler would win and a pot of money would make her father's eyes shine again. Everyone would want his services as a stallion and the sovereigns would come tumbling in.

Jack and Martin might come home! If Nat could be persuaded to drop the threat of prosecution against them . . . surely he would be satisfied with just pursuing Ellen? Nat might turn into a nicer man without his father's bullying.

Clara rammed these hopes into her reeling brain, kissed Rattler on the nose, blew out the lantern and went out into the evening. A wind from the west had blown the rain clouds apart and some stars were shining brilliantly as if to cheer her spirits. Perhaps it was Nicholas up there, galloping through the clouds on his pony Prince as he always said he would, together in paradise – Nicholas who had seen the good side of everything even when death was so close. If only she could speak to him ... she had no friends now, when she needed them. Yet Miss Charlotte had once confided closely in her, professing envy at what she called her freedom, and Clara had shared her closest secrets with Jane at the vicarage, who had nursed and loved Nicholas – two friends she had avoided lately.

Perhaps Ellen would be spared, for her youth and her good family. Perhaps Nat would pardon Jack. Perhaps ... Clara tried to think more positively and not cry like the feeble woman she knew she truly was. Not to think of Prosper, not ever, to feel her heart really breaking. That was the path to despair.

She walked down to the river to settle her mind, and stood by the ford watching the dark water, listening to the familiar burble of its busy progress towards the village. She loved these moments when the quiet perception of her rooted loyalty to the farm soothed her spirit, when she knew that whatever, whoever, came and went, the river would flow on, the stars would shine over the topmost branches of the wood and she was a part of the land. That was her comfort.

The child gave her a kick and she laughed.

'Come quickly, little beast, and let me get on with my life.'

Nothing could be so bad as now. It was bound to get better.

5

When Eb Grover was buried no one from the village attended the service save for the squire and his wife. Lord Fairhall was said to be abroad, the miller in Norwich, the landlord from the Queen's Head at a meeting with the brewer. The pews were sparsely filled by relations from Norwich and a sprinkling of farmers. When for Nicholas the church had been full to overflowing, for Eb six rows of pews alone were filled.

But the churchyard, after the hearse had pulled up, the body manhandled – with difficulty – inside, and the mourners ensconced, gradually filled up with the village people. They filtered in, grinning and excited, and stood in a band around the boundary walls, as far from the open grave as possible. It was said that a written note had been thrown in the grave saying 'Bed for a bastard' but there was no sign of it now.

Thank goodness, Clara thought, it was well away from her mother and Margaret, under a yew tree by the door, and away from Nicholas's grave by the gate to the rectory. She did not want the evil Grover body fluids and bone dust contaminating her loved ones. She had gone down to watch, drawn by curiosity like everyone else, although no one else from the farm had come. She passed the time of day whilst they waited with several homely housewives who commented kindly on her figure, asked her her dates and commiserated with her severance from 'poor Martin, exiled by old Grover'. Several of them hinted that he might come back, along with Jack, now Grover was dead. None of them doubted that her baby was his. Maybe it was, but Clara didn't think so. What were they going to say when she produced a brat the image of Nat Grover? The women she spoke to did not mention Ellen, the subject was too painful, but Clara knew that her sister was already something of a heroine in the village. No longer that 'naughty little Garland girl' but 'poor lamb, may she be spared'.

'Clara! A pity our Nicholas isn't here to see this. He would love it, wouldn't he?'

Clara turned and saw the solid, familiar figure of her friend Jane behind her, once housemaid in the vicarage.

'Jane! How lovely to see you! Oh yes, I cannot help but think of him when I'm here. I could not help myself coming. And you? Who gave you time off?'

'My monstrous mistress, the miller's wife. I am her parlourmaid, can you believe? She's here herself somewhere so she could hardly deny me. We get little enough entertainment in this village. Get your Rattler going again, Clara, and give us some excitement. It seems your family provides it all, what with your Jack and now Ellen, and you setting yourself against the farmers with your horses – what would we do without the Garlands?'

'We could do without this latest, for heaven's sake! Ellen's like to die for it, and even Eb's not worth that.'

'Oh Clara, I didn't mean to make mock of it – I didn't mean it that way. Ellen is a star for what she did. It's as if the whole spirit of the village is lifted. But it will bear heavily on her and on you all, that goes without saying. But it was an accident – surely they will see that?'

'Who knows. Waiting is awful. I can't think about it any more.'

'Oh, poor Clara! Bear up. When your child is born—'

Jane broke off as the pall-bearers appeared at the doors of the church, staggering under the weight of the coffin. Everyone fell silent. Ill-played organ music issued out into the cold air and the family and friends emerged to trail down the path to the open grave. They were taken aback by the large crowd that met them, expecting to be alone, and Clara saw the dismay on Mrs Grover's face. But Nat beside her straightened up. He knew full well what the humour of the crowd was and faced it defiantly. He was a challenging figure with a new weight of responsibility palpably upon him. Mellower since his father's death? Clara doubted it. She was impressed by his presence, as were all the villagers who seemed suddenly cowed, their cruel delight quenched by the impressive figure all in black, even the gypsy eyes which Clara felt she knew so well. How those eyes had coaxed her that day, nine months away! And as if invoked by her unbidden memory she felt the long anticipated turn of pain in her belly, cruel and sharp. At last! With the pain came a wild surge of exultation. Oh, how she longed to be free again, her own self! Come again, she willed the pain, as if she would have the child spill out in the very churchyard before its father.

The Grovers and friends collected round the grave and the bishop intoned the solemn words. None of them were weeping, it was noted. The two young daughters even exchanged a giggle. Nat stood facing the silent crowd, his hat in his hand. Clara wondered if he could feel the hostility of his neighbours, recognize the insolence in their stares. What a heavy inheritance he bore, coming after his vile father! She admired his courage in facing them, head up, when he could have stood bowed with his back to the sneers. He was not listening to the bishop. His eyes were roving attentively over the crowd and Clara knew he was looking for her. She had been stupid to come, to give him that satisfaction, yet she was glad he saw her, glad when his eyes caught hers and stayed. She lifted her chin, and at the same time the cramping pain came again, making her bite her lip.

'Jane,' she whispered. 'The baby's starting!'

'God in heaven, what timing!' Jane put her arm round her. 'I'll come home with you.'

'Wait till Grover's in the ground. I don't want to make a disturbance.'

Jane's arm hugged her.

'Ask Mrs Grover for a lift back!'

They both stifled a laugh. The Grover carriage stood waiting at the gate although the distance was scarcely worth harnessing a horse for. Presumably there would be a wake at the house. Their guests would have to walk.

The service finished and the gravedigger shovelled the first spadefuls of earth on the coffin. The family and mourners straggled down to the gate and Nat handed his mother into the carriage. And as it drove away and the visitors set out on the road, some wag at the back of the village crowd shouted out a 'Hip hip hooray!' There was laughter and then 'Hip hip' again and this time a ragged hooray came from the crowd. The third time and it was full-throated and joyous. The crowd then started to break up, most of the men making for the Queen's Head and the women wandering off in chattering groups, the day's excitement over.

Clara stood shivering, moved more by her exchanged glance with Nat than by the crowd's cruelty. She did not know why she was drawn to him in that way, when she hated him and all he stood for . . . yet he too sought her glance. His baby was now struggling to be born, and she was convinced it was his, and knew it would show the world shortly that it was a Grover by its dark colouring and gypsy eyes. Martin and his whole family had reddish-gold hair and that's what the village would be expecting.

'Oh Jane!' She was frightened now.

'Come on, we'll walk home slowly. Or if you like, I'll go and fetch Anne and the cart to carry you.'

'I can walk. It will be ages yet. I just wish—'

Oh, what did she wish? Too much to put into

words, only not to be in the turmoil she was in now.

'Everything has gone so wrong,' she whispered.

'Come, it will get better. Don't fret.'

Jane was staunch, so strong. She had had little joy in her life, after all. She had loved Nicholas too and held him in her arms when he died. Clara always remembered her little triumph in that and had been glad for her, sorry for herself. Jane had only a sick father and no one to care for her. She had always had to work hard. She was sixteen, much the same age as Clara.

They walked back to the farm, no more pains coming and Clara afraid now that it could be a week before the thing was born. She had heard such tales – how the old girls loved to relate the terrible stories of prolonged labour and death in childbirth: it was their favourite subject.

'There, going to that funeral was enough to bring anyone's pains on,' Anne said briskly when they got back home. 'Sit down by the fire and get yourself warm and I'll make you a drink.'

'I'll have to go back, else I'll get the sack,' Jane said. 'But I'll try and come tomorrow and see how it goes. Good luck!'

Now the time had come, Clara forced herself to stop worrying like a sick hen. She was young and fit and determined to make no fuss. Anne turned the men out of the house and sent Sam for Dr Roberts but he was up at the squire's place attending to a bad hunting accident.

'Not the squire, I hope!' Anne was alarmed.

'No, some follower we don't know. He was taken to

the manor, the nearest place. Roberts said he'd come when he could but I said there was no hurry.'

Sam had seen four children born and knew the way of it.

'Miss Charlotte said she'd come,' Sam added.

'Oh no!' Miss Charlotte was the last person Clara wanted to observe a little Nat Grover come into the world.

'Well, rather her than her mother or sisters,' Anne said. 'She's the only one who cares for anyone in the village. She and the squire himself, they play their part. The others – huh!' She shrugged dismissively. The squire's wife was certainly no Lady Bountiful. She and her two elder daughters thought only of their social life, wining and dining and visiting London and Bath in the season and toing and froing to dress-makers and milliners in Norwich. Charlotte avoided all that, preferring to go hunting with her father.

The afternoon drew to darkness and Clara's pains gathered pace. She lay in the cold bedroom determined to let no groan pass her lips. Anne brought her hot bottles for her feet and cold cloths for her face and kept calm, as if she had delivered babies all her life. Had she? Clara had no idea. It was so easy for horses! Twenty minutes at most. Clara gasped and almost screamed, bit her lip hard and gasped again. She heard Anne talking to someone, could not see, could not think. Oh, the brat, to hurt so! It must be as big as a house! I hate you for doing this to me! But who did she mean? If it was Prosper's would she be loving the pain, crying with joy instead of despair? Oh no! I can't bear it!

Did she cry out, did she scream? There was a scream from somewhere, a loud and lusty wail which could well have been her own, but wasn't. A laugh and chatter.

'Why Clara, it's a girl! What a surprise! We all thought it was going to be a boy.'

'Give it her,' said the other voice. 'It's so lovely to hold it straight away. All the pain is worthwhile. Oh, the sweet thing! Look, Clara, the image—'

The baby squalled, wrapped in a thick towel, and was passed to Clara's bewildered arms. The image of who?

'The image of you, Clara. Just look! The absolute image!'

It was Miss Charlotte bending over her, laughing. Anne was smiling, lighting more candles.

'What a lovely birth, Clara, so quick and easy! Dr Roberts has still not arrived.'

Clara could not believe it was over. Charlotte said it was only seven o'clock, the evening not the morning. The baby was in her arms, and now Clara did not hate it at all. A fierce sense of possession made her grasp it firmly: it was no longer the unwanted interloper, but the very fibre of her being. Her feelings overwhelmed her. She wept and laughed together.

'Like me?'

It was true. The baby had soft brown hair, not black or ginger, and eyes the grey-green colour of her own, not gypsy eyes or Ramsey blue. It was a Garland baby, a secret baby. No one would guess its

63

father. It was more like Prosper if it was like a man but more like her than anything.

'Oh the darling thing!'

Better than any foal. Clara could not believe it.

Her father returned with Dr Roberts and they came upstairs with glasses of brandy and drank the baby's health. Charlotte dressed the baby in her little clothes, and the pretty jacket made by Ellen, and wrapped it in the old shawl they had all been wrapped in in their time. Anne combed out Clara's hair and propped up her pillows and they all sat round the bed and talked and laughed. Clara found it hard to remember what her feelings had been after the funeral, so low and despairing. Now she seemed to have no cares in the world, only an amazing feeling of being filled with a sort of brightness, indescribable, of entering a world where there was only the huge great puzzle of life and death and no inbetweens, and for now it was life, the magic of birth. Death could wait. Life was suddenly on another plane.

'I can't believe how I feel,' she whispered to Charlotte.

'I can guess. I love seeing babies – animals – born. It seems to make sense of everything.'

'I didn't want her!'

Charlotte laughed and held her hand. 'I'm glad I came, butting in. It was such a lovely birth.'

'I'm glad you came too.'

Charlotte never seemed patronizing but always a person on their level, a rare grace in the snobbery of the time. To know one's place was fiercely taught and rarely ignored. But there were always personalities that transcended decorum and Clara already understood this, mainly through Rattler. Owning a potentially great horse gave her acceptance into rich farming families like Prosper's; she had discovered this in her rounds with Rattler as a stallion. When Charlotte departed, these thoughts flitted through her mind, and as she nursed her new tiny belonging she remembered that the little thing was going to be a boy, to ride her horses. It would be a nuisance, a drain on her concentration with the horses, an unwanted embarrassment. And now suddenly the baby was the light of her life. Her love for the baby almost stifled her, putting every other thought out of her head as she kissed her fuzzy head and examined her tiny fingers. She was like the old sour mare Tilly when she gave birth, changed to sweetness! Twelve hours ago she had been lamenting her life with Jane. Now in her familiar draught-ridden bedroom, Clara snuggled down under the blankets with the child against her breast, and her happiness was a fire that warmed them both, defying the icy rain that beat on the windows. For once she truly felt able to thank God for what had happened, the first time she had felt the urge of religion since her mother died.

With the baby's birth, the trauma of Ellen's departure was alleviated. It was a diversion from the terrible facts that faced them. Clara lay on the old sofa in front of the fire and nursed her baby and refused to think of Ellen. Jane managed an hour off to make a fleeting visit.

'She's not a scrap like Martin, but the image of you. How lovely! What are you going to call her? Some horse name, I suppose, like Daisy or Blossom?'

Clara laughed. 'No, she's to be Susannah. Ellen chose it.'

'A good name. Susannah Bywater. I still find it hard to think of you as Mrs Bywater.'

'I do myself. It was just a good turn of Nicholas's, thinking ahead. No one can call her a bastard. She will be properly in the church register as of married parents.'

'It's lucky the register doesn't have to say who the true fathers are.'

'There's many would be caught out there!'

'You must ask me to the christening, Clara. And maybe the old Rev Bywater won't be too frail to take it. She's his own granddaughter officially, after all. But he couldn't face burying Eb – he made himself out to be too frail for that. He told me he was going to cry off.'

'He's sunk very low since Nicholas died.'

'Yes, poor old chap. He will follow him soon, he has no more will to live.'

They didn't speak of Ellen. But when the squire called it was to tell them about Ellen's trial, not to admire the child. He gave the baby a man's bemused inspection and congratulated Clara, but then he sat at the table with Sam and a glass of port to discuss business.

'Ellen is in Norwich Castle gaol, and will remain there until her case comes up at the Quarter Sessions, presided over by judge and jury. I shall have no say there, I'm afraid, save to give her a good character. I have spoken to Nat and he says it is impossible to withdraw the charge, given the seriousness of the crime. It was in play, perhaps, but the result was mortal. He has his mother's wishes to respect, of course, and Eb's family who are powerful in Norwich.'

'So when will this trial be?'

'In a few weeks' time.'

'And she will be in gaol until then?'

'Yes. There's no getting her bail, I'm afraid. With Jack's escape, the name Garland does not go well with the authorities.'

'And when she comes to judgement, what do you think the sentence will be?'

Clara could not believe her father was asking this question, the one none of them had so far dared mention.

The squire looked grave. 'It is a hanging offence, as you well know. But she is only thirteen, of good family and with no other offence behind her. It will pay you to hire a lawyer to plead her case: that it was a prank, after all. No one can believe that a child with a home-made catapult meant to kill a man. It was a chance in a million. A good lawyer can get that over to the jury. I can find you one when the time comes.'

'A lawyer? I'd never have thought that was necessary! The facts are there for all to see.'

'She can hardly plead her own case, such a child. Against the Grovers? Eb's brothers will be in court and they will show no leniency. They have witnesses to the attack and will produce the men in the post-chaise who were at the scene. I am afraid you are up against very brutal opponents. We all know what Ebenezer Grover was like and I am afraid his brothers are no kinder.'

'What about Nat? Does he go along with them?'

'I have spoken to him and he says he has no influence with them. I sense – although I should not say it – that he is relieved to be rid of his father. The farm goes to him, the brothers have no say there.'

'But to his elder brother, legally, if he turns up?'

'To Philip, yes. But I doubt we will ever see him again. Nat said they have had no word, not ever, even to his mother.'

'It's a bleak picture. And Barney – poor Barney too.'

'I told her he would lead her into bad ways,' Anne said. 'But of course she never listened.'

'Barney would take the blame, he told me. It was his catapult. But the witness saw Ellen fire it. I think they will be held jointly responsible.'

'Barney offered to take the blame,' Clara said. 'He isn't all that bad!'

'No. He's a ruffian but he's got a kind heart. At least Ellen has a friend by her in gaol.'

'Would that the Grovers knew what kindness was!'

'Oh come,' Sam said shortly, 'when your bread-winner is killed, why should you be kind? And Jack fired his threshing barn. Why should they feel kindly towards us?'

Sam spoke the truth, bitterly, and silenced his wife. The squire sighed. It was his job to keep his neighbours in peace with each other, and not an easy one. Starving peasants took his game which outraged him, yet he could see their children crying for food. He tried to solve as many injustices as he could without taking to the courts, but sometimes it caused great acrimony. He had a reputation for softness. His wife was forever scolding him. But he had seen terrible things in his early life, fighting at sea under Nelson, losing his arm at Aboukir Bay, and now in his middle age he preferred peace. He was devastated by the fate that had befallen pretty little Ellen with her cheeky ways, laughing or crying about the village, never still, bright as a button, but he had had no choice but to indict her for trial. At least the village people understood that. He half-smiled, remembering the cries of hip hip hooray in the churchyard. What a terrible epitaph for any man, over his grave!

He stood up to go, relieved to have the visit ended.

'Come to me at any time. I will stand by you at the trial.'

'You are very kind,' Anne said sincerely.

When he had departed she reiterated this statement. 'At least we have a good man for squire. He could easily have been in cahoots with the Grovers. Most of these rich families hang together.'

Sam shrugged and blundered out into the yard to continue working. He could not discuss the thoughts that filled him.

Anne said to Clara, 'At least he's not taken to the Queen's Head again. I worry for him so! I think we should visit Ellen in prison, but I'm afraid it might break him to see her so.'

'I'll come with you,' Clara said.

'No. You have the little one to feed and the journey will be too cold to take her.'

'Ellen would love to see her!'

'And you? You've had troubles enough yourself. Forget Ellen, get back to your horses. You've your own life to live.'

'You can't go alone. It will be awful.'

'Miss Charlotte said she would come with me. And in that case we'll have a comfortable carriage to travel in.'

'To wait outside the gaol! Oh, to bring her home – if only she could have bail!'

Clara was amazed at Charlotte's generosity. She was sure Charlotte's mother would be furious with her for prison visiting. But she knew Charlotte defied her mother and guessed that her father took her part.

There were several long weeks to wait before the trial. Clara recovered her strength very quickly and was soon back riding, determined to get Rattler fit for a new match when the weather improved. If they could find a rider for him . . . Clara knew she would never be allowed to ride him herself in a match as she had once, not now that she was a married woman with a child. She had been a child herself then. Scarcely a year ago – it was hard to credit! She would not challenge Nat with his lovely Crocus and she doubted if he would challenge Rattler after what lay between them. But there were plenty of game farmers out there who would answer a challenge, if they dared to get beaten.

It was wonderful to be slim again and able to bend and twist. She had a lithe, strong figure and the happiness with her child had given her a new bloom, a radiance she had not shown before.

Rattler, in spite of her neglect, looked magnificent. He was now mature, heavier in build than Nat's Crocus, but with great quality in his conformation. He was high-spirited, enquiring into everything with his large, kind eyes, not particularly handsome with his bony, slightly Roman nose but showing character. He needed careful handling but there was no bad in him, just spirit. He stood fifteen hands, a dark bay in colour, brighter round the muzzle, with hard black legs. Clara rode him round the fields in her boy's breeches but in public rode side-saddle.

'You're a woman now. You've got to heed convention,' Anne reprimanded.

But at dusk she rode him on the road astride, training him in his racing trot, the fastest he could go, as fast as a good hunter could gallop. The longer his stride the smoother he rode, so sometimes she laughed aloud at the feel of the cold air whistling past and the warmth of the great machine beneath her. If she saw anyone they scarcely had time to notice that it was Clara Garland astride again like a boy. The more she rode him the fitter he became and the more work he demanded, but her father encouraged her, knowing there was money in the horse. Anne was only too happy to have his mind deflected from brooding over Ellen and loved looking after Susannah in Clara's absence.

But how they could find the right rider for him in his matches occupied Clara's thoughts. If only Jack could come back! Sometimes she thought it might be worth approaching Nat to ask if he would give up the Grover determination to prosecute him, but Father said to wait until Ellen's business was finished. He thought, but could not bring himself to say it, that if Ellen received the ultimate sentence Nat might soften in regard to Jack. Clara guessed this herself.

She had not seen Nat at close quarters since the funeral. If he was at all human she guessed he would have wanted to see the baby to find out if there were any signs that it was his, but he had not called. Word had probably gone round that the baby was the image of herself, so he would have heard that. Did he wonder? Clara had no idea what men thought about siring children. They seemed to do it so easily and pass on without regard, leaving the mother to the grief, poverty and scorn that came with illegitimate birth – or so it seemed to Clara's observations. She wondered if her Susannah meant nothing to Nat. It seemed so, judging from his lack of curiosity.

It was said in the village that the regime on his farm was now slightly kinder, the workers being allowed to eat their bait in the barn out of the weather instead of in the hedgerow, and when the weather was very bad he sent the smallest children home. His work force was smaller too, owing to the success of the threshing machine. But no one spoke more kindly of him, in spite of his concessions.

One morning, two weeks before Ellen was to appear in court, Clara was riding (side-saddle, in her quite smart habit) home from the village having delivered some orders from her father, and met Nat on the road. As they had to pass, Nat on horseback too, there was no way to avoid each other. Clara thanked God that she looked respectable but felt her heart start to pound with nervousness. She felt the colour coming up into her cheeks, wondering what his response to her would be: the sister of his father's murderer, possibly the mother of his child, the sister of the man that fired his farm? She played all those parts.

She thought he looked rather like she felt as they came face to face.

'Why, Clara!' His glance took her in sharply, top to toe. 'You look well. Motherhood becomes you.'

'Getting out to ride again becomes me better.'

She stared back, unable to deny that her heart was beating faster with looking at him. Why could she hate him so and be so vulnerable at the same time? – all her instincts wanting to please him, make him smile, make him admire her, and her head telling her to turn away, be cool, he was the enemy. It had always been the way between them. How much easier to hate him if he had not been so attractive, with that flirting, teasing question in his dark eyes and the tentative, challeng-ing smile. He dressed so well, apparently careless and yet with undeniable flair, to show off his fine figure and bearing. She wondered he had not joined the army and bought a commission to wear a colourful uniform: how magnificent he would look! Farming gave him no opportunity to show off. She wondered if, now the farm was his, he wanted it.

'How is it, with your mother and your family?'

'All lamentations. And yours too, I daresay.'

'Yes. I prefer to come out, keep with the horses. I know where I am in the stable.'

'And what with the child? A girl, I hear.'

'Yes. Susannah. She's very sweet.'

'Whose is she, Clara?'

'She's mine! The image of me, they all say.'

She flared at him, surprised that he had broached the subject so quickly. Yet, of course, he must be long-ing to see her, no doubt convinced he was the father. It would be unnatural if he wasn't. How many others had he sired? she wondered.

'I know no more than you,' she muttered, to be fair. 'There are no signs either way, no red hair, no black. Thank God for it, I say. But I confess I'm not sorry I bore her, although I didn't want her. Now she's here – it's different. We all love her, and she takes our mind off what is to happen to Ellen.'

'What happens to Ellen is entirely her own fault.'

'Yes, nobody denies it, although she never meant it. How could she? It was just a prank, to sting the horse.'

'My uncles are very determined. Don't blame me, Clara, if it turns out for the worst, for I have no say in it. I am pushed about by events as much as you. My father was lord in our house, as you know, and I now have the farm to run without advice. He took it all on his shoulders and used me like a dog. I am ignorant about so many things. I would say this to you, but not to everyone, although they have eyes to see. I never thought to be a farmer, in my heart, but choice doesn't enter into it, even now. It never did.'

Clara was thrown by these unexpected confidences and did not know how to reply. It was true that his father had treated him without affection, purely as an extension to his own authority, giving Nat no role of his own. Only the horses had been Nat's own speciality. Even there he had not been as successful as Clara, mainly – in her opinion – because of the way he treated them. She thought his horse Crocus was as good as Rattler and even had the beating of him, should he be ridden and treated with the skill and tact required. He was a nervous, high-mettled horse, and Nat was a forceful and unsympathetic rider, which did not make a winning combination. She would give a great deal to have the lovely Crocus in her stable. Seeing him curvetting to Nat's heavy hands as they conversed, she saw the pure quality and beauty that Rattler – darling Rattler! – could not compare to. Rattler was all character and heart and only beautiful in his strength and arrogance, but Crocus was a prince apart. She did not want to match the two of them again, for neither deserved to be beaten.

'You will flourish when you find your way, I'm sure,' she said lamely, and made to ride on. That he should complain, with his vast acres and wealth and independence! But he had no loving family as she did and had no friends to depend on, so wholly had his father commanded him. He must feel now like a man with no prop. She thought then of Prosper's large and agreeable family, all working together and enjoying what they did, laughing, teasing each other round the big kitchen table, the atmosphere so contented even when they were complaining about the price of corn. She longed for her own home to be like that, but without Jack and Martin it had fallen apart, and now Ellen too . . . her troubles if she dwelled on them were worse than Nat's. She knew that since Ebenezer's death the village was waiting with its usual prurient curiosity to see how Nat was going to turn out: whether he would continue with the same overbearing, savage cruelty his father had practised or whether he would mellow without the old man's influence. She had sensed his indecision, heard his fears. It was remarkable how much he had revealed to her.

She went home and reported back to Anne.

'One could feel sorry for him, in a way,' Anne said. 'He's only a lad after all, and cruelly raised. If he feels lost it's not surprising.'

When Clara took Susannah to her breast she looked for any sign that the baby was Nat's, and saw nothing. Yet now, she did not feel the usual unease but more a sneaking, fragile contentment.

Later, Anne said quietly, 'If he softens, maybe there's a chance for Jack coming back.'

Clara did not dare reply.

6

Clara knew that Ellen's plight was terrible. When Anne had visited her in Norwich Castle gaol with Miss Charlotte, she had come home crying and would not speak to Clara of what she had found. Clara shut herself away from Anne's conversation with Sam, concurring with Anne's reluctance to upset her with bad news. It was bad for a baby's milk, they all understood, for a mother to get upset and Clara was a nursing mother. She did not pursue it.

But when the time came for the trial, in March, Clara knew she had to attend, in spite of all advice to the contrary. Sir James the squire offered to take them with him to Norwich in his carriage. Sam wanted to drive there independently, but their cart was uncovered and the weather was bitter and he gave way to Anne's common sense.

'He will think it very strange if we refuse. After all, he has hired a lawyer for Ellen and briefed him well – however would we have managed that on our own? I know it will be difficult—'

They would not be at ease in the carriage with the squire whereas on their own they could rant and weep. Maybe all for the best, Clara thought. She dreaded the appointment and could not believe that even the Grovers relished it, certainly not Nat. Could they be so evil, to wish death on Ellen? Yet the law was so harsh. People, including boys as young as ten, were hanged for stealing quite trifling articles. Many kind people did not press charges for this reason and left it to the local magistrate to sort out privately, without going to court. But Ellen's crime was far beyond local wits to cope with. She was to be tried before judge and jury with all the panoply of pomp and theatre that was supposed to impress and deter the lower orders from wrongdoing.

Travelling in the comfort of His Nibs' coach (Nicholas had always called the squire His Nibs), Clara had time to contemplate her own future; uppermost in her thoughts was the prospect of travelling Rattler once more as a stallion around the district. If his first foals, due at the end of May, were as brilliant as she hoped – expected – there would be a demand for his services, and if before then he could win a decent match against a proved competitor it would advertise him at just the right time. Who would ride him? Oh, Jack, she breathed, laying her forehead against the cold glass of the carriage window . . . if only dear Jack could return! If the worst panned out for Ellen, Clara determined to ask Nat to allow Jack and Martin to return without punishing them. How could he refuse now there was no evil Ebenezer standing over him? His burned barn was mended, his threshing-machine replaced, his farm thriving – what more did he want? If Ellen was sentenced to death and Jack was still banished Clara saw no hope for her father, sinking deeper by the day into despair, but if Jack were to come back from his wretched tin mine in Cornwall, then there was a chance for them all. Their farm cried out for Jack. She longed for his company, the sibling always closest to her. She had never had time for her sisters, she had to admit it, and only their awful fates stirred her to a loving compassion. But Jack – Jack was almost as dear to her as Prosper.

Prosper . . . now her thoughts drifted away to where they were forever roving – to Prosper who would now be in India. In a few months' time his first letter to his family might arrive back at Great Meadows. She did not dare to hope that he would write her one. True, he had declared his love for her when he left, but how could a young man be expected to remember a passing passion when he was faced with a new world, a new life and probably new female friends? Clara had no conception of what this Indian life was like. She knew nothing about India, scarcely even where it was, only that it was hot and a long way away. She would ride over to Great Meadows as soon as she had the chance, and perhaps be able to read the letter he was bound to send there. One would hopefully arrive in June, the journey each way taking five months. Or perhaps he had posted one from South Africa on the way out, in which case it would be much sooner. Oh, how ignorant she was! She must learn about India, find some books to read so that she could picture his life. Maybe the squire knew about such things; he was well-travelled and was said to have a fine library. At least she could read well enough. She wasn't a total village maid without learning. She was bleakly aware that her station in life was well below Prosper's but at least he was the seventh son and not depended on to make a good marriage, even should he be thinking of marriage. Which he wouldn't be.

Clara straightened up with a jerk, her thoughts so ridiculous. What an idiot she was! She looked across at her father, talking in a low voice to Sir James. He looked unfamiliar in his best attire, not formal like the squire's, but country best, farmer's best, worn for market and church. And the Assizes. The well-sprung carriage rode smoothly over the road, horsed by the handsome grey pair that made all Sir James's errands. If Rattler made them some money this year she would buy her parents a proper carriage to ride in, with a roof and sides, not as good as this one but at least where one could ride out of the weather. The usual excitement of approaching Norwich was this time replaced by dread. The men's voices fell to silence and Sam sat twisting his hat in his hands, grey-faced.

It was a bright day, if cold, and everyone was going about their business without care, laughing and chatting. The world went on, the biggest platitude of all. Through one's own doom and disaster, the unaffected crowd moved as usual, oblivious. Clara longed to run away down to the market square and hide from the ghastly court business but when their carriage pulled up by the forbidding castle gateway, she got down calmly and stood waiting while Sir James instructed his coachman where to take the horses.

'I daresay we'll be an hour or two. Go to The Bell and we'll come to you there.'

What had she expected?

She had tried not to think about it.

She had not thought about it.

Now, faced with it willy-nilly, she began to realize what Ellen had suffered.

When they threw me in the cart with my hands cuffed behind me, I turned my head and bit the gaoler in the calf. I bit so hard through his felt trousers that I nearly broke my teeth and the taste of his blood was like nectar. After that they hit me again and I remember nothing until I heard Barney's voice: 'Hey up, Ellen. Come to! We're in Norwich. Look at it!'

I was sick and dizzy, propped up against the window. My lips were caked with blood and my nose was thick and running but I could not move my hands. My whole body was stiff and cold. I groaned. My head ached like fury.

'Barney,' I croaked.

They must have picked him up from the squire's. The two gaolers sat opposite.

I started to cry, I felt so dreadful and Barney said, 'Shut up, Ellen. It's all right, we're nearly there.'

He wiped my nose on his sleeve and asked the jailers if they would undo my hands but they refused.

'She's a wild cat. We're not letting her loose.'

Barney's legs were chained together, I noticed, but he was more comfortable than I was. The two gaolers were smoking stinking pipes and the draughts whistled in through the window cracks as the cart rattled and swayed over stone cobbles. I sniffed and choked and buried my face in Barney's tweed collar. I hadn't seen him since the squire took him away. I wished I was dead.

'At least you get a meal in prison, and a roof over your head,' Barney said. 'It won't be so awful, you see.'

That might have been his idea, but it wasn't mine. The prison was in a castle on a great hill in the centre of the town and as the horse toiled up the slope to the gates, the walls rose up in the darkness higher than any building I had ever seen. My teeth chattered with horror.

'I want to go home!' I had no pride, no defiance any longer. I just ached to be anywhere but where I was.

The gaolers mocked me. 'Home! This is home now, dearie! Welcome!'

A prison had been built inside the keep of the old castle. It was like you were a monkey shut into a cage, with a barred door and a jangle of keys and a stench of human manure like I could never have imagined. I had a floor space just big enough to lie in and a bucket and a jug of water. They put chains on my legs like Barney's but let my hands free. There was a board bed with two dirty blankets, but no mattress, no pillow. No nothing! A faint light came through the barred door from away down the corridor, and the only sound was of moans and sobs and sometimes screaming and shouting as from mad people. I could not believe this had happened to me. I sat on the boards and cried and cried.

After a bit, a woman's voice said, 'Give us some peace, dearie. We want to get to sleep.'

I screamed, 'I want to get out of here!'

'Don't we all, dearie? Be a good girl now and settle down. It'll be better in the morning.'

I gradually lost consciousness, but whether it was sleep or not I could not say. When I awoke I was stiff all over and my ankles were already sore from the chains. I was freezing cold and couldn't stop shivering. It was a gaoler who had woken me, opening the door.

'Out you get!'

A great crowd of prisoners jostled and shoved at a table where wooden bowls of gruel were being handed out. I was so hungry I elbowed my way with the best of them. Thank God amongst the crowd I found Barney and we pushed our way to get a seat at the table together. It was a terrible rabble we were among and there seemed to be no one to tell us what to do. As we were new, as soon as everyone had eaten (mostly like pigs in the trough) we were subjected to a grilling. Revolting filthy men pawed at me and Barney bravely tried to push them aside. But he was only a little starved boy. I screamed, thinking a gaoler would come to help, but they didn't seem to bother. It was a stout woman who flailed in.

'Get off her, you louts!' Her language was dreadful. She had great bare red arms like a washerwoman and flung her fists like a man. She hit one of the men square across the jaw and nearly felled him.

'Leave her be, you filthy pigs! She's a child, for Gawd's sake!'

They slobbered away. I sat sobbing again.

'Hey up, Ellen, stop making such a fuss,' said Barney, who seemed to take everything in his stride. I suppose he never normally got such a good feed as that gruel.

The washerwoman lady said, 'You've got a brave lad to look after you, what are you crying for? My name's Meg and I'll see you both right. Kids like you shouldn't be put in with a rabble like us. It's a disgrace. But you've got to learn to stick up for yourself, gel. Kick and scratch. I'll show you how.'

Meg was the woman in the next cell. I found I had made a friend.

'This is a funny prison. Very lackadaisical they are here. No discipline. You can't get out, that's for sure, but you can do what you like most of the time. No work, no improving the mind, not like most. Only the treadmill if you're troublesome.'

She went on, 'They're building a new one outside this keep. I suppose that's why they don't bother in here. Going to be a model new place, they say. I might be in here long enough to sample it, one day.'

She laughed. She was immensely fat which made her conspicuous, and amazingly jolly considering her fate. How anyone could be jolly in such a dreadful place was beyond me. I could not stop shivering although I tried not to cry any more.

'What do we do?' I stammered.

'Do? Do? Whatever you like, dearie. Walk about in the yard. Chat. Pick lice. Scratch on the walls. 'Ave you

84

got someone to pay for easement – get your chains off, like, get you a mattress?'

I gaped. Whatever was she talking about?

'Your nearest and dearest, lovie – if they pay the gaoler they can make you more comfortable. If they don't you'll find yourself in a cell with a lot of mad women shortly and half your clothes ripped off your back. You've got family, I take it?'

'Yes!'

But what did they know about prison rules? Nothing at all.

However, I think it was the squire -- he knew. Because that night there was a mattress and a pillow on my bed and the gaoler unlocked my leg irons so that I was free. And in the morning Barney had no irons on and he said he had been given a cell to himself with a mattress and a pillow. Had he paid for us?

I can't tell you how strange it is to settle into this awful life. To think I had been discontented with my lot, complaining all the time! After my stepmother had visited with Miss Charlotte, I got two more blankets and better food, but it didn't make any difference to seeing out every day in that vile place among all those vile people. A few rich men had private suites and received friends often, but some of the hopeless poor devils were locked in a dungeon down below where there was not a speck of light, and the water leaked down the walls onto a sodden straw-strewn floor. One of the young men told me about it. And I heard all about the treadmill, where a lot of the men had been chained by the wrists for six hours a day, climbing up an unending staircase. They were rested for ten minutes each hour, else they would not have survived. The treadmill ground the prison's corn. Women were not put to this, thank God. For I wasn't a good prisoner and might have been a candidate. I learned to fight for my rights, for my food, for my clothes that might have been ripped off my back, and my good boots. We lived like animals. The weakest went to the wall.

Barney was sharp, using the wits he had survived on all his life, and the great bulk of Meg guarded us to a certain extent. Some people lay in a corner and gibbered all day. Some played cards and gambled, some fashioned little bits of wood or stone into ornaments, many argued and fought. We could sit out in the yard inside the prison walls and look up at the blue sky, but the birds flying across, so free and careless, and the white clouds like great dandelion clocks floating over made me cry. You could just hear the voices of freedom way below and the clatter of horses' hooves. It was awful to picture the people in the city below, all untroubled, shopping and laughing and drinking in the friendly inn. And there was a lot of noise close outside our walls where old buildings were being demolished to make way for the new model prison. Even these workers were free men. However hard they worked and moaned and groaned, at least they were free to go home at the end of the day to some sort of hovel where the air was pure and the place their own. But not us.

And what did we have to dream of, Barney and I?

A hanging was the most likely, and when I got to thinking about this and went out of my head with fear, Meg took me in those brawny arms and rocked me like I was a baby.

I didn't want to hang!

7

Ellen looked terrible, like some feral animal dragged from its lair. She was dirty, her clothes in tatters, her hair snarled in a dull mat down her back. She was led into the dock by two warders and stood wild-eyed, white-faced. Behind her, Barney stumbled into place, roughly pushed by another warder. They both had fetters on their legs which clanked dully in the parched, evil-smelling atmosphere of the court room.

Clara felt as if she would faint. She had tried not to anticipate this day, to picture what she knew in her heart was happening, and now she was unprepared for the shock. She had already taken in, with awe, the amazing number of official people scurrying about with sheafs of papers, chatting with each other, darting to and fro, and the grim rank of Grover relations who sat behind them. Ebenezer's brother was talking to a man in a white wig who Clara supposed was his lawyer, and the two men in the post-chaise and their driver were sitting on a bench by him.

Sir James explained to Clara who they were, and pointed out a calm, silent man who sat near the dock as the defending lawyer who would speak up for Ellen.

'He cannot deny she did it, only try to persuade

the judge that it was an accident, a prank that went wrong. He will plead for mercy. He is very experienced and I put my faith in him. He knows all the facts. I have briefed him and he has spoken with Ellen.'

A huddle of motley men sat chatting to one side who Sir James said constituted the jury. They looked an ignorant lot to Clara and she only hoped their collective hearts would soften towards Ellen. If only she looked more agreeable, in her old laughing way! But she looked hunted and vicious; Clara scarcely recognized her. What loss to the world would it be if they hanged her? Very little if looks were anything to go by. Clara felt sick with fear. Anne sat very straight beside her, grasping Sam's hand, both silent, their eyes on the judge. He appeared elderly, short-sighted by the way he was handling the papers before him, but his face was kind enough, rough-hewn, not sour. He must have children of his own, Clara thought, even grandchildren – surely he would have pity on Ellen? If the jury found her guilty, as surely they would, it was in his hands to decide her fate, in his heart to show mercy. Clara found herself praying to God again. She would be back in church if she wasn't careful, toeing the line with the rest of the population. Her father had stopped church-going in his family when his first beloved wife died, and after Margaret's death Clara had lost faith too. God was not love, it seemed. It made no sense.

Nat was sitting with the post-chaise men. Clara did not want to meet his eye, but they were well apart, the observers separate from the well of the court. It was like watching a play, she thought. They had no chance to make their pleas and must sit in silence watching the story unfold, mere spectators. She found she was shivering, although it was not cold. She shut her eyes as one of the men with wigs read out the indictment.

She knew the story well enough. The prosecutor described it, hinting that Ellen intended to kill Grover because he had persecuted her brother. Ellen's defending lawyer made short work of this theory, describing the home-made catapult, the chance meeting with Barney, the dare Barney had made with her to frighten the horse. Children's play, he called it. The post-chaise men were called to say what they had seen and the driver gave evidence that it was Ellen who had fired the stone, not Barney. The judge questioned him on this, suggesting that it was more likely to have been Barney, but the driver was sure. The judge shook his head sadly and Clara felt a shift of optimism at this sign of sympathy. Dr Roberts was then called and said stoutly that the chance of the stone killing Grover was one in a million and quite obviously an accident. He was not impressed by the authority of the Grover lawyer and said in his opinion the case should never have been called: the death was a pure accident.

'A prank with a grave consequence,' said the judge.

Clara guessed that the busy doctor had been pressured into giving evidence by the Grovers for he surely would not have volunteered. They were all scowling at his opinion but none of them were able to stand and prove Ellen's intent to murder. They had instead to listen to Ellen's lawyer's speech in her defence, which was concise, hard-hitting and extremely eloquent. Sir James had hired a splendid man, Clara decided.

The judge seemed to agree, for his summing-up was very brief.

'Members of the jury, it is for you to decide whether the defendant is guilty or not guilty of killing Ebenezer Grover. You must talk among yourselves and when you are ready let me know your answer.'

At this, he yawned and got up from his chair. Everyone stood up, but when he did not appear to go anywhere, other than to stretch and chat to his minions, a murmuring of conversation broke out amongst the gathering.

'What happens now?' Anne asked Sir James.

'Nothing much, until the jury is ready. The judge does not expect them to be long about it, obviously.'

The jury were in a huddle on the floor, some talking and gesticulating, others staring gloomily, silently, into space. Ellen and Barney were sitting down between the warders. Ellen would not look towards them, but stared at her feet. She looked very small and thin and Clara, twisted with pity, could not bear to look at her. It was hard to believe this was happening at all. After Jack's escapade and his flight, and now this, it seemed that their very ordinary uninspiring family had a curse on it. What have we done, Clara asked herself, to go through so much misery? She longed to be out of the place, back with her baby in her arms, blotting out this hateful charade. She looked towards Nat and saw that he looked no happier than her, sitting beside his dreadful mother who was done up in her absurd best as if she were going to a ball. Mrs Grover all her married life had aspired to society – but in vain – and Clara guessed she was furious to see them sitting with the squire. Her husband's death had not grieved her, obviously, as it had grieved no one, but that did not lessen the usual Grover greed for redress. A kindly family, even after as grave a tragedy, would not have seen a child come to court for it.

The judge came back to his seat and they all rose for him. The jury stood to attention, blank-faced. The judge sat down. They all sat down. The judge waited for the shuffling to stop and then addressed the jury.

'What is your verdict? Guilty or not guilty?'

There was no hesitation.

'Guilty, my lord. But, in the case of the girl, with a recommendation for mercy.'

It couldn't have been otherwise, but Clara felt a sickening, desperate disappointment. She dared not look at her father. Ellen, standing, made no move. Barney was stony-faced.

The judge pursed his lips, shuffled his papers.

'The sentence I pass is hanging for the boy, and for the girl transportation to Australia for seven years.'

Transportation! Anne cried out, Clara gasped and hot tears blurred her vision. She did not see Ellen's reaction, nor Barney's, but reached out for her father's hand. She felt the squire's arm round her shoulder.

'We will try for a pardon, don't despair,' he said. But his voice was heavy.

'Clear the court! Clear the court!'

They stumbled, unseeing, from their bench. Sir James steered them, else they would have found no way amongst the rabble outside the doors and the phalanx of grim-faced Grovers. Clara was aware of Nat beside her for a moment, his hand on her arm.

'I'm sorry, Clara. I'm so sorry. I had no say in it, believe me.'

She did believe him but shook him off.

She saw Eb's brother, red-faced with pleasure, Nat's mother laughing.

'Damn you all!' she hissed.

She embraced her weeping father. 'Dad, bear up! She's not to die, that's the main thing. Think on it, it's not death.'

'Poor little Barney, he's got no one,' Anne said softly.

It was all despair, muddle, tears. They could not see Ellen, it was forbidden.

'Oh, it can take months, to get them on a ship,' a warder told them. 'Buck up, you'll see her many times yet.'

The hallway was full of people thrusting in for the next case. Ellen's fate had been sealed in a bare half-hour. They were shoved and elbowed in the throng but Sir James pushed a way through for them into the open air.

'Come,' he said. 'The Bell and a stiff drink, sir,' he said to Sam. 'We must think to the future. She's not to die, that's the main thing. We could even say there is cause for celebration. I had feared the worst.'

Afterwards, Clara realized what a debt they owed to Sir James for his help – the lawyer, the journey and now his care when the three of them were in helpless disarray, blind with tears. In the cold, sunny March air, they came to their senses and for a moment, looking on the cheerful town, Clara felt her heart soar with relief that the awful period of waiting was over. It was true what Sir James said – Ellen was not to die. Clara knew nothing of transportation, save that it was a time-honoured method for ridding the country of criminals. They got rid of them, quite simply, to an empty country on the other side of the world. It was considered a brilliant solution to a difficult problem, there being very few prisons in the land, certainly not enough to contain all who deserved to lodge there. Clara tried hard to think of the consolations. Prosper, after all, went on an equally demanding journey from choice, and who could tell that the future for Ellen might not be so terrible.

In spite of Clara's positive thoughts, it was not a cheerful party that came to the inn. Sir James ordered a table and a square meal and a stiff brandy for Sam, and in the cheerful warm hubbub they gradually came out of shock. It was no worse, after all, than they had expected, and the awful uncertainty was over.

'There is always a chance for a pardon and certainly I will fight to get Barney's sentence mitigated,' Sir James said. 'He's a stout little beggar with a good heart in spite of having no family. He doesn't deserve to die. I will put a word in where it might be useful.'

'They're a cruel family, the Grovers,' Sam growled. 'It's our misfortune to have them as neighbours.'

'Yes, it's a pity they bought into our neighbourhood. We'd be a lot happier without them. The old man Grover, Ebenezer's father, made his fortune over Holkham way and always had a nose for rundown places when they came on the market. He was a bad 'un too, right from the start.'

Anne said, 'Perhaps Nat will be an improvement on his forebears. He didn't seem to have much stomach for this prosecution, not like the rest of the family.'

The journey home was gloomy and mostly silent. When the carriage jolted up their drive to deliver them to their door, Sam grasped Sir James's hand to shake it and said hoarsely, 'I can't thank you enough, sir, for all you've done for us, more than in your line of duty, I think.'

'I wish the outcome could have been happier, Garland. But don't despair. We might save her yet. There are ways. And it is victory of a sort, not to die.'

'Thank God for it.'

The baby Susannah was screaming her head off in the arms of old Mrs Ponder who had stayed the day to look after her. Mrs Ponder had been their housekeeper before Sam had married again.

'She'd take nothing, however I papped up a gruel

or warmed the milk. She's a little minx and no mistake.'

But somehow the child's bawling took the edge off the misery that engulfed them and it was a relief to be feeding the baby by the fire, with Mrs Ponder taking fresh bread out of the oven and boiling up the kettle, bustling to comfort them. She heard the news with a shake of the head, pursing her lips. She had always called Ellen 'a handful' and obviously thought – though did not say – that she had expected trouble.

'And that poor homeless boy – he's to hang? He surely never deserved that, poor lad.'

With Susannah content and back in her cradle, Clara went to see to her horses. She went into the stable and into Rattler's stall. His nostrils rippled with pleasure as she put her arms round his neck. His muscles flexed hard against her hand.

'Oh you handsome beast! All the farmers will want you for their mares when they set eyes on you.'

She determined to ride over to Great Meadows to call on Prosper's father. He could well know of a suitable horse to challenge for a race: a horse with a good reputation, so that beating him would be worthwhile, a feather in their cap. And maybe there would be news of Prosper. It would not be out of order to pay a visit. Susannah could be weaned in a month or so and give Clara back her freedom. Much as she loved her child, being bound to her in the house was not an attractive proposition to Clara. Fortunately, Anne relished the role. Clara realized she had some luck in her life, after all.

'You are going to make my father happy, Rattler. For now that is your job in life.'

Making plans was a healing business. Already her spirits were rising. On an impulse she fetched Rattler's bridle and led him out into the yard. She was in skirts and, hitching them high, she climbed onto the edge of the water-trough and slipped onto his warm bare back. He half-reared away, keen, and she shortened her reins and laughed. His trot was so long and smooth that having no saddle was not a hardship. With all the training he had received he never galloped now, but only lengthened the all-powerful trot. She went down the drive and out onto the road, away from the village, to scatter her miseries in action, exhilaration, breathing in the earthy, foxy smells of the evening and seeing the first stars faintly proclaiming the end of a dreadful day. She would not think of Ellen. She had her own life to live and had had enough of disaster.

8

It was a warm, sweet morning a few days later when Clara rode over to Great Meadows, twenty miles away. She made out she was showing off Rattler to the Mayes family and to find out if there would be a demand again for his services – although it was plain that everyone would be waiting to see what his first crop of foals were like before they had him again. Anne encouraged her to go. She knew the real reason, for she had seen Clara and Prosper together before their parting, and it was plain to anyone with eyes in their face that they were gloriously in love. Why Clara had to make such pain for herself was a mystery to Anne, to love a boy on his way to India, but then she could see that it was impossible not to fall in love with someone as lovely as Prosper, who seemed to have every attractive attribute under the sun: looks, a kind heart, humour, ambition, a respected family. No doubt he would be quickly snapped up in India, where rich girls had nothing to do all day long save look for men. He could aim a lot higher than Clara, after all, who had little to commend her beyond her great spirit, which was – in Anne's opinion – worth all the other attractions put together. Clara was a fighter. Maybe if she decided to fight for Prosper, she would win.

Clara rode side-saddle in her habit, with a neatly-tied stock and gloves. She felt like Miss Charlotte, save for having no hat. Charlotte had gorgeous hats for riding in, little bowlers tipped forward, with bits of veiling – she always looked lovely. Clara was proud that Charlotte was her friend, although she always had to resist an urge to curtsey when they met.

The twenty miles spun away and they came to where the lane breasted a slight rise and the Mayes' farm lay below in its natural bowl of beautifully tilled fields and woods. The house was old and looked as if it had been born out of the soil, so perfectly in accord with its surroundings, its orchard and gardens. To Clara, whose own home looked as hard-worked as its inhabitants, it was a model place, a paradise farm, her idea of perfection. She made Rattler walk the last stretch so that she had time to satisfy her vision, aware of a mounting excitement to be where Prosper lived.

The family had not forgotten her and she was received with great kindness by Prosper's mother. Rattler was put in a stable and Clara invited into the kitchen to be plied with fresh bread and cheese from the dairy. The men were all out working and she was pleased to be alone with Prosper's mother.

'We have a letter from him. He's been there two – three – months now. It's mostly about the journey and his impressions – it makes my head whirl to think of him so far away. I've never been farther than Norwich, after all, not even to London. He's not much of a one for writing letters so I daresay this will do for a while. He does mention you somewhere, if I remember rightly. Tell Clara not to forget me, he says, which is a little high-handed from someone not likely to be back for at least four years. Does he expect you to dance attendance on a memory? You're so young, Clara, and all that's happened to you, so much sadness . . .'

She rattled on, and all Clara could think of was the phrase, 'tell Clara not to forget me'. So she did matter to him; she wasn't just a passing whim! With so much happening to him, so much to put in his letter, it must mean something that he remembered her. She would have loved to have read the letter, but it wasn't produced.

Of course she had to answer questions about Susannah, and about the trial. Ellen's fate had been well broadcast and everyone knew that she was to be transported. This by many was considered a worse fate than hanging.

'There's no one I've met who regrets the death of Eb Grover. The child did everyone a service, and of course there's no way it could have been other than an accident.'

Clara was pressed to stay to lunch and the family all welcomed her, and then Rattler was taken out and admired and Clara was shown the in-foal mares. In another month she was to return and see the produce; she would be welcome at any time.

'And how about another match, now the weather's right?' Mr Mayes said. 'It's a good time to show the horse off and he looks fit. There's a horse – a mare –

over Bungay way that's highly thought of and her owner very cocky. Challenges anybody to beat 'er and no one's taken it up yet. I think your Rattler could have the beating of 'er.'

'Yes, we're looking to find a match for him! Who is this man?'

'Name of Chignall. The mare is by Performer. Tell your father – Hugh Chignall. Tell him you'll match your Rattler with her and you'll have a great turn-out, I'll warrant. It'll be a fine advertisement for your horse, just at the right time of year.'

'If he wins!'

'Of course he'll win, my dear! He's that bonny and you know the game well, you and your father. You go home and tell your father now, to go and see Hugh Chignall. It'll give him something to think about beyond your poor lass in prison.'

'But I've no rider without Jack.'

'That was the day you rode him, eh? And beat young Nat! How we did all enjoy that day! But now you're a grown woman with child it wouldn't be seemly, I daresay, and Chignall wouldn't agree to it, to risk being beat by a woman, my God!'

The old man's red face broke into cracks of joy at the thought and Clara had to laugh too, although it was her dearest, most hopeless dream, to ride her own horse in his competitions.

'One of my boys would ride him for you, my fifth boy – I call 'em by numbers myself, I get so muddled. Number five, he's a good rider and steady, wouldn't lose his head. Gabriel, he's called. If you make this match I'll send him along and you see what you think of him. Mind you, you won't have any difficulty getting a rider, not for a horse like that.'

'Yes, but I won't have anybody riding him, spoiling him. But I would like it if Gabriel were to try him. If we see Mr Chignall, I'll let you know.'

'You go and see 'im, gel, let's have something to look forward to. And I'll send word when our first foal arrives.'

Clara rode home, her thoughts tangled with all the new ideas suddenly in her head. Oh Jack – if only he were back home, what a difference it would make to them all! What a weight off her own back, to share the troubles, the work, how to handle Rattler's future. But the idea of a brother of Prosper's riding Rattler attracted her, especially if it would keep her in closer touch with the family. She thought she remembered Gabriel: a teasing, careless boy, not unlike Prosper but no way as gorgeous. He was two years older, nineteen.

Coming back onto the village road, nearly home, she met Charlotte riding her mare Fairylight, coming from the turnpike. She pulled Rattler up to meet her and they rode on together.

Charlotte said, 'My father's got a reprieve for Barney. He's to be transported too. Isn't that good news? So if Ellen has to go, at least she will have a friend with her.'

'Oh, thank goodness! For Barney – that's great news.'

'Have you thought, now Ebenezer's gone – I wondered—' Charlotte hesitated. The horses were walking, and Charlotte had to press her mare to keep up with Rattler's stride. Clara hooked him back momentarily.

'What have you wondered?'

'That you should ask Nat if Jack can come back.'

'Oh yes, of course I've thought of it! I think of it all the time, but I'm frightened to ask. I thought after the trial I'd ask – well, now it's over and I want to call on him, but I keep putting it off. I don't know where I stand with Nat. But we need Jack so. What do you think he'll say?'

'I don't know. But I think you should ask. He can only refuse you, after all. You'll be no worse off.'

'His mother will say no!'

'But does he take any notice of his mother? He did of his father – he had no choice – but his mother's such a stupid woman. Even he can see that. And he seems to be more his own person now, I've noticed. He came to talk to my father last night, something about shooting rights over his land, and he seemed much more human than he used to be, not so high and mighty. I think it's well worth your while to approach him.'

'We want to make a match for Rattler. I was talking to Mr Mayes about it and he said there was a horse belonging to a man called Chignall at Bungay. But we have no rider without Jack, and I can't bear to see anyone else riding – we really need Jack if we're to match Rattler.'

'Nat will offer to ride!' Charlotte laughed.

'Oh no, he's a terrible rider, you know he is!' Clara

protested. 'So hard on his horse, no sympathy at all. He would ruin Rattler.'

'That's true. Just say your father needs Jack, which is the truth. Try him, Clara, don't be afraid. Or get your father to ask him.'

'Father would never do it.'

'Well then, you've got to, that decides it. Tomorrow!'

Clara's mind was churning when she reached home. She saw to Rattler and went in to see her father. He was cheered by the squire's news about Barney and they discussed that for some time, and then he enquired after her visit to the Mayes. She told him the news about Hugh Chignall and was thrilled to see the old gleam come into Sam's eyes.

'I know Chignall. A right cock 'o the dunghill is Hugh Chignall. So he's got a good horse, has he? We'll have to go and see it, my girl. See if he's worth taking on.'

'Mr Mayes said so. If word's got that far he should be.'

'We'll go tomorrow.'

Thank goodness, that meant she could postpone her visit to Nat.

'Oh my Gawd, wot 'ave we 'ere?'

'Black Rattler. You've heard of him, I daresay?' Sam was cool and proud. 'We fancy beating your mare, whatever distance you choose.'

'Eh, that's rich! You've not seen my 'oss yet.'

Chignall's eyes were needling Rattler as he spoke,

up and down his legs, taking in the muscle over his quarters, the long slope of his shoulders. The man looked like a gypsy, in loud dirty clothes and a red rag of a scarf round his neck. He had cropped bristly red hair and narrow dark eyes with a decidedly evil expression, the sort of person – Clara thought – she would go a long way to avoid.

As she was riding Rattler side-saddle, she had to accept his sneer: 'A right lady's 'oss by the look of 'im.'

'Yes, he's very mannerly,' Sam said calmly. He was riding Tilly, whom Chignall obviously recognized. She looked as mangy as ever, for all Clara's care, her dirty-coloured roan coat almost white, her hip bones sticking out like a cow's and her expression mulish, underlip hanging.

'The old mare's past it now, I reckon?'

'Yes. She's had her day.'

'Well, I'm looking for a good 'un to beat. There's little competition for the likes of mine, she's that good. My lad'll bring 'er out to show you.'

They were in a dirty, cramped stable yard behind an inn. Two boys were shovelling out manure and Chignall shouted to one of them: 'Bring Linnet out to show the gentleman.'

The boy went in and after a few minutes punctu-ated by shouting, banging and swearing, a horse shot out pulling the boy on the end of its halter. Chignall went up and heaved it to a halt, thumping it round the ears, at which the horse stood out, obviously frightened, and gazed at them with nervous, white-rimmed eyes. It was a gangly, roughly-made bay mare, but with an undoubted aura of power about it. It was lean and fit and ugly and exuded a nervous energy that suggested that it could, indeed, be a worthy competitor. By comparison, Rattler looked like a thoroughbred.

'Who's she beat?' Sam asked.

Chignall reeled off some names, none of any fame, and said no one in the district would take her on because of her reputation, but he mentioned several farmers that Sam was familiar with who could vouch for her worth, and Sam decided to volunteer for a match. The two men went into the inn to discuss terms and dates and Clara was left to mind Tilly and await events.

She rode up and down a lane behind the inn, leading Tilly, letting the horses stop to browse on the fresh hawthorn shoots in the hedgerow. Life was beginning to get back to normal and with her father showing signs of coming out of his depression, her spirits too were rising. At least Ellen, and now Barney, were not to die, so the worst cloud had passed over. She had Susannah, Prosper had sent her a message and if Nat were to allow Jack to come back . . . then life would be on an even keel again with good grounds for optimism. Rattler would beat Linnet; his foals would be gorgeous, they would make lots of money . . .

When her father came shouting for her, he was slightly tipsy and grinning with the prospect of the match ahead.

'Our Rattler'll beat that underbred nag by a distance! And Chignall says all the bets will be for her! The man's a maniac. Eh up, Tilly, let's get home.'

And the old mare, turned for Gridstone, went into her amazing trot, Sam riding like the young man he once was, and Clara, in her dreams, had to shout at Rattler to keep up. They were home in under the hour, some sixteen miles.

'It's Tilly we should have put against Linnet, not your young upstart,' said Sam as he pulled off her saddle in their home yard. 'That mare's by Performer. Good blood.'

Clara smiled.

'Now for Nat,' she whispered to herself. They were on a rising spiral of good luck and she must use it while it lasted.

9

The Grovers' house had been expensively improved in recent years and from being a tumbled Tudor, homely place, now had a new severe frontage in the modern style with symmetrical sash windows and a door in the middle with a fanlight over and stone pillars holding up an elegant porch. It had a gravel sweep for carriages, but nobody used it. They all went round the back and into the kitchen just as they did at Small Gains. This was where Clara made for now.

It was late afternoon. Clara knew Nat was home for she had seen him ride in, so took her chance. The longer she put it off the worse it would be. She was tidy and in a clean skirt, her hair braided back. No one at home knew what she was doing. She dreaded meeting his mother and when she knocked at the door prayed that this awful woman was not going to answer it. But of course Mrs Grover did not lower herself to answer doors. The maid answered, a poor little thing whom Clara knew as one of Martin's cousins. Servants at Grover's were reputed to have a terrible time and only lasted a few weeks.

'I want to speak to Nat – to Mr Grover. Is he in?'

'He's in his study, miss – ma'am.'

Clara smiled. 'I don't feel like a ma'am. Can you tell him I would like to see him?'

She stepped inside and the maid scuttled away. Clara waited. The hallway was just like Small Gains, only bigger, full of the same muddy boots and muddy jackets, sacks of potatoes, dog baskets and broken harness. She knew Nat would be surprised; she had not seen him to speak to since the day in court.

He came out in person. He had no jacket on and his cravat was pulled loose, his feet in stockings, without boots. He looked as embarrassed as Clara felt.

'Is anything wrong?'

'No. I just want to ask you something.'

'You'd better come in. My study—'

He led the way through the big kitchen where a cook and some maids were working and through a passage to a small room in the unimproved part of the house. It was untidy; a large desk covered with papers took up most of the room and there were shelves of ledgers and books, and candles already lit to alleviate the gloom. A wood fire burned in the hearth. Nat went to it and kicked a log into place, then turned round with his back to it.

'I'm trying to do the books. The taxes drive me mad and all the legislation for Enclosures and what not. I'm not a man for desk work.'

'No, my father neither. My stepmother does it for him.'

'Having a school mistress in the family must be very useful.' He smiled and Clara was immediately aware of the old quickening of the blood at his presence. The way his eyes seemed to caress, his lips invite, the tumble of his uncombed black hair – there was such a powerful attraction face to face, she could not deny it. She did not know if she alone had a weakness before him or whether he had the same effect on everyone. Certainly poor Margaret had been helplessly in love with him. He had been known (according to Nicholas) to make advances to Charlotte, but Clara found it difficult to envisage enquiring about this to Charlotte herself. She presumably rejected his advances, for Clara had never seen them together.

He gestured to a saggy armchair beside the fire and invited her to sit down.

'I don't want to disturb you if you're busy.'

'No, I would like to be disturbed. I can't imagine anything nicer. Shall I call for some tea and cake? It's about the right time.'

Tea at four o'clock was the new fashion. Clara laughed, the habit considered ridiculous in her home.

'No, really. I'm not used to tea.'

'No, well, my mother – you know – she likes to be fashionable. I don't take it myself. I'm usually outside till dark. What is it you want to talk about? Is it Ellen? I hear that Barney is to be spared hanging. I must say I am pleased at that.'

'Yes, that's good news. We're all very relieved. But it's not about that, or Ellen. It's about Jack.'

'Jack?'

'I am wondering if there is any chance of his being able to come home, without your prosecuting him still.'

She felt herself trembling as she spoke. It meant so much, and she expected so little. She did not dare look at him.

'It's for my father,' she whispered. 'He lost Margaret, and now Ellen. He needs Jack. We all need Jack.'

Nat did not say anything. He turned round and stared into the fire.

Then he said, 'It's not easy. My mother – my uncles—'

'But you're the master here now.'

He scowled. 'I would like Jack to come back. It's past history now – we've got a new barn, a new threshing-machine. He wouldn't be so stupid as to repeat his tricks, I assume. But the old people—'

'They've had their pound of flesh, surely, with Ellen? Isn't that enough?'

'Yes, I think it is. I told you. I wouldn't have had her in court if I'd had my way.'

'Then show them who runs the place now. It's your farm now and the decisions are yours.'

Having found the courage to broach the conversation and now seen Nat's unexpected irresolution, Clara found her voice, no longer a whisper but full of command.

'They made you go after Ellen – you admit it. You've got to show them you are master here, else they will start running the farm for you. This is your chance. You know how much it means to us – it's everything to my father, to have Jack back.'

She knew from village hearsay that Eb's brother

Isaac had suggested that he took over the farm 'until Nat was of an age', but she knew too that Nat had refused. That was something. Fortunately Isaac lived some forty miles away. She had expected a curt rejection and now felt a fierce optimism.

'Please, Nat! Can't you see how much it means to us?'

She stood up and faced him, her face flushed with determination. He did not say anything but just stared at her.

'Oh Clara!'

What on earth did that mean?

'Don't you see that we could be friends, with Jack and my father – now your father is gone – why do we have to be enemies all the time? Why can't we start again? Ellen – that is so dreadful, you've injured us enough surely? – but we could put that behind us—' Clara's words stumbled out, almost of their own accord. She had not planned on such an appeal, only a dignified request, but now she seemed to have lost control. It was too much, to keep such feelings held back.

'We need Jack so badly! My father is heartbroken, to have lost so many! Can't you see how it is for him?'

Nat stared at her, his cheeks flushed. Clara saw how he wrestled to rearrange his brain, organized all his life by his terrible father.

'You are the master now,' she reiterated. 'Show them that you can do what you want. Jack would be your friend if he came back. We are no threat to you – surely you can see that? We've nothing. We just want

112

our lives back. It's nothing to you to give us this – but everything to us. Can't you see?'

She should have been a preacher! She knew they declaimed like this in the little tinpot church on the other side of the village, all hellfire and loud singing – the people who did not want to sit quietly with the squire and his lordship in the back pews in the proper church. Her blood was up and running and she guessed she was red in the face and looking pretty stupid. But she could not help herself.

'Oh, Clara!' Nat said again.

His voice was soft and almost trembled.

'My father would never—'

'Your father's dead! The best thing that ever happened – you admit it, Nat! Say it yourself! He was a wicked man and wicked to you! You are free now. Don't be so frightened to be yourself at last!'

She was close to bursting into tears now, and turned away from him. 'I'm sorry – I'm sorry to say such awful things, but I can't help it. The villagers all cheered when he was buried. You know it's the truth.' Her voice was choked and she was shaking. She had never meant for this meeting to turn out like this and wanted to be away now, back to weep on Anne's shoulder. She went to the door and turned.

'I didn't mean to say these dreadful things. But only about Jack – please think about it, for my father's sake. I must go now.'

She hurried out down the passage and Nat came after her, silent. They went through the kitchen and to the outside door. Clara opened it, but Nat put his hand on her arm and said, 'Tell me, before you go, is your little girl mine?'

The change of subject threw Clara.

'Susannah?'

'Is she mine or Martin's. You must know!'

'How can I know?'

'Oh come, she's not red-haired like all the Ramseys. I think she's mine. I care about this, Clara.'

'She's mine, that's all I care about. But give me an answer about Jack, and I will bring her to you and you can find a likeness if you can.'

Clara knew that the baby was Nat's by, sometimes, a fleeting likeness in her expression, the increasing darkness of her green eyes. She had never spoken of it, and nor did her parents, for it was a subject of such delicacy it was best left alone.

'Visit us with your answer to my question and we will make you welcome, and you can see Susannah for yourself.'

'Very well.' His voice was soft; there was no aggression or arrogance.

Stumbling away down the drive, Clara tried to make sense of her visit which had gone so awry. But perhaps revealing her emotions had moved him more than the intended dignity she had meant to display. She was not ashamed. But she was very shaken, and glad to unload her feelings on to Anne, who was getting the supper ready.

'Charlotte told me to ask him.'

'By heaven, you're a brave girl!' Anne said, astonished at hearing what she had done. She hugged

Clara who now could not stop the tears pouring down her cheeks. 'But how wonderful if he agrees! It had never struck me to ask him – how strange! Did your father ever mention it to you?'

'No.'

'You must tell him – or perhaps not, if it raises his hopes and Nat refuses.'

'No, that would be dreadful.'

'He'll be back soon. Wash your face and look normal.'

Clara composed herself and took Susannah out of her cradle to feed her. She was a good baby and did not cry much, merely chortling contentedly to herself when she was awake. (More like happy-go-lucky Martin than Nat!) To Clara, horse-oriented, she was still something of a nuisance, getting in the way of her work, and without Anne she would have found the business of motherhood insupportable. But when she came to handle the funny little thing in the tranquillity of her home, she was always overcome by the strange warmth of mother love, something she had never been able to conceive of before Susannah. It was as if the whole world melted away before the bonding of herself and the baby and nothing else was of any consequence. Very weird and rather unsettling, but a lovely feeling. It occurred to her then that the business of being made to tremble just by the smouldering look on Nat's face was Mother Nature's way of assaulting her senses, to push her into having a baby again. That was the whole business of nature, whether it was humans or animals. Falling in love was mere biology. So why, when she didn't love Nat at all, not like she loved Prosper, did his look make her feel so helpless? She could not understand this. She would never love Nat, even if he reprieved Jack. He wasn't kind like Prosper, or understanding and gorgeous like Prosper. Yet he made her feel for him, made her heart beat faster, her face flush up. Why? She wanted to ask Anne, who had known passionate love in her earlier life, but she did not dare confess to her these feelings. Charlotte might understand, or Jane. But she doubted it. She was sure Charlotte had never lain with anyone.

Nat did not come.

Clara had expected him but he did not come. Her father meanwhile was making plans for advertising a match between Rattler and Chignall's Linnet, and making a rough draft for an advertisement to put in the paper listing the places Rattler would visit to serve mares.

'I don't think you can travel Rattler yourself this year, with the littl'un still at your breast. Sim will have to take him.'

'Oh no, I want to go! Sim got so tired last year.'

'We can make the journeys shorter.'

'I want to go! I can wean the baby by then.'

'Well, there's time. We'll see. But you're sixteen now. It's time you behaved more like a lady. It's not women's work, seeing to a stallion's cavortings.'

'You know Rattler behaves better for me than anyone! Just my voice, he knows it. He needs me.'

'Come, Sim knows the horse as well as anyone. And I was thinking, Clara, that mare of Chignall's – if she goes well I wouldn't mind buying her. We could breed a few ourselves now we've got the stallion.'

'Oh, Father, she's ugly!'

'Yes, but, as a brood mare, she's got a great big backside on her, and heart room aplenty. That's what matters. Put her to a bit of quality – who knows? But we'll see her go first.'

'If she's as good as he says, she'll be a lot of money.'

'We'll beat her fair and square and talk to him afterwards.'

That her father was talking like this, emerging from his trough of despair, was a wonder to Clara. He was smiling, thinking ahead. There was a life besides Ellen, now the fear of her death had receded. Tales had come that transportation offered hope, at least, and the sun always shone in Australia. Some convicts made good, some saved enough money to come home.

The Garlands held on to the good stories. There was great sympathy in the village for them, and still hate and scorn for Nat Grover who had taken on his father's mantle in their eyes. If he were to forgive Jack, it would make his name more liked in the village; such a gesture would go a long way to change people's minds. Clara wished she could relay this good argument to him, but she did not meet him.

'There's a stranger coming up the drive,' Anne said to Clara. 'Anyone you know?'

Clara carried Susannah to the window and looked

out. A young man on a handsome hunter was just riding into the back yard.

'It's Gabriel Mayes.'

Clara tried to keep her voice calm, but Gabriel's arrival jolted the memory of Prosper with such pain that she almost cried out. Prosper had ridden into their yard like that on his mare, Cobweb, the last time she had seen him, before he departed to India. Gabriel was not unlike Prosper – the same easy seat in the saddle and lithe, slender figure – oh, if only! Clara felt creased with longing, seeing him. She had always supposed her love would fade, but it was harder now, remembering, than it had ever been. If only she could know it was the same for Prosper, remembering her!

'Perhaps he has news of their foals,' Anne said.

Clara gathered her wits together. 'Of course, that will be why he's come. Oh, good news, I hope!'

'He wouldn't have come if it wasn't.'

It was true. Gabriel had come with splendid news: their first colt by Rattler was big and active and well-made, and there was good news from another farm where he had visited, a good filly and even better colt, save the mare had died in the birthing of it.

'But it's being raised by a pony, along with her own. They've got her to take it. And the farmer's wife there is teaching it to take gruel from a bucket. They think the world of it. My father told me to let you have the news, so that you can bring Rattler back.'

'Good. We'll get his travelling arrangements put in the newspaper. We'll work it out tonight and get notices printed.'

'You'll make good money with him now he's proved.'

Sam and the men came in for their dinner and Gabriel stayed and Clara sat listening to the farm talk. Her father was well pleased with Gabriel's news and asked what Clara had not dared: 'And how's young Prosper doing in India? Have you news of him?'

'We get a letter now and then – twice since he's been gone. He was never one for sitting down with a pen. But yes, he seems happy – it's mostly about going on tiger hunts, not much about work.'

'Life here will seem very dull after that. Is he planning to come home, or make a life out there?'

'He doesn't say. It's too soon, I think. He only went because he thought there was nothing for him here.'

A deep disappointment settled on Clara at this statement. No message for her, no intimation that he had left his heart behind in her keeping. He had forgotten. How could she compete with tiger hunts?

They went on to talk about Ellen's transportation. She was still in Norwich gaol, waiting for shipment, and Gabriel said he had heard of prisoners making good and coming home when their time was done. Many people had told them this to cheer them up, but the stories were very vague. They had been unable to trace anybody who could produce a person who had come back. Anne had tried, but in vain.

They then discussed whether Gabriel might have the riding of Rattler in any forthcoming match, and he agreed to come over and see how he got on with riding him if a date for a match was made. Clara kept quiet about Jack. She thought now that Nat was going to ignore her plea. No doubt if he had discussed it with his mother he had been beaten down. She must keep her mind on her horses, forget Prosper, her plans for Jack, think of buying Linnet and engaging Gabriel as a rider. There was plenty to think of.

10

A servant from Grover's delivered a hand-written message to the door of Small Gains three days later. He asked to take an answer back.

Anne opened it and read, 'Nathaniel Grover would request the pleasure of the company of Mr and Mrs Samuel Garland and Mrs Clara Bywater to drink with him at seven-thirty tomorrow evening.'

She showed it to Clara. 'It must be about Jack. What else? But why the formality? Surely he could just have called in and said yes or no?'

'Very strange.' Clara was equally puzzled. 'Maybe it's because I said we all ought to be friends, instead of enemies. He wants to chat.'

'It's possible. We've hardly ever passed the time of day with him for all that he's our nearest neighbour.'

'We should get an answer at least. He can hardly ask us to drink with him and then say no, don't you think?' Clara felt her excitement rising. 'Surely it's to say yes, and we'll all drink to it?'

'Yes, that seems likely. He wants to make it a friendly gesture. We'll go, and we'll have to warn Sam what's brewing, what you've been up to.'

They both felt a rising excitement as the servant departed with the affirmative answer.

'Have we got to dress up? What in, for heaven's sake?'

'And who's going to look after Susannah?'

They got the giggles, trying to work out suitable clothes from their hopelessly empty wardrobes. It seemed impossible that Nat would summon them merely to put paid to their hopes, so optimism seemed justified. When Sam heard the story, he immediately caught the excitement.

'I don't believe it! Jack back! Clara, what have you been up to? You never said—'

'But steady on, don't count your chickens—' Anne warned.

'Well, what are we to drink to, if the answer's no? Drinks are for celebration. It's surely not to drink for telling us no, and sending us away with our tails between our legs?'

Her father was so excited at the thought of having Jack back that Clara was frightened for how a possible setback might affect him. Yet she could not see what Nat was up to, unless it was a friendly gesture. He had taken such a long time to come to a decision when it was such a simple thing, yes or no.

The next evening, they had their supper and then a good wash in the kitchen, and Clara went to find the best clothes she had, which were still her mother's cut-downs refurbished by Anne. Anne was a clever seamstress but even she could not disguise the old-fashioned lower waists and full skirts. Waists were now up under the bosom and skirts hung straight and narrow. Useless for a farmyard! Clara would rather have had a new riding habit than a new dress, and made do now with a straightish dark red skirt with a ruffle round the bottom and a blouse of Anne's with a front of cream lace. She unbraided her hair and brushed it out loose, then pinned it back from her face. She was too old now for loose hair but she knew Nat liked it that way, and it took too long to do up cleverly at the back with a few dangly bits round the ears, as was now fashionable. She would be at it all night.

'Much too pretty for Nat Grover,' her father growled at her.

'Well, we're clean, at least,' Anne said. She was not unhandsome herself, with her calm, upright carriage, smooth, pale complexion and shining brown hair pulled back in a chignon. They were a family not to be trifled with, Clara thought optimistically as they set off down the drive. She knew her parents were as nervous as she was. But no one spoke, save Sam remarking on his turnip crop coming through nicely, and they arrived at the Grovers' door at exactly seven-thirty. They chose the front door this time.

Sam pulled the bell handle. 'Well, here goes. For better or for worse.'

A maid in uniform let them in and they found themselves in the new-modelled hall, very spacious and airy with its white plaster fallals and little gilt chairs.

'I doubt they'd hold a full-grown man,' Sam

muttered as the maid went off to fetch Nat. 'It used to be a right cosy hall, this, with a fire burning and all dark panelled. It's a crime to turn it into this.'

'Hush, Sam. You're out of date. This is Mr Adams' work.'

'I'd sooner be in a stable.'

Clara got the giggles, but now Nat was coming to meet them across the wide space. He too was dressed in his evening best, which was far more impressive than anything they had managed. His cravat was high and severe under the collar of his black cutway jacket, set with a diamond pin, and his cream breeches and shining black evening boots were very fine, up to the squire's standard. Clara could feel her father thinking, He fancies himself, but she was so easily impressed: she felt her colour rising and her voice stumbling even as she bid him good evening.

Nat took them into the sitting room which was Mr Adams again, all white and pale blue and a carved marble mantelpiece which Clara could see her father eyeing, estimating the price as if it were a milch cow. Thank goodness there was no sign of the perpetrator of all this glory, Mrs Maggie Grover the ex-dairymaid, and they sat down, relieved, on the brocade-covered sofas with the little gold legs in front of the fire. There were more candles burning in the room, Clara noted, than the kitchen at Small Gains would use in a month.

A servant set down a decanter of port and a dish of little biscuits on the table beside them. Nat poured and handed the port and struck up an innocuous conversation about trotting matches with Sam. Clara was impressed with how easy her father seemed, not at all thrown by the grand surroundings, but talking solidly of famous sires, on home ground with the subject. Yet he must be dying to get to the point, Clara thought. She sat silently beside Anne, trying to be equally unfazed by the unaccustomed grandeur. Certainly their home was nothing like this, but it had a cosy welcoming air which this house lacked, for all its elegance. But perhaps, if they made some money by Rattler, they might aspire to some new furniture or a carpet?

Sam was talking about Chignall's Linnet, and the prospect of taking her on with Rattler.

'She's not a pretty beast, but she's well-made. I was saying to Clara, we could do with buying a mare of her sort, and perhaps breed some more of our own. Tilly's never come in foal but the once, in spite of running out with the stallion. And that was a poor beast she dropped. She's not cut out to be a brood mare.'

'I would like to see a match between your horse and Chignall's. She's very well spoken of.'

'We lack a rider, that's our problem. I think that's why Clara mentioned to you the possibility of getting our Jack back home.'

'Ah—' Nat's expression changed and an obvious nervousness showed in his face. 'I have been giving the matter my consideration. My family is against the idea of course, but Clara tells me I must show who is master here.' He gave a faint smile.

'Best to start how you mean to go on,' Sam remarked, as if the matter was of little consequence.

Clara felt herself squirming with impatience to hear a straight answer.

'I have come to a conclusion that may not be acceptable to you. That is the reason I have invited you here tonight, for it isn't a straight yes or no, and you will need to think on it.'

'So what is this conclusion?'

'I am asking you, Mr Garland, for Clara's hand in marriage in exchange for Jack coming freely back to Small Gains.'

Sam's composure was overtaken by such a sense of shock that his jaw literally dropped. Clara could not believe what she had heard. There was a complete silence in the room. The candles fluttered in a faint draught. Nat downed his port as if in relief that his words were out.

Then Anne said, 'Oh, my dear,' and reached out her hand to Clara's.

Nat was pale, and he turned away to hide his emotions. What they were, Clara could only guess at. He was surely not in love with her? How was that possible, when all their meetings had been so fraught and angry? Their first and only coupling had been a case of blackmail. He was using the same ploy again, blackmailing her. It had worked the first time and no doubt he thought it would work again. Not very original but, if he wanted her, devilishly clever.

'Your – our – child needs a father,' he now said to her.

'Oh!'

As if he cared! Or did he? She could not fathom

his feelings at all, seeing him now as an imposing, masterful land-owner, commanding the lower orders as his father had before him.

'You don't love me,' she said. 'How can you ask this?'

'I want you to think about it. I didn't expect an answer tonight. I just want you to know that, however you plead, I will not change my mind. It is a bargain if you like. It could be a good one for you, Clara, to be mistress here. Think about it.'

He poured more port and Sam reached for his glass gratefully.

'Aye, it'll need a deal o' thinking, I reckon.'

Clara saw that his hand was shaking. Her own head was reeling and she wanted to go, find some cold clear air to help her recover from the shock. Perhaps Nat too found it difficult to carry on with polite conversation after dropping his bombshell, for when Anne got up he called the servant to fetch their coats.

Anne said, 'We must take our leave. You have given us such a surprise we can only discuss it amongst ourselves now. I don't think any of us could chat politely about other matters, the shock you've given us.'

'No. I understand. But I look forward to hearing your answer. It means a great deal to me. Clara can call here at any time to discuss the proposal, if Mr Garland gives his permission.'

He looked at Clara in such a searching way then that she could not meet his eyes, and turned away to take her coat from the servant. He had not lost his power to make her feel trembly in that strange way, but she did not think that was truly love. Not like Prosper. Oh Prosper! she wanted to scream.

When they got out into the drive and the door was shut behind them, the cold evening air revived their shattered minds.

Sam said, 'He's not old enough to marry without his mother's permission and I can't see her giving it. She'll want better for him.'

'There's none better!'

'You know what I mean. To climb up, someone of Miss Charlotte's ilk.'

'If he loves Clara, he can wait until he's twenty-one, then his mother will have no say. The farm is his, after all. It's common knowledge that Grover left it to him in his will, not to his wife.'

'It's entailed to the eldest son. That's Philip, if he ever turns up again, which is unlikely. So if it's Nat's, it's a rich man asking for our Clara's hand. Do you want him, Clara, that's the question?'

'Do you want Jack back?'

'Oh my God, yes. Of course I want Jack back.'

'It seems then that it's decided for me,' Clara said.

Anne said fiercely, 'It's your life, for heaven's sake, Clara! It can't be decided in a moment, to do this for another's sake and not your own. Do you love him? Has something been brewing between you that we don't know about?'

'No! I lay with him that time to save Jack's life. That's the truth. And never again. I've hardly spoken to him since.'

'And did that coupling give you mind to love him?' Sam asked roughly.

Clara was silent. The true answer was yes, yet she could not bring herself to say it.

'You should not ask such a thing,' Anne said.

'She's of an age to marry,' Sam said. 'Who else is there round here save a village oaf? And she with the man's child already.'

'Are you making her mind up for her already?' Anne was angry now. 'What sort of a man is he, to be father to her children? He's no better than his father as far as we know, and that man was a tyrant. Is there any sign that Nat is kind and caring and fit to be Clara's husband? Clara is pure gold, Sam, and it's not for you to throw her away on a man not fit, Jack or no Jack.'

'She must make up her own mind,' Sam growled.

But Clara knew perfectly well that most marriages were decided by parents, rich and poor alike – although mostly rich. Well-born rich girls had little chance of marrying for love, being traded for money, estates or titles like cattle on the market. After her marriage to Nicholas, the only one she had ever thought of was to Prosper, and that was a pipe-dream. It was true that she was not easily marriageable any longer, with her baby daughter and her lack of domestic obedience. She was known as 'should've been a boy' all over the neighbourhood. Of course – so long ago now, it seemed – she was going to marry Jack's friend Martin but that had been a childish thing. But to marry Nat – it was something that for the moment she could not contemplate. It would have to sink in.

Anne said, 'We cannot make any decisions immediately. Even Nat understood that. So many things come into it. Let it settle, Sam. We must all sleep on it.'

But Clara knew that her fate was settled long before she laid her head on her pillow. She could not deny her own family its future, which was Jack. Small Gains desperately needed Jack, and her father above all. So she had no decision to make.

But to consider her future . . . her brain could scarcely embrace all it meant. In the stupidest way, the only thing she remembered before she fell into an exhausted sleep was: if I marry Nat, I will take charge of his gorgeous horse, Crocus.

11

'Clara, it can't be all bad. He's young and handsome and rich and you will still have your horses. And scarcely leave your family, just crossing the road.'

'But I love Prosper!'

'Prosper is never likely to come back. They don't, from India. They like it there, with all those servants and shooting big game and lots of women looking for husbands. Or they die. You have to be practical.'

Clara had met up with Charlotte out riding, which happened often and was how their friendship had ripened. Nat had not yet got his answer, yet the whole village seemed to know what was afoot.

'I must say, I wouldn't hesitate,' Charlotte said. 'You must know he showed an interest in me, but my father would not hear of it. He absolutely forbade me to see him. Of course Nat was only smelling out the ground, so to speak, to see if there was a possibility – our land adjoining, you see, so much to his advantage, and his mother so creepily wanting to better the family with links to my father. But he didn't love me, Clara. I think he truly loves you.'

'But he's not very nice, admit it.'

'Well, now his father's gone there's hope for him,

131

I'm sure. I know lots of girls who marry men they loathe, but they make a success of it. They have children, which is nice, and if there's plenty of money and you don't see much of your husband, it's quite all right. My eldest sister is marrying a man of sixty-four, can you believe? But he's got a title and an estate and she thinks it's wonderful. He's a widower and of course his children – they're grown up and waiting for his money – they're furious! She's got all that to contend with and she doesn't mind a bit. I think she's absolutely raving mad. But I suppose she's getting past her marrying age, twenty-five, and it's better than being left a spinster. Myself, I like being at home. I don't want to get married.'

'Anyone would love you, Charlotte, if you gave them a chance.'

'I get suitors but no one my mother approves of. She sends them all away. She wants me to marry Edmund.'

Lord Fairhall's son, Edmund, lived next door to the squire's acres and was definitely a sweetie, but only interested in his studies in Oxford and playing the organ.

'I couldn't love him though. I want to marry for love, but it's very unlikely. Like you and Prosper. Does he write to you?'

'No. I have to confess he doesn't. But he sent a message in a letter to his mother, to tell me not to forget him.'

'Oh, but if he can't be bothered to tell you himself – then you must forget him, Clara. He's such a charmer he's bound to be snapped up over there. And after all, you only knew him for a little while.'

'Yes, a week, when I stayed there. But it was so lovely, Charlotte! I will never forget it. How perfect he was, everything he liked and thought about – it was just like I thought myself, like we were sort of – of twins. You didn't have to say anything really. You were just together, like one person.'

'Were you one person? Did you?'

'No. No, we didn't. It didn't seem right somehow. Almost as if it might spoil it. I wonder, sometimes . . . I can't work things out. Prosper is very like Nicholas, you know, and sometimes I think Prosper is Nicholas as he should have been if he had stayed well. Maybe that's why I love him so, because I loved Nicholas.'

'I loved Nicholas too.'

'He wanted to marry you! He always told me I was only second best, after you.'

'I know. I told him I was too old for him. We did have jokes with Nicholas, didn't we? He was always so joky, right up till he died.'

Not at the end he wasn't, Clara thought, but did not say. Not when they got married, the day before he died.

'*He* wouldn't like me marrying Nat.'

'No. But you have no choice, have you? There's no way Nat'll let Jack come back if you refuse. He's too proud.'

'What about the mother-in-law I'll get? I've been thinking about it.'

Charlotte laughed. 'But the horse, Clara! Think of

Crocus. You must send the mother-in-law away. You can't live in the same house with the rest of the family. It wouldn't be possible. But it's your right to send them away. They all want to live in Norwich, anyway, so it won't be difficult.'

Clara was weary of turning all the arguments about in her head, especially as she knew she was going to agree to marry Nat. Part of her, quite naturally, could get excited at the thought of being rich, of having a carriage to drive, grooms to do the stable work, even nice clothes, but she could not get the thought of Prosper out of her head. Sometimes she wondered if she was just living a dream, that because he wasn't there she had turned him into some rosy hero on a pedestal. She hadn't seen enough of him to know about his worst nature. She thought he didn't have one, but how could she know?

Anne thought that they should get to know Nat a little better and asked him to supper.

'He'll have to get used to our humble ways if he's going to be one of the family,' she said plainly. 'Note that he hasn't asked us to eat with his family at his place. I daresay his mother won't allow it. In fact, I should think she's furious at this whole business.'

'Are we going to give him an answer at this supper then?' Sam asked.

'That's up to Clara.'

'Yes. It's yea or nay time, Clara. He needs to know.'

'You know I'm going to say yes,' Clara said.

She had known from the very moment his proposal had been made that she had no choice but to agree. She had brought it on herself with her plea to him for Jack's return. But how she felt about it . . . one moment she was excited, thinking of the new life that opened up before her, and the next in despair at abandoning her dream of Prosper. And how did she know whether Nat had lost the cruel ways his father had taught him? He was arrogant by nature and his father had ruled by physical abuse. Nat was used to a beating and in his turn used his whiplash out in the fields. It wasn't how things were run at Small Gains. If she stood up to him, he might use the same physical power over her. It was common enough in the village, wife-beating. But then she thought of Jack – dear, strong, shining Jack – and she knew that, whatever her fears for herself, she was bound to agree to the bargain and get him back.

'We need this business settled,' her father said. 'If Jack's to come back, he can travel Rattler for you, Clara. The time is ripe for the horse to be about his job.'

'I want to travel him!'

'If you're engaged to Nat, I doubt he'll agree to that.'

Clara wanted to scream. Anne shot her a warning look. 'You'll have to behave like a lady, Clara, if you're to be mistress of Grover's.'

Prosper wouldn't have wanted me to behave like a lady, Clara thought fiercely, remembering their race up the long hill behind his house. And was her father intending for Rattler to stay at Small Gains for Jack to travel and Jack to ride in his matches? It sounded like it. Yet Rattler was *hers*. There was so many things that enraged her about this bargain. Yet she had brought it on herself.

They made the kitchen look as neat as they could for Nat's supper party, and Sim and Bob went down to the Queen's Head to be out of the way and Susannah was put in a clean frock in her little wooden cradle and propped on her best embroidered pillow.

'If you leave for across the road, I'm certainly going to miss the little one,' Anne said sadly.

'I can bring her every day. And soon she'll have a pony and come herself.'

They put out double the candles than usual, and there was a joint of mutton, a bottle of port and a bottle of Anne's sloe gin as well as the ale. Clara dressed carefully for her 'intended', as she thought of him. She must surely get a clearer picture of him tonight. But she wasn't so cold-blooded that the sound of his horse's hooves in the yard didn't set her pulses racing again. God, he was lovely enough in most girls' eyes as an intended! Why did she have to have so many doubts?

And when he came in, she had another rush of emotion and it struck her with a blow that she was *lucky* – that the deal she had made was with such a handsome, attractive man, not an old lecher as it might have been. Suppose Ebenezer had lost his wife and suggested she married him in exchange for having Jack back? What would she have done then? The thought, so capricious, almost made her gasp. She knew lots of girls were forced into such marriages just in order to get some sort of a life. Oh, she was lucky! Could she not appreciate it?

But her feelings were so mixed that she could not join in any conversation at the table until the dinner was half over. It was only then, over Anne's marvellous spotted dick, that her father said, 'Well, I reckon you are due for your answer from Clara. She'll give it you now and we can make plans.'

Clara then looked up and did not miss an almost agonized expression on Nat's face as he turned to her.

'It's yes, of course,' she said.

And then was humbled to see how his face broke into such a joyful smile and she realized how different he looked, how rarely he had smiled in the past. His natural expression was always a scowl.

So she smiled back at him, and the bond was sealed.

Her father poured the lovely sloe gin into their best glasses.

'Here's to you both, and to our absent Jack!'

And Clara realized the deed was done, no more wondering and wishing and mooning over Prosper. Life was real, life was earnest, and she was to be married to the most handsome man in the county, married into riches and comfort.

'There are a few provisos,' she said.

'And on my side too,' Nat countered.

'Well, come, let's have them,' Sam said. 'We need a proper contract. Better now than recriminations later. A firm promise for Jack not to be prosecuted.'

'That is a promise. I shall say welcome to Jack.

What does Clara ask of me?' He looked worried.

'First, that I cannot live in your house with your family. Your mother hates me. Either we have another house or your family leaves.'

Nat smiled. 'That is not a problem. They are moving to Norwich. You must know that my mother and my family are very against our marriage, but no matter. We shall be well rid of each other.'

That was a great relief to hear. Clara wanted nothing to do with the rest of the Grovers.

'That's very good news. The second thing is my horses.' She looked challengingly at her father as she spoke. 'Rattler is mine and he will come with me. And you will not ride him in his matches,' she said to Nat. 'Gabriel Mayes is to ride him.'

There was a surprised pause round the table at her words. She wasn't sure herself what made her say this, but recognized a rather desperate ploy to keep in touch with Prosper's family. She knew Gabriel was a sympathetic rider, but so was Jack.

'Not Jack?' her father said.

Nat lifted his chin, aware of being found wanting. 'And you,' he said, 'will not be riding astride when you are married to me.'

'Oh!'

Anne said softly, 'You're not a child any more, Clara, and certainly not a boy. There are certain conventions you must keep.'

'I can't train Rattler riding side-saddle!'

Her father laughed. 'You'll have to train him in the dark, my dear, or out in the fields where no one can see you. Or a groom can train him. You'll have grooms now, Clara – think of it!' Sam had drunk plenty and could not see any problems. 'And as for Rattler; your property, such as it is, becomes Nat's when you marry. It's the only dowry you'll be taking.'

'Rattler is *mine*! Nat must understand that!'

With the drink and her sudden fury, Clara's eyes spat fire. Nat looked at her and laughed and she remembered suddenly his taunting her, holding her back from kicking and scratching and saying that was what he loved about her: her fiery spirit. She almost sobbed: 'He must never be sold, never! You must promise that, Nat! He is *my* horse!'

'You love him better than me,' Nat was laughing. 'Calm down, I will never sell him, agreed. You may ride him – side-saddle – whenever you like. And you may ride my Crocus too, if that will give you pleasure.'

'Yes, that will please me.' Clara had to give in, but not with good grace. The thought of not bombing through the lanes astride Rattler was a great blow. To do the long distances side-saddle would be sure to damage his back. She knew Prosper would never have stopped her riding the way she wanted to.

'It's a good thing Nat will be taking you in hand, Clara,' Anne said, smiling. 'It's not too severe, what he's asking. You can't imagine Sir James allowing Charlotte to ride astride.'

Clara did not argue, but resolved to ride Rattler astride when Nat was away, or at night-time.

To show her spirit was not cowed, she then said,

'And I don't want babies all the time. I've my own life to live.'

This stopped them all in their stride.

'Clara!' Anne was shocked. 'What a thing to say! For a young woman – what is marriage for?'

Clara wanted to point out that Anne had had no babies, but held her tongue.

Nat said, not laughing any more, 'I want a son, Clara. That is my right.'

Sam growled at her, 'You'll do your duty by your marriage, my girl. Any man would expect that.'

Nat said evenly, 'We can withdraw from this arrangement if you wish. This meeting is to thresh such things out. If we don't agree, we can part and forget it.'

'The lass has no right to make a stand like that!' Sam said roughly. 'It's as Anne says, marriage is a duty. Children are what it's for. You're no daughter of mine if you speak in such an unnatural way.'

'I just mean not dozens, like the Ramseys.' She was fertile enough, if one coupling with Nat had produced Susannah. 'Not every year, for ever.'

She had hated the burden of her pregnancy, stopping her agility. She was haunted by Mrs Mayes's words to her, that having her first child at sixteen was the biggest mistake she ever made. She had made that mistake already and knew that, much as she loved Susannah, she was not a doting mother.

'I don't want dozens, but a few, yes,' Nat said.

'You'll get what God chooses to send you, no doubt,' Sam said. 'So enough of your silly talk, Clara.'

140

Clara shrugged. 'Very well.' She knew she had no choice. She would ask Jane if she knew the tricks for not getting pregnant. Jane was up to that sort of thing. It struck her suddenly that she could bring Jane into her employment, which made her spirits rise again. Marrying Nat would bring new powers. Now the idea was in her head, it seemed to improve along with her commitment.

'I will be a good wife to you,' she said meekly.

Anne gave her an oblique look, wary, but Sam reached for the bottle of port and said, 'Good girl! We'll drink to that then, and call the evening a success. And with your permission, sir, we'll send for Jack to come home?'

'If Clara's promise is given, yes.'

'Clara?'

'Yes, I will marry you.'

She could not miss the look on Nat's face at her words, as if he had just received the most desired but dangerous present. It made her laugh. Maybe it would help to have another glass of port herself.

When Nat departed, Clara went out with him to fetch Crocus. It was a soft spring night with a heavy dewfall and a canopy of stars streaming across the sky, and as they crossed the yard Nat took Clara's hand and pulled her to a standstill.

'I am so happy – I can't tell you!' he whispered.

She saw his face with the moonlight shining on it, hesitant, anguished.

'I do so want you to love me.'

She did not know whether to be moved, indignant

or heartbroken. Nothing about this betrothal made any sense to her feelings which remained pulled in all directions. But she could struggle no more. When he bent to kiss her she offered herself demurely, lifting her head and putting her arms round him.

'I will do my best, I promise.'

And to her relief he kissed her gently, tenderly, with nothing like the passion she had once witnessed between him and her sister Margaret. Perhaps in this arrogant boy there were hidden depths of tenderness and consideration that she could discover. Who could tell? She had given in now; she had to be optimistic.

At least with the marriage would come the horse, the lovely Crocus. And she laughed to herself when they went away down the drive, to think that she was more happy to be marrying Nat because of his horse, than for any other reason.

12

Dearest Clara,

You will think me remiss in not writing to you before this, but all I can say is that I have been thinking about you all the time, so much so that I feel sure you have been aware of my feelings all across those miles of rolling ocean, all my thoughts sailing towards you filling the clouds overhead. Do you remember when we raced up the Summer hill at home and lay by the trout stream the day before you left? I think of you all the time. I long to see you again.

Your loving Prosper.

'Huh! What sort of a letter is that?'

Jane flung the dog-eared sheet down on the kitchen table.

'Clara, you are mad to go on thinking about him! To marry Nat and be a rich lady is the biggest stroke of luck in the world. Now that Ebenezer's gone, and his awful family, you have that lovely place all to yourself and Nat will surely turn into a perfectly reasonable husband without his father on his back all the time.'

'The letter came the day after I promised Nat,'

Clara groaned. 'I cannot go back on Nat. But how do you think I feel?'

'Prosper should never have written this rubbish. He's totally irresponsible. He makes no advance to you. He just wants to keep you hanging in there.'

'It's beautiful. It's a lovely letter!'

'You should burn it.'

'Never! I love him!'

'Clara, I never thought you to be so stupid. Jack is coming back – that is what you wanted, isn't it? Everything is panning out in your favour and you moon about like a twelve-year-old over a boy you scarcely know.'

Everything Jane said made sense, but Clara could not acknowledge it. Clara had shown the letter to no one else, not even to Anne, the only person who had witnessed Prosper's love for her. She knew perfectly well that to go on maundering over Prosper was stupid. Perhaps she had made a mistake in telling Jane that she would employ her at Grover's after the wedding, for the prospect had cheered Jane enormously. Jane couldn't wait for her to get married. She was always asking when.

'We have to wait a decent interval after Ebenezer's death. Six months at least. And then there's Ellen . . .'

Clara found it hard to speak of Ellen, who was still in Norwich Castle gaol waiting for her transportation. Anne visited her at frequent intervals, but she would not take Clara with her and Clara was ashamed to feel glad of this arrangement.

'We can't make a date. We don't know when Ellen

will go, and if we make a date it might get mixed up with Ellen's going and us saying goodbye, which is going to be terrible – you can see that.'

Jane sighed. She longed to exchange the miserable miller's abode for what promised to be a fantastic job at Grover's. She had heard enough gossip about the situation, waiting on the miller's wife, to make her head whirl. The whole village was agog at the way things had turned out and was taking sides as to the pros and cons of Clara marrying Nat. The inevitability of it was obvious, given the circumstances, but they could only guess at Clara's feelings. They were not to know that Clara's feelings were as muddled as their guesses.

'I want time to myself to think it out. I'm not in a hurry.'

'You can't back out!'

'No. I've given my word. Jack is coming home.'

'And Martin?'

'No. Martin is staying. He's got a Cornish girl now and has forgotten me, thank goodness.'

'That's lucky for you. He wanted to marry you before he went.'

'Yes, well, I didn't want to marry him, so at least there's no tears shed there.'

When Jack came home, Clara felt better about the whole thing. The joy in her father's face, the sight of dear Jack again, so strong and as full of life and fun as he had always been . . . her doubts evaporated. Whatever her future with Nat there was no way she could have denied the happiness that suddenly engulfed their home. He jumped down off the mailcoach outside the Queen's Head; his bundle of belongings was thrown down after him, the mail exchanged and the coach was off with scarcely a halt, leaving an ecstatic group hugging and kissing in the stable yard, with Jack's old drinking pals cheering in the background and nosy village women pressing in to welcome 'our little Jack' back to the fold. It seemed then to Clara that the village was family, and she a part of it. It would not be like that when she was the mistress of Grover's.

They went home, and over dinner Jack heard all about Ellen and her fate, and the gloom descended as always. Clara felt a familiar resentment dragging down her own happiness – first Margaret's long descent into death and now Ellen's awful future – as if her own well-being was shackled to these disasters and her spirits sucked dry by her sisters' tragedies. And then the equally familiar shame at such selfish feelings. She stood up, rattling the empty plates.

'Jack, come and see the horses! You won't know Rattler after a year, and now he's due to travel as a stallion again – I've got him so fit – he looks fantastic!'

Jack grinned. 'Still riding astride like the devil – I know you! Nothing's changed. Come on, show me your darling.'

And then Clara felt all her doubts dispelled as she went down through the fields with Jack, just as if he had never been away. He was the same Jack, laughing as always, his pure strength seeming to dwarf all around him: lean and agile with his mop of blond hair and bright blue eyes, just like Margaret, just like their mother. No wonder their father loved him so!

'We've been promised a match with Chignall's Linnet – that's a mare, very well thought of. We went to see Chignall and have got to arrange a date. Father's got a mind to buy her, but I think she's an ugly thing. He says we should have our own mares and breed a few, but it depends how much she'll cost. A good deal, especially if she goes well in the match. She won't beat Rattler though, that's sure.'

'I hope I haven't got to ride Rattler. I haven't ridden since I left home. I'll never sit down for a week if you make me ride.'

'I asked Gabriel Mayes to ride. I didn't know, then, that you'd be coming home. And I don't want Nat – he's too harsh with them.'

'Oh, Nat! Are you sure you're doing the right thing, Clara, saving me at your own expense?'

'It's for Father, you know that. And yes, I can't back out now. I will make a go of it. It will be all right. Nat has mellowed since his father's death.'

She had no real evidence of this, for Nat was still known as a hard task-master by his employees. She saw little of him, for he was much occupied with getting his mother and siblings moved to Norwich, besides the heavy work on a spring farm. Only he could work the mechanical drill, and with the weather ripe for sowing he was slaving all day long.

'I don't know about Nat mellowing, but I know I've mellowed, Clara. We should buy a drill and a threshing machine. Since working in that damned tin mine I'm all in favour of labour-saving. The more machinery can help us the better.'

'Jack!' Clara could scarcely believe his change of mind. Less than a year ago, he set fire to Grover's threshing machine to make a stand for the poor workers it was replacing.

'Yes, you can laugh at me. But I've learned a bit of sense working down in Cornwall. There's more jobs now in making the machinery – that's where the future lies, in industry. You know yourself how poor we farmers are down here compared with the workers up north where all the factories are. That's where the money is, up north.'

'You don't want to work in a factory, surely?'

'No. I want to be here, on the farm. But, believe me, I've changed my mind about the use of machinery. Nothing would give me more pleasure than to see a threshing machine here in our barn.'

Clara found his change of heart hard to take in, but knew that her father had called him a young idiot for joining the machine-breakers. Her father had been envious of Grover's machinery.

'I want to make this place as good as Grover's, Clara. If Rattler's going to make money this season, could you see your way to lending it to Father to set this place on its feet? I know it's your horse, your money, but we could pay you back in time. And if you marry Nat you'll be more than well provided for. You won't need money.'

Jack's conversation was knocking Clara sideways.

In his year away he seemed to have grown five. He had always been full of ideas and ambitions, but now instead of being wild they seemed to have sense behind them.

'Yes, you can have Rattler's money, apart from enough to buy our first mare. Chignall might want a packet for Linnet, but I want a mare, Jack, and so does Father. But if this season goes well and we win a match or two, we should be able to put some aside.'

Clara laughed. It was wonderful to be with Jack again, leaning over the gate and looking down the bright water meadows to where their horses were grazing: Rattler and old Tilly, who now kept close to him and squealed with rage if they were parted; her runty son Good Fortune and dear old Hoppy.

'The mare's showing her age at last.'

'Yes. For all she runs out with Rattler now, she's never got in foal again.'

But when they visited Hugh Chignall again to arrange the match and make an offer to buy his mare if she turned out as good as he had boasted, he said she was sold. He wouldn't say who had bought her, but laughed.

'You're too late, mate. I got my price from a generous gentleman. Too good to turn down. So there'll be no match, I'm afraid.'

Sam swore.

'Is she still in the county?'

'No. She's gone up to Yorkshire.'

Sam went home annoyed, and Anne told him she had news that Ellen was leaving for Australia in three days' time, on the ship *Queen Eleanor* from King's Lynn. They were to go and see her depart.

*   *   *

Clara did not go to see her off. Her parents went, and Jack. They travelled to King's Lynn on the public coach and Clara was left with Susannah. The family misery blanked out the beauty of the May morning. Even Susannah's charm and her engaging new smile could not lift Clara as she sat at the kitchen table thinking of Ellen's awful fate, re-reading Prosper's note and brooding over her future. She tried to think of the good things: Ellen was not to hang, Jack was back, Prosper had not forgotten her, but she knew it would take several weeks for the shock of Ellen's departure to lift and for life to return to normal. It was like a death, really, with no expectation of their ever seeing her again. Now the moment had arrived, Clara could not stop herself grieving.

'Your auntie Ellen, you will never know her,' she said to her baby, but Susannah only smiled.

Clara was surprised to hear horse's hooves in the yard and, terrified it might be Nat finding her alone, she shrank behind the window, peering out between Anne's pots of herbs. But it was Gabriel Mayes.

She ran to the door, pleased, her cares lifting suddenly.

He swung down from his horse, smiling. 'I'm glad to find you at home, not out riding. You're well, I hope?'

'Oh yes.' Clara explained the family situation and Gabriel was full of sympathy. Clara brought out a jug of ale and he sat with her talking, telling her all the good things he could think of about living in Australia, which weren't many.

'But there, Prosper went to India of his own volition, and that is even hotter and nastier from what I know. He might have to come home again, as our mother is not well and seems to think she's not long to be with us. She wants to see him. We tell her she's fine and leave the boy alone, but she seems to be in a decline. She's lost her spirit. We all know Prosper was her darling, her last baby, so perhaps his going has had this effect.'

He took a swig of ale. 'But that's not what I came about. I came to see when you're bringing your fine horse over our way again, for everyone wants to use his services again, his foals are so fine. Has word not got to you?'

'We made the dates for this week, but then we got word about Ellen which upset our plans. But yes, as soon as he gets home, Jack will bring him.'

'And his match with Chignall's Linnet? We've heard no more.'

'Chignall's sold her! He won't say where. So that's no go.'

'That's a pity. But there's a few out our way will challenge him. Ralph Herbert has a new horse he's very hopeful about, says he'd like to try him against a good 'un, to see how he compares. And there's his famous Red Emperor – he's sound again now and the ground is right for him and he's ready to wager him. Hunting's over for the year and we're all ready for a bit of fun. So I came to see how the land lies.'

Gabriel was the tonic Clara craved. The news that Prosper might come home again whirled round in her head even as she discussed plans for Rattler. Yes, Jack would take him on his round of stallion duties and as soon as these were completed he would take on any comers.

'And do I still have the ride, or will Jack take it?'

'No. Jack doesn't want to. You will ride.'

'Good. I must come over and try him out. See how we suit each other.'

'You can take him now, if you wish. I can't ride him today, with no one to look after Susannah. Oh yes, do!'

Gabriel was only too pleased and the wretched day for Clara was suddenly transformed. The sky was cloudless, the breeze soft as a caress, the mating birds singing their heads off in the flowering hedgerows. Even Ellen on her ship would have a fair breeze and calm seas. They saddled Rattler, and Gabriel departed away across the fields at the famous trot, sitting like an angel and giving Rattler all the confidence and sympathy that Clara could wish for. Did all the Mayes boys ride as well as Prosper? It seemed so, for Clara could not fault Gabriel.

Poor declining Mrs Mayes certainly bred good stock. At the back of her mind Clara could not forget Gabriel's news of Prosper's possible return. She stood out in the driveway with Susannah on her hip, watching Rattler's huge backside powering away into the distance, all her black thoughts dissolving as fast as Rattler's hooves hit the ground.

13

Clara shivered with excitement at seeing Nat's horse, Crocus, waiting for her in the driveway, wearing a side-saddle. He was led by Nat from the hunter he rarely rode.

'All yours for the day! Don't be afraid, he's been schooled in side-saddle for the last two weeks.'

Jack, riding Rattler, laughed at Clara's expression. The three of them were to ride together to the Mayes' farm, where Rattler was to be matched with Red Emperor. Clara was not allowed to deliver Rattler herself as in the past. She was an affianced young lady, and must ride side-saddle in a habit with hat and gloves. But for the opportunity to ride Crocus, she was not complaining.

'How fine he looks,' she said to Nat.

'You will marry me for my horse, I've heard it said.' But Nat was laughing.

'Yes, and you me for mine.'

'No, for you alone, Clara.' This time not laughing. He gave her a bunk up into the side-saddle and she took up the reins reverently. She adored Nat's horse Crocus, a little chestnut trotter with a thoroughbred head and shy, sensitive manners that went strangely with his brave heart. He was nothing like Rattler. She had never ridden him before.

Anne and Sam and the baby, and one-armed Billy, had gone on ahead in the cart pulled by Hoppy, but the three of them soon caught up and passed them, flourishing their whips. Rattler and Crocus trotted side by side, powering down the dusty road, and Nat had to canter fast on his hunter to keep up. Then Jack pulled Rattler back to half-speed to preserve his energy for his race and they progressed in a more seemly fashion. Clara loved the feel of Crocus, smoother than Rattler and very sensitive in the mouth, more so than Rattler, which was surprising considering the wear and tear of Nat's heavy hands on the reins. It was carefree and fun, suddenly, the three of them riding together like good friends with none of the old aggression souring the atmosphere.

'We can make a date for our wedding, Clara, now the business with Ellen is settled,' Nat said to her.

And Clara did not disagree. The business hung over her and the sooner it was settled, the better her head would feel. She had promised. There was no getting round it, whether Prosper came home or not. Seeing Jack laughing on Rattler was a great consolation, and seeing her father's cheerful face at the imminence of the match.

'Before harvest time,' Nat suggested.

'Yes, we'll make a date. Here, in the village I want it, just simple.'

'Yes. No cathedrals.'

'No angelic choirs!' But no bridesmaid either – how Ellen would have loved that!

Clara smiled at Nat and could not help but agree with Jane's estimation: she was lucky to have such a rich and handsome suitor. Her feelings for him were uncertain. But for Prosper, she would have loved him. However with a date fixed, her head would clear and she would find sense at last. It warmed her to see Jack and Nat together, laughing, as if they were old friends. If only her marriage could unite the two families and all the warring be over, that would be worth any sacrifice on her part.

When they arrived at the Brewer's Arms, the inn near to Great Meadows, there was a great gathering already, the ale flowing, money changing hands, riders and carts converging from all directions. The match was to take place up to the turnpike and along it as far as the next post-house, the White Hart, and back the same way. Their adversary, Red Emperor, was holding court on the green outside the inn, and Clara could not help but admire him as she rode up on Crocus. He was of the same stamp as Rattler, powerful and slightly coarse, a dark chestnut with no white on him. He had a very patient air, unlike Rattler. His rider was his owner, a middle-aged farmer who doffed his hat to Clara and Jack, his eyes running critically over their horses.

'Great to have this opportunity, ma'am, to see if my old horse still has the power to keep up with a young 'un. He's nearly had his day now, like your old Tilly, but he won his last two matches. His will is as strong as ever.'

Clara could see that, by riding Crocus, she was setting all the gossip aflame once more, advertising her liaison with Nat. How they all stared and whispered! And Jack was eagerly pointed out, back from the far side of the moon by their reckoning. Clara suddenly thought, with impatience, that maybe Ellen's lot was not so dreadful, to take a chance in a wider world. And not so strange, that Prosper had chosen to go to India.

Gabriel was there waiting for his ride, along with his father and several brothers, all welcoming and optimistic. Clara got down from Crocus, not intending to forgo her usual job of checking Rattler's tack all in order, seeing his rider into the saddle and leading him to the start. Gabriel had practised him along the road they were to ride now, and was confident of beating Red Emperor.

'But don't take anything for granted!' Clara warned him.

She was as nervous now as always. Little Billy held Crocus for her. Sam and Nat went to lay their money on and Jack went for a drink. There was the usual fairground atmosphere, everyone out for a good day, a great posse of riders barging around ready to ride behind until the racing pair were out of sight. Even the blood horses at a gallop couldn't keep up with the trotters after a few miles but they enjoyed trying, or having private races on their own. A match day was a holiday, almost as good as the harvest horkey.

'Hold back! Hold back! Don't crowd them!' shouted the stewards.

Ralph Herbert lined Red Emperor up beside the inn sign and Rattler joined him, knowing that it was a race, prancing on his hind legs. But Red Emperor stood placidly. Gabriel held Rattler with difficulty.

The starter dropped his flag. Rattler strode away and Red Emperor, to Clara's surprise, went with him from his quiet standstill, straight into a long, practised trot.

'He's a good 'un, Clara,' her father said. 'I might lose my money.'

'I hope not!'

'Maybe he'll tire. But he knows his job.'

'At twenty, Rattler will know his.'

Clara could not bear to be beaten. They had nothing to do now but wait out the whole twenty miles, about an hour.

'Shall we ride out and meet them?' Nat suggested, when half the time was gone. 'You could turn and keep up with them on Crocus for the last few miles.'

They left the crowd and set off down the road, not in a hurry. Clara felt Nat's eyes on her. She had avoided being alone with him and he had never pressed her, not even tried to court her as would have been his right. In spite of being glad of this, such tact rather surprised Clara, even made her wonder how she would feel if he kissed her. At just seventeen she knew she should be into marriage by now. They would make the date before the day was over.

The road was busy with people coming out to watch from neighbouring houses, and there was much toing and froing. Nat consulted a gold watch at his waist pocket and said, 'They're about due by now. Let's pull in here.'

They could hear shouting and cheering and in a few minutes the two horses came in view together, scarcely a length between them.

'I knew it was going to be close,' Clara whispered, agonized. She had hoped Rattler would be well ahead.

'He's leading.'

'But look how steady Emperor goes! He doesn't look tired.'

'Nor does Rattler.'

As they approached, Crocus pranced beneath her, knowing a match when he saw one, his neck breaking out in sweat. Clara soothed him. As they came past, Gabriel saluted her, grinning anxiously, and Clara let Crocus into an eager trot behind them, not close but to keep them well in sight. He went so smoothly: she was distracted for a moment into admiring him yet again instead of watching Rattler. She thought he wasn't going quite level – had he picked up a stone? What devil's luck if so. But perhaps it was her fevered imagination – he must win! Perhaps Gabriel was keeping something back for the finish. He was an intelligent rider, more so than Jack if the truth be told. Oh, if only she had been able to ride! She knew Rattler's every heartbeat, his very breath, his mind.

Crocus swept her along, keeping a steady distance, and the throng ahead of them thickened as the end of the race came nearer. A mile to go and the two horses were side by side. If their riders had any breath left they could have carried on a conversation without trouble. Now Clara could see the Brewer's Arms on the road in the distance and the huge crowd waiting on the green.

'Oh Gabriel!' she breathed.

Involuntarily, she lengthened Crocus's stride so that he, a fresh horse who was good enough to have won this race himself, started to catch up. Then, as the cheering started to echo across the fields, she saw Rattler start to inch ahead, just a little at first and then, as if lifted by the cheers, he powered on and left Red Emperor clean behind. His tail whirled, clods and stones flew, and he raced to the line several lengths clear.

Pandemonium broke out. Clara gleefully sent Crocus on, cheering at the top of her voice, and reached the finish at the same time as Emperor. She thrust Crocus through the crowd and slid from the saddle. Gabriel jumped down and she embraced him.

'Wonderful! Wonderful! How well you rode!'

She flung her arms round Rattler's neck and he covered her habit with a great snort of froth, nuzzling her affectionately. He was not sweating at all, but excited, triumphant. He knew.

'My wonderful horse, my treasure! I love you!'

She buried her face in his mane, trying not to cry. She couldn't remember ever being so happy, to have 'made' this wonderful horse all by herself, from a foal, when she saw his stride as a baby. He had never let her down.

Mr Herbert slid regretfully, stiffly, from Emperor's saddle and put his arm round her shoulders.

'You've a splendid beast there, my dear. Well done.'

'But your horse ran him so close! He's great for an old fellow. You must be proud.'

'Aye, I would not swap him.'

Clara put up her arm to stroke Emperor's damp neck. He knew he had been beaten. She could see the look in his eye and her heart was sad for him.

'It was a great match. They were very equal.'

Billy walked Rattler round to cool him off while Clara joined in the celebrations. Her father and Jack were ecstatic. Gabriel was thrilled with his first success and most of his brothers and his father were there to have a drink with him. As they stood chatting, Nat put his arm round Clara in a proprietorial fashion. She introduced him to the Mayes family.

'I think you all know Nat. We're to be married soon.'

They raised their glasses to him but Clara saw no joy on their faces. No doubt they knew all the gossip and the reason for the marriage and one of them said, 'You're a lucky man, Mr Grover, to capture Clara.'

'I think so too,' Nat said smoothly.

There was a short silence. Were they all thinking of Prosper?

Clara broke it by saying, 'Gabriel tells us Mrs Mayes is not very well. It's not serious, I hope?'

Mr Mayes said, 'Aye, she's gone into a gloom since Prosper left. She says she's not ill. She won't see the doctor, so what can we do about it? It's a woman's thing no doubt, and she'll come out of it sooner or later.'

They rode home as they had come, with Jack on Rattler who showed no sign of having already covered forty miles, half of them at full speed. Clara could not keep her proud eyes off him. *Her* horse! Nat must never forget that.

14

Nat would not wait until after the harvest.

'Six months is long enough to respect my father. June or July is the time for a wedding.'

'Oh come, what if the hay isn't in?' Jack said. 'No one can waste a day even for a wedding if the weather's right. You've got to keep June clear and most of July in case it's bad.'

'The end of July then.'

'In the village church,' said Clara. 'And make sure Edmund is around to play the organ. And that Sir James isn't away, and Charlotte. I want them to come.'

'What, and the mother and sisters too!' Jack laughed.

'No fear! Only them.'

'You won't get many of my family, you'll be pleased to hear,' Nat said. 'My mother is totally opposed to the idea and none of my uncles will come. But I'm of age. It doesn't matter.'

Nat rarely came across to Small Gains, being wholly preoccupied with running his large farm. Like his father, Nat was overseer rather than worker, apart from drilling with the machine. He kept his large gang of villagers hard at the job. Sam Garland would not employ children nor women save at harvest time, but had a few loyal men who probably did as much work as Nat's raggle-taggle bunch in the same time. Although Nat was easier than his father, there was still a strong resistance in the village to the Grover name, and Nat could not help but be steeped in Grover ways. As Clara got to know him better she saw that the ingrained sense of superiority was still there, along with its disregard for his workers' problems, sorrows and inadequacies. He sacked poor women if they were ill, bullied his little boys, expecting men's work from them, and would strike a man across the back with his whip if he was malingering.

'It's the only way he knows,' Sam said. 'You'll have to teach him better, Clara.'

But Anne said, 'You can't change a person's nature, just by marrying them.'

Clara knew that her family was partly against the marriage but would not renege from a promise. For herself, she felt strangely uncertain, unable to resist the attraction of Nat's presence, yet unsure of being able to love such a nature. They were scarcely ever alone together for which she was grateful, for she did not know how she would respond if he were to make advances to her. She made a determined effort not to think of Prosper, for she knew only too well how she would respond to him: with all her heart and soul and senses, beyond reason.

The days to July passed quickly. Susannah sat up in her cradle and laughed and played with the toys they made her: a stuffed doll with knitted clothes, a clean-picked pair of sheep bones tied together to rattle, a wooden box with wooden clothes pegs to put in and out . . . she was a contented, perfect child. All the same, Clara dreaded having another child now that she was active and thin again. Much as she loved Susannah, she recognized that hers was not a maternal nature. She would rather care for her horses than a baby.

'Jane will look after her,' she told Anne. 'She can bring her down to you every day so you will not miss her.'

'While you ride out on your horses?' Anne sighed. 'You're a funny one, Clara. Perhaps Nat will have other ideas.'

'What will he want me to do? Embroidery? Play the piano? He knows he cannot tame me to indoor things.'

'You will have a large house to run.'

'He has a housekeeper.' Clara was dismissive.

Anne could not help but show she worried about Clara's future.

'It's give and take, you know. I don't think it will pay you to oppose Nat. We know only too well his Grover nature. Don't be headstrong, Clara. You will not win against Nat.'

'He's supposed to love me!'

'If you please him.'

'I cannot change how I am.'

That makes two of them, Anne thought, not happily. Charlotte was determined that Clara should be the bride of the year in their small community, and produced a very beautiful, expensive wedding dress which she got from a friend.

'It's exactly your size, Clara. You will look fantastic in this. It's a gift. My friend wants it out of her sight.'

'Why?'

'She was jilted, three days before the wedding.'

Clara was shocked. 'It must be unlucky! How can I wear it?'

'Oh, surely you're not superstitious? This lovely dress yearns for someone to wear it. What would you do – throw it out with the rubbish?'

Even Clara could see this was stupid. She had been going to wear a dress Anne was planning to make, but Anne could never make anything as lovely as this: a sheath of satin and lace all set with tiny beads in flower shapes. It fitted her to perfection, reaching to an inch off the ground.

'And these little satin shoes to go with it. Do they fit?'

'I don't believe it! Nat will faint at the altar when he sees me.'

'Well, you know he will look lovely too. He's a very smart dresser. He has a manservant who used to work in London. He does hair and everything.'

'Perhaps I can borrow him!'

'No. I have a maid for hair. She will do yours beautifully.'

'Oh Charlotte! I can't believe this is happening to me! I would rather stay here as I am really – and yet, you know, the thought of being rich, having that big house, a carriage – I'm not such a bumpkin that it does not excite me a little bit.'

'You'd be unnatural if it didn't, don't be stupid! And Nat too, of course.'

Clara wasn't sure whether she detected a touch of envy in Charlotte's voice.

'I'm not sure about Nat.'

'How could you be? How can anyone be?'

The weeks went past, full of work. Rattler served half the county's mares and was challenged to another match when the harvest was over. Clara put the money on one side, amazed at how the little pot was filling. A good stallion could certainly make money. Rattler's name was already known all over East Anglia. Then the hay harvest was in, a good one and not too late, and the next date for the village was the wedding.

Charlotte, to Clara's amazement, volunteered to be a bridesmaid. Clara would never have dared ask her. So they asked Jane too, and Charlotte's dress-maker made their dresses, both in the same shape as the wedding dress, but simpler, in peach-coloured silk.

'We're not going to steal your thunder. No jewels, no fripperies. What is Nat going to buy you for your wedding present? Diamonds, I hope.'

'Don't be silly! Why should he buy me a present? He's getting me.'

'It's usual, to give your bride a present.'

Clara didn't know any of these things. When Jane managed to scrounge an afternoon off, the three of them had a very giggly time trying on their dresses and experimenting with hair styles. Jane was very dark, almost swarthy, and Charlotte had a mass of beautiful soft golden curls which she could make into the most fashionable style without any trouble. Fashionable hair was very complicated. Clara despaired of hers. It was thick and more frizzy than curly but – when washed clean of the stable dust – shone with reddish lights, dark and glossy.

Charlotte said, 'I will bring my hairdresser when we come to dress, and she can do us all. We must start in plenty of time.'

The day before the wedding, Clara got everything ready. There was to be a reception in the garden at Grover's and Nat's cook had taken on the job of making a wedding feast for what was expected to be the whole village. Everyone was invited. The weather was warm and steady and the tables were set out with benches as for the harvest supper, with just one fine table for the family and important guests – the squire and Lord Fairhall and his son Edmund and the poor old Rev Bywater who was determined to take the service in spite of his frailty. He had already married Clara to his son Nicholas scarcely a year before. Clara could not believe how quickly her life was moving.

In the evening, having talked to the cook and servants she would shortly be in charge of, she walked out into the garden at the front of the house to look around at the trestle tables and benches all set ready on a finely scythed grass sward. Beds of roses were in tumbled bloom on either side and some finely-clipped yews hid the garden from the road. Clara had never been there before, and sat down on a bench that was a permanent feature with a bower of roses trained over the top of it. It was very elegant, no doubt a whim of Mrs Grover – the *dowager* Mrs Grover, as from tomorrow. Clara smiled. Clara Grover. Not a pretty name. Only seventeen, and it would be her third name. Clara Garland, Clara Bywater, Clara Grover. Then . . . Clara Mayes, she whispered. If only! That was the nicest name of all.

The scent of the roses, funny blooms striped in red and white, and a lovely mauvy-pink one that drooped over her head, was soothing and delicious. They had no garden at Small Gains, only the orchard where they sat out on the rare occasions when they had nothing to do. Perhaps she would sit here with nothing to do: there were grooms in the stables who would do all the chores she was so used to. Her rough hands would grow white and smooth. Was it possible? The sun was going down over the woods behind their farm and the yews cast long shadows across the lawn. A thrush was singing, a dog barked in the village, otherwise all was silent. I am happy, Clara convinced herself. It is not like leaving home; I am still close to all the people I love. I am still part of my home farm. I am not going away, like poor Ellen. They would think of Ellen tomorrow – how she would have loved to have been a bridesmaid! Ellen, and Margaret, her mother and Nicholas, all gone. Yes, she was lucky to be sitting in a rose-bower on the eve of being married to a rich and handsome man. A little quiver ran through her. Was she?

'Clara!'

Nat's voice came from the stable yard. He had been at work all day and had just come in on Crocus. She got up and crossed the front of the house to the driveway that came up from the road. The stable yard stood immediately across the driveway, conveniently opposite the kitchen door at the side of the house. The young groom Peter was taking Crocus into the stable.

Nat was smiling. He looked tired and hot, his cravat pulled loose and his hair sticking sweatily to his head.

'I want to give you your present,' he said. 'You will be surprised.'

She was, having expected a small jewel box, exquisitely wrapped. But out of the stable Peter led a bay mare and stood her square before Clara.

'It's Chignall's Linnet!' Clara shouted.

She was so excited she ran to Nat and threw her arms round his neck.

'Oh thank you, thank you, thank you! What a wonderful present! Oh, how wonderful!'

Nat lifted her off her feet, laughing, and took her up to the mare. Clara put her hand gently up to the mare's neck and stroked her. The mare flinched away uneasily, showing white round her eye.

'Oh, she's nervous, this one,' Clara breathed. 'I saw it before, at Chignall's. What have they done to her? Did you buy her from him? She never went to Yorkshire?'

'No. I told him to put you off. She was here all the

time, in that little hidden field behind the threshing barn.'

'Oh, what a present! We can put her to Rattler straight away – it's not too late, and next year – oh next year, our first foal, our own! My father will be so pleased. Oh, Nat, you are so clever, to think of such a marvellous present.'

Nat said, strangely, 'I can buy you with a horse? With your brother? I want you of your own free will, Clara.'

Clara looked at him, chastened. She could think of nothing to say.

'You can cry off,' he said roughly. 'It's not too late.'

The odd thing was that Clara thought of the wedding dress being discarded for the second time. This made her laugh.

'No,' she said. 'I don't want that.'

His face softened immediately and he smiled. 'Oh Clara, I never know how it is with you.'

'It will be all right,' Clara said shakily. After the laughter she found that tears were trickling down her cheeks. 'Truly, it will be all right.'

How the Rev Bywater ever made it to the altar, Clara never knew. She wanted to hold him in her arms and say, 'My father-in-law, I love you. You will soon be with our dear Nicholas. Just hold up for today, to marry me again.' What stupid thoughts! She was stunned by seeing Nat, so fine and gorgeous, waiting for her, and seeing his face showing how stunned he was at seeing her out of her stable clothes and turned into the vision that Charlotte and her hairdresser had wrought. She drifted towards him on her father's arm, not sure that anything was real. The little church was full of flowers, most of them wild and gathered from the meadows, save for two great vases of white lilies on either side of the altar. Their scent sweetened the whole church. (Nat's gardener, perhaps. He had a greenhouse round the back which Clara had never even looked in.) Edmund's beautiful organ-playing was like a caress to Clara's disordered thoughts. She must stay sweet and serene like a proper bride, with all the crowded church looking on and the Rev's stumbling voice to follow. She held out her hand to Nat's. As the ring slipped on her finger (her old one having been removed the night before) she knew the deed was done. She said all the words that she had said last year to Nicholas, but her voice trembled on the word 'obey'. She would obey reason, but not otherwise. Nat would understand that, she felt sure.

The sun streamed through the church windows as they walked back down the aisle hand in hand. How the villagers gawped! She saw their expressions, awed and amazed at how the hand of God directed operations in their tiny community – which most of them had scarcely left in all their lifetimes. It was no time since they had jeered at Ebenezer's funeral in the same place – and now this! Then they started smiling, because the young couple were so handsome and looked so happy, and then they were all out in the churchyard laughing and gossiping, and the bell-ringers played a great jangle of celebration on the cracked old bells. Clara and Nat stood and received congratulations and kisses from family and those who considered themselves friends, and then they moved off down the path towards the waiting carriages.

'Wait a moment,' Clara said.

She left Nat and crossed the grass to where her mother and Margaret lay under the same stone, and she pulled several flowers out of her bouquet and laid them on the grave. Then she crossed to Nicholas's grave and laid the rest of the bouquet on it and whispered, 'I'm sorry, Nicholas. I know you're not approving, but you can see how it is. Look after me.' She stood up and saw Nicholas's father standing there. She put her arms round him.

'You'll come back with me? I will look after you. And Nicholas is looking after us both.'

'Yes, dear boy. I cannot help thinking of him.'

'And me too.'

She led him slowly back to their carriage. Nat's two chestnut carriage horses, used in the past by his mother and now hardly used at all, were very fine. Behind them was the squire's carriage with his two snow-white geldings, and behind that Lord Fairhall's single-horsed, rather tatty phaeton. Sam and Anne and Jack rode with the squire, and the bridesmaids squashed in with Clara, Nat and the Rev, and the little cavalcade moved off up the road followed by most of the villagers.

Now the food was all laid out and the tables decorated with roses, the garden looked beautiful. Everyone ate and drank, the squire made a speech, very short. Peter the groom led Rattler onto the lawn with a garland of flowers round his neck, and everyone cheered and Sam, who was rather drunk, sent a man for Tilly and everyone cheered some more. Then Edmund who played the organ showed that he could play the violin too, and the dancing started. Nat said he couldn't dance.

'You'll have to learn now you're a married man,' Charlotte told him. 'Life is not all farming, you know.'

'I wish to God that was true!'

Nat's vehemence surprised Clara.

'Why, are you not happy with running the farm?'

'I always wanted to go for a commission in the army but my father would not let me. He wouldn't pay for it. I've always wanted to get away.'

Both Clara and Charlotte were astonished.

'That's a fine thing to say the very moment you've got married,' Charlotte remarked.

Nat smiled. 'Don't worry. There's no war to fight in now, so being a soldier isn't really an option. Officers are all now being put on half-pay. They'll hardly take new recruits.'

'And it's your own farm now. You're not working for your father any more.'

'No. But farming is very boring.'

Clara had never thought of farming as being boring but, compared with fighting in the battle of Waterloo, she supposed it was.

'Making money's not boring,' Charlotte said shrewdly.

Nat shrugged. 'No. But making it with turnips is boring.'

They laughed.

Charlotte said, 'Clara will farm it for you. You go off and deal in stocks and shares in Lombard Street with your turnip money – that's how you make more money. Or go bankrupt. It's very exciting, I'm told.'

'I haven't the head for that. I never got an education, after all, apart from how many gallons in a bushel and suchlike.'

'I got an education,' Charlotte said. 'I can play the spinet, I can sing, I can do drawings in water-colour, I can sew and embroider, I can talk French and Italian, I can dance a quadrille, I can play a hand of bezique, and croquet. And what good does it do me? I never want to do any of those things.'

She laughed. Clara was very impressed.

'I can't do anything!'

She had always taken her position in life completely for granted, never wanting more nor less. She was surprised to hear of Nat's dissatisfaction, amazed to hear Charlotte's list of talents. She could think of no more to say, but at this moment, Jane, dancing with Jack, came spinning to a halt beside them.

'Such a lovely party! Here you are parading your horses, but where is your little Susannah? She should be here. What have you done with her?'

Clara frowned. She had discussed with Anne what to do with Susannah at the wedding celebration. Clara had not wanted her on show, mainly because she was beginning to look more and more like Nat every day.

Anne said it was her imagination; she still looked like her mother, but Clara did not agree. She did not want the whole village seeing the child and giving them fuel for even more gossip, and had decided that she be left at home for the day in the care of Mrs Ponder and old Sim. Now with Jane's challenge, she realized that she was being a little high-handed, trying to ignore a blatant fact.

Nat said, 'Yes, she should be here. I want to see her. Why don't you go and fetch her?'

He did not ask Clara but appealed to Jane straight. Many of the villagers were departing, the sun now low in the sky and animals at home to be fed, children to be put to bed, so Clara did not question the demand. As from now, Jane was to be the child's nurse so it seemed a natural request – or demand, from the tone of his voice.

Jack said, 'I'll come with you. She knows her uncle Jack.'

Or was there more to it than that, Clara sensed, seeing the way Jack looked at Jane. God in Heaven!

When they came back, Nat would have taken the baby on his knee but Clara held out her arms, aware of many spectators still, most of them still dancing or lolling about with too much drink inside them. She set her on the warm grass and picked daisies for her. Rattler and Tilly still grazed on one side with their grooms, and soon an inebriated Sam came up and picked up the baby and held her on Rattler's back. Charlotte and Jane stood laughing.

'I am tired of this wedding,' Nat said suddenly to

Clara. 'I want to be alone with you. Shall we go in?'

It was hardly a request, more a demand.

'Very well. But first—'

She went to her parents and embraced them. She was close to tears and so were they.

'God bless you, Clara, for what you've done,' Sam murmured. 'But there's always a place for you at home if you need it, you know that.'

'Be happy,' said Anne. She took the baby Susannah into her arms. 'I will bring her up to you tomorrow, when Jane starts work. But you won't want her tonight. God bless you, Clara.'

None of them cared for this sort of emotion and blinked it away quickly with a show of smiles and laughs, but the feelings ran deep and would not be forgotten. The older guests, the squire and Lord Fairhall had already departed, taking the vicar with them, so Clara had no excuse now to prevaricate. Nat was waiting for her, holding out his hand. He led her into the house and shut the door behind them.

Then he took her roughly in his arms and said, 'You are mine now, Clara. I love you, but you will do what I say. You will be a good wife to me and bear me sons, that is the bargain. Then we shall be happy.'

Clara could think of no answer to this that she dared give word to. She thought of dear Nicholas whose name she no longer bore, and dear Prosper whose name she never would, and sighed deeply. If Nat thought it was for happiness, so much the better.

PART TWO

15

I said I wanted some excitement in my life. God in Heaven, when I saw the sea and the ship I nearly died of fright. All that water – and that was only King's Lynn where you could see water on the other side – and they said you went nearly all the way with no sight of land . . . and why did the ship not sink? It was heavy surely, with us three hundred convicts on board and all our food, and live animals too – sheep and hens and pigs – and a regiment of soldiers to guard us and all the crew, a wicked-looking surly lot who looked even worse than us, if possible. We were to be four months on this ship, stopping only once, I was told, all the way round the world! Four months! I thought then that I would rather have been hanged.

Seeing my parents on the quay, come to say good-bye, was terrible. I truly wished they hadn't come. I couldn't contain myself, weeping, weeping, and clinging so hard they had to drag me away. I heard Anne say, 'No word of this to Clara – thank God she didn't come!' My father looked pitiful. That I had done this to them – I couldn't believe it. It is too painful to remember. I knew I wasn't the same person now as the one they were weeping over and that stiffened me: I had learned a lot in prison and knew ways of looking after myself that they would never know, and ways of surviving that they would never need to know. That was my only consolation, that they were weeping for someone who didn't exist any more. I would never see them again.

On board we were put in chains, and great cannon-ball things were shackled to our ankles in case we thought of jumping overboard and swimming for it. Moving around, we had to drag this weight with us which cut our ankles sorely. A sailor told me it was only while we were in port, but that was long enough. My parents had brought me good clothes but most had only rags, and the stuff I couldn't wear was filched from my bunk almost immediately. We slept on bunks below, four to a bunk, six feet square. They were in two rows with a walkway down the middle. There was very little headroom and the only air came in from hatchways above which had iron bars over them. These were to be battened down in bad weather so we would all be in complete darkness. My parents had paid for me to be given better provision when I was in Norwich gaol, but now I was in with the worst and without privilege.

There were forty of us women, and mostly they were prostitutes, destitutes, idiots and old crones. I was hard put to find anyone likely to become a friend, but I managed to get in a bunk with a woman I had spoken to in Norwich called Emma. She was to be sent out for thieving food. She had had three starving children who were now in the workhouse. She wept a lot, not unnaturally, but at least she still had her brain. She was only twenty-one. Her husband had been killed in a mining accident. The only one near my age was Milly, a prostitute. She was fifteen or sixteen and a bit of a joker. She said Australia was lovely, all sunshine. Better to starve in the sunshine than in the rain. She was all skin and bone and coughed a lot, but had a smile that slashed across her face like a wound. She was looking for likely sailors immediately.

Of course Barney was on board too, but the men were in a separate hold, and until we were at sea we did not mix.

Luckily it was summer, so when the ship sailed I suppose it was as pleasant as it is likely to be on a ship. We had our chains and cannonballs taken off and were allowed up on deck. I wasn't sick, but many were, the first few days. It was disgusting below, but I was hardened to stench and disgustingness. The first couple of weeks were the best of the voyage but I didn't realize it then. I still had a terror of being at sea, of seeing no land at all, anywhere, but it eased off, this terror, as I saw how matter-of-factly the sailors took it. It was their world. Some of them had known nothing else nearly all their lives.

When we got to know them, some of them were quite human and pleasant and, of course, us females got a lot of attention. Sometimes, too much. Two sailors quite early in the voyage were flogged for being found with a woman, hidden under the ship's tender, and that was a very nasty interlude. We were all mustered to watch the punishment, convicts as well as crew, for it was to be a lesson to us all.

Of course we were accustomed to seeing floggings in the jail, but it seemed very unholy, somehow, when it happened at sea, with the sun shining and the dolphins running under the bowsprit. There were soldiers on board to guard us, and they made a thing of it with a roll of drums, and the poor sailors, one after the other, were tied with their arms outstretched and flogged with a cat-o'-nine-tails till their backs were running with blood. Neither of them made a sound, although when they were cut down they both near fainted with the pain. I shut my eyes. Emma was sick. Everyone was very silent, but when it was finished and the men carried below it was all back to normal, with shouting and laughing again. One of the sailors, a jolly lad the same age as me called Robbie, told me sometimes a flogging would kill a man.

'That was only twenty lashes, nothing really,' he said. 'You get five hundred and it can kill you.'

'Five hundred!'

'They flog the convicts too, you know. You better watch out!' He laughed.

'Not the women?'

'I've seen a woman flogged, yes. Mind you, she deserved it, we all thought that. Screaming and fighting day and night. They shut her up in irons afterwards and she couldn't do any harm then. Mostly, flogging is for stealing food. That's a very bad thing to do. Some of the convicts don't know that, but we do.'

We got enough food, but it was pretty disgusting most of the time: salt meat and suet puddings mostly. But our water ration was very strict, two pints a day each, and when we sailed south and got into hotter weather this was never enough. The only thing we thought about all day was the next ration of warm, sour-tasting water. At supper there was a ration of port which cheered everyone up, but I never got used to the muzzy effect it had on me. I think the crew and soldiers got rum too, but we didn't. Drink seemed a big thing amongst the crew. I think the captain and his officers had smart dinners each night in their elegant quarters, with a lot of wine to drink and every comfort just like home. When the weather was good, that is. When it was rough, that was a different matter. The food slid and jumped all over the table and everything spilled. We got used to gobbling it as fast as possible, one hand to eat and one to hold on to the table as it tilted from side to side.

Robbie told me we were lucky. 'This ship has a good captain. Captain Reeves. He is very fair. Look how he lets you on deck all day. Some of 'em are frightened and keep the convicts chained and battened below nearly all the time. The stench is frightful. And women give birth down there some-times, all in the filth, you wouldn't believe.'

But I believed anything, as the voyage went on.

We came into what I learned were called the doldrums, a part of the sea where the wind stopped blowing. It was incredibly hot by now, and the ship just sat swaying without moving. The sails hung down and all the ropes slatted and chinked and nobody had any-thing to do save sit and sweat. It was really terrible. One of the old women in our quarters died, and we all had to attend her funeral on deck. She was sewed up in a canvas shroud and the captain read the burial service just like it was in the church at home. The officers were all ranked up to attention in their best uniforms. Seeing them there on parade I thought them a very smart bunch and was sorry we were never allowed to consort with them. The prostitutes were all making quips even while the captain read the Bible. The soldiers in their bright uniforms (even in the heat!) were also on parade for us women to goggle at. It was quite a jolly diversion. But when the canvas bundle was slid over the side of the ship I could not help thinking: poor old lady, to land up here amongst the whales and the crabs so far from home, when she belonged in a pretty Norfolk churchyard with the daisies and buttercups over her and a daughter to visit sometimes to keep her grave neat. I had never got to know her, but she had seemed harmless enough. I think a lot of convicts were just derelicts sent away to keep them from being a burden on the parish. Apart from us murderers, that is. I was the only murderer on board, and pointed out with respect at times. I was aware of it.

Before we moved out of the doldrums, quite a few were hoping for death, myself included. But at last, one morning the top-most sail imperceptibly filled, flogged, dropped, and then filled again. Everyone watched silently, hopefully. The captain came on deck and stood with his first mate, looking up at the sky. A tiny ripple stirred at the bows. Then, several minutes later, the huge limp balloon of the mainsail gradually lifted itself like a great recumbent animal shrugging off sleep. It sighed into shape, fell limp, and then stirred again. The top-sail filled right out, and then the mainsail bulged again, and this time lifted itself right up and filled. We all felt the soft breeze on our cheeks. The captain smiled and then everyone broke out into a roar of pleasure, sailors, soldiers and convicts all, and the ship started to move and the glassy waters to crinkle, and at last we were out of the doldrums.

Robbie said it happened every trip. 'Everyone hates the doldrums, worse than a great storm. You wait, you won't mind a storm after sitting in the doldrums.'

'But we've already had a storm. What do you mean, wait?'

'We've had nothing yet! Wait till we round the Cape. Unless we're very lucky we'll have some great storms down in the Southerlies.'

I didn't know what he was talking about. What was the Cape?

'It's the tip of the African continent. We have to go round it to get to Australia.'

Australia was still a lifetime away.

'What's it like, Australia?'

'We go into Sydney cove, and that's where you're landed. I've scarcely been ashore there. It's only a few government houses and prison blocks and rough houses where you have to live. But quite pretty, with nice trees and streams and things. And very weird black people, all naked. It's their place really but we seem to have taken it over. Not fair, when you think about it. They shoot the convicts with bows and arrows quite often. It's quite understandable.'

That was the first first-hand description of where we were going that I had ever heard. It wasn't very comforting.

'How many times have you been there?'

'This will be my third trip.'

I was curious. How could he be happy to do this three times?

'You like being a sailor?'

'Yes. My father was a sailor. He was killed at Trafalgar. My grandfather, all my uncles – all sailors. It's in our family. I would rather do this than work on a farm. Farming is very boring, the same thing over and over. I don't say working on a convict ship is the smartest thing, but we have a good captain, which is very important.'

I liked Robbie. He was more intelligent than most, and seemed to have a mind beyond sex, which was very rare. Most of the sailors were after only one thing, and many got away with it in spite of the risk of flogging. But as I was a murderess I think they were a bit wary of me. I was also, after my time in jail, good at ways of discouragement. If I ever lay with a man, it was going to be someone worthwhile. Someone rich and respected. I had vowed that to myself long ago. The Barneys of this world were not for me.

Barney was jealous of Robbie. 'Why are you always talking to that tar? Has he got eyes for you?'

'No. He's just sensible, that's all.'

'I'll square him off, if you like. Tell him what's what.'

'No, it's only talk between us. He tells me things.'

'Like what?'

'When we put into Rio, we're battened below for the whole time we're in port, with the soldiers standing guard night and day.'

'Blimey! And how long is that?'

'While we take on provisions.'

'More water, I hope. Oh hell, what a prospect! I suppose they know some of the men are planning to jump ship in Rio.'

'Fat chance. We'll be in chains and cannon-balls again.'

This proved true.

I did not see either Robbie or Barney again for some time. It's not much use describing the horrors of being shut below in the broiling temperature of Rio (wherever that might be) in chains, night and day, with a load of mewling, puking, stinking women. Some things you try not to remember. During that time, it was my fourteenth birthday.

We thought of those days later when we were battened below in the storms of the southern ocean. We thought the time in Rio was a holiday compared with being in the pitch dark, clinging for one's life on to the side of the bunk with gouts of water pouring down from the leaky hatches. So this is what Robbie had been warning me of? The sea laid about us in huge grey heaving mountains over which our poor ship laboured and plunged and rolled. Water broke over the lower decks continually and the poor sailors had to work there at all times, pulling in sheets or letting them out, clinging like limpets to the life-lines that were rigged. When we were allowed out I used to try and find a high place, even up the ratlines a few rungs and watch it, for it was magnificent in a way, something one never dreamed of in a Norfolk village. None of us – save Jack – had ever even seen the sea. When the men went right up the masts and out on the footropes under the yards to shorten sail, I watched in horror as they tossed against the sky, swaying right out over the water with nothing but a rope under their feet and a wildly-flogging sail to hold on to. Robbie said you got used to it. It was a matter of pride to go right out to the farthest end of the yard, the bit called the Flemish horse, where you were clean above the sea, a spot in the sky with the wind screaming to tear you off. I thought Robbie was a real hero.

The soldiers didn't much care where we went on the ship now we were settled into the last leg of the trip, and the younger ones of us who weren't weeping below were able to chat with the male prisoners on deck at times. They were a sad crew, most of them, as scared of the sea as the women, and I didn't come across any I fancied. Barney told me about the ones he knew. Some were quite old and a few of them well-educated men, mostly transported for debt, not really wicked at all.

A strange thing happened one day, when Robbie was aloft. He wore a gold ring on his finger which he had taken from a corpse, and when his hands were so cold aloft he lost it. He said he felt it go but could do nothing about it. Two days later I found a gold ring on deck, lodged in a coil of rope. I quickly picked it up, making sure no one saw me, and in the night I put it on my toe, underneath my stocking, for safe keeping. I didn't tell Robbie, for I thought it might come in useful later on. I suppose I stole it, but it didn't worry me.

We were all dreading getting to our destination, yet dying for the journey to finish. Being cooped up in so small a space, day after day . . . there was a lot of fighting among the men and punishments. For something not so bad as to deserve a flogging, you were put in what was called a cramping box for a few hours – squashed in with head bent and legs crooked up and that was not very nice. Women had that too. Or you were shut into the forepeak alone in irons for several days. I was careful not to get into trouble. But at least this part of the journey was better if there was nothing else on your mind; calm and sunny and fish to catch and no more terrible storms.

The journey took four months and a bit.

When the first call of 'Land! Land ahoy!' came from the boy up the mainmast, my heart gave a lurch. The sailors all cheered but us convicts remained silent. Better the devil you know . . . I knew I was frightened. I had learned that because I could read and write, I would probably be 'assigned' to somebody as a clerk or servant. And it depended entirely on whether you got a good master or a bad one, because you had no rights. You were a convict. No good complaining or running away. We all knew that running away was impossible. At least, the running away was easy, but the travelling and living in that wild land on your own was impossible. They said there were clean-picked skeletons all over the place within several miles of the harbour and its settlement. I don't know where all these stories came from or even whether they were true, but Robbie told me quite a lot.

'All the rough men are sent building, road-building mostly, for the government. They work in gangs, in chains. Or else they go as servants, slaves or whatever, to convicts who've done their time and got settlements. You might get that.'

'To another convict?'

'Aye. They mostly stay when they're free. Got no money to pay a fare back. They're given land and enough tools to make a living. Lots of them have got rich and lord it, servants, carriages and all. And some have got big farms in the outback, all sheep, making money.'

'What if you run away and hide on a ship going back to England?'

Robbie laughed. 'You don't think they all try that? Well, before the ship sails the soldiers go through it with bayonets, sticking into every corner and cranny and on some ships they use sulphur to smoke it all out so the hideaways have to come running out. I've seen it often, every time we leave.' Robbie had lots of stories. 'There's times men have got on a ship and when the captain finds them, he dumps them on some island in the Pacific, anywhere. He doesn't care. Could be uninhabited, no water, nothing. Imagine! And if a man does make it back to England, he only gets tried again and his sentence doubled and sent back here.'

It didn't sound a bit encouraging.

But Robbie said, 'You might be lucky. Keep your fingers crossed. You might like it. It's wonderful weather, and very pretty.'

Well, I was bored at home. Playing truant with Barney was how I got into this mess. I didn't know what I wanted at home. But I did used to cry a lot in my bunk at night for homesickness, thinking of my parents and even snotty Clara. It didn't make sense. Once land was sighted I longed to be there, with firm ground under my feet. To get some fresh water and wash my hair, which was in great tangles down my back like a wild horse! To smell flowers and hay! Oh, to jump in a fresh-flowing river and feel the water flowing over my stinking body! The blue blur on the horizon hardened as the ship swept in a fair breeze to its final destination: everyone on board had a new zest and there was singing and dancing amongst the tars and soldiers and a huge dinner on our last night and double rations of grog. We anchored off in the moonlight, battened down, and the soldiers kept watch. I lay in the hot dark in my bunk for the last time, and prayed. I was bad at prayers like all my family, and this time I did want God to give me a reasonable berth, so I prayed and prayed, and even promised to go to church if He was good to me.

It did seem at first sight like a paradise we had come to, a huge natural bay in from the bright sea, surrounded by forests, and at the far end a small town of higgledy-piggledy buildings with fields and tilled land around them and more forest beyond, and a harbour filled with ships. It was a pretty sight, prettier than anything I had seen in England. All the same, we went ashore heavily chained together in a shaming way and filed into a grim building to be written into a book and questioned, and then we were locked in a prison. At last we had plenty of water to drink and enough to clean ourselves up – those of us who wanted to, which wasn't by any means all. A lot of the women were very apathetic after the voyage and seemed to have lost any spirit they might once have had. Or maybe they had never had any. Milly, my friend the prostitute, was lively enough though and we bonded together, ever hopeful.

'Maybe we'll get a place together.'

And Barney too, I hoped. One needed friends in this place.

We were interviewed eventually, one by one, and our fates were decided.

I was young, strong, and a farmer's daughter. I could milk and make cheese and kill hens. Most of the convicts came from city slums and couldn't do anything of use to this growing farming community, so I was considered quite valuable. The reading and writing didn't come into it. The demand for convict labour from the settlers was insatiable, apparently. They complained that the government creamed off all the fittest men for road-building, and as most of them were making farms out of raw bush they needed labour.

The men in the office looked up our record. 'That woman up beyond the barracks – what do they call her? – Fat Hams Annie – she's been down again wanting people. Anybody, she said. More than our job's worth to fall out with her.'

They laughed and shook their heads.

'Send this one then. It's a female but strong by the look of 'er.'

'My friend could come too,' I said. 'He's strong.'

'Strong ones go on the chain gang.'

'He's only twelve.' I didn't want to go to Fat Hams Annie on my own. Her name was enough to put anybody off, for a start.

'We're only doing women. She'll have to apply for him herself. Stands a chance if he's only twelve. It's a bit young for the chain gang.'

And Milly, I thought. I'll get Fat Hams to apply for them both. Milly wasn't much good for anything.

The outcome was that I went up the hill to Fat Hams Annie, and she roared down to the recruiting office and got both Barney and Milly at my instigation. Whether I did them a good turn or not was another matter.

Little did I know that Fat Hams Annie was worse

than Norwich gaol and the transportation ship put together. And we had no redress, because we were convicts. The seven years that stretched ahead looked like a lifetime.

16

Clara walked up the drive to her old home, Small Gains, to see how the extension was getting on. It was three years since her marriage to Nat, and with the money made by Rattler, her father was building on a new parlour and bedroom above. Anne was thrilled.

'At last, I shall have a quiet place to sit and sew and play with the children, without the men's coming and going in the kitchen. And a new bedroom – what a Godsend! You are so good, Clara, to give us Rattler's money. He's always been your horse, after all.'

'I was brought up on the money Tilly made. It's quite fair,' Clara said. 'And besides, you know I don't want for anything.'

'Let's sit in the orchard out of the muddle. I'll get some ale. Where's Susannah?'

'She's gone to find Billy. You know how she dotes on him.'

Clara swung the two-year-old Robert onto her hip and went out through the gate into the orchard. In June the grass was long and bright with flowers, ox-eye daisies and borage and buttercups. Soon Sim would scythe it for hay, but not until the flowers had seeded. She sat under the apple tree where the bench was and remembered sitting there with Margaret in the last summer of her life when she had been so desperately in love with Nat. How strangely everything had turned out!

'More in love with him than I have ever been,' she thought with a sigh, and remembered Charlotte's gloomy prognosis of marriage – usually for one's family's advancement, arranged by parents, rarely for love. Charlotte had still evaded all her parents' wiles to marry her off, and was fancy free, fast becoming an old maid. She was twenty-two to Clara's twenty. She called often at Grover's, and was now Clara's fast friend, although Nat and Clara were never invited to the hall for social functions. Charlotte's mother considered them beneath her.

'Oh, she's a dreadful woman,' Anne dismissed her. 'Just like Nat's mother. I don't know why it's the women who are such snobs. The men don't seem to care so much.'

'Thank goodness. Nat doesn't care. He doesn't seem to have any friends. None ever call. But he rides off in the evenings and goes drinking and gambling in town and doesn't get back till gone midnight, so he must have friends there. Not ones I want to meet though.'

'He drinks too much.'

'Yes. He says he's bored. He hates farming.'

'He's a strange one! Why doesn't he go hunting and meet some decent people that way? Or sell up if he hates it so – save he wouldn't get any price for farm-land today. It's in the doldrums, like everything in the countryside. All the money is made in the cities these days.'

'I couldn't live in a city. I'd go mad.'

'No. Being rich isn't everything. Is it, my little love?' Anne bent down and swung Clara's toddler into her arms. 'Are you going to be a rich farmer one day, like your daddy?'

The dark-eyed baby crowed with delight, kicking his bare legs.

'You have lovely babies, Clara, for all you hate having them!' Anne was laughing. 'Everyone says you'd rather have foals!'

Clara laughed. 'Yes, I would! Linnet's new one is gorgeous.'

'This one's gorgeous too, aren't you, my bonny boy?'

Clara was eternally grateful that her stepmother doted so on her two children, taking them off her hands. Much as she loved them, she did not want to spend much time with them. If Anne didn't have them, Jane was always there to look after them at home. Thank heaven the second child had been a boy, to please Nat. Clara wanted a rest from child-bearing and Nat was satisfied for the time being. Robert was walking now and was a very strong and healthy child, like Susannah. At least Nat had no qualms about her suitability as a brood mare. Babies in the village died like flies in the winter but Susannah and Robert were never sick.

'If you keep them here today, I'll ride over and visit Mrs Mayes. Gabriel says she's no better. They're all worried about her. He says she seems to have lost her spirit.'

'You know they say she's written to India for Prosper to come back?' Anne spoke hesitantly.

'Yes.' Clara could not bring herself to say any more. Gabriel now worked for Nat as farm bailiff and Clara heard all the news from Great Meadows. Gabriel said his mother wanted to see Prosper before she died.

She went home, got Crocus saddled and set out for Great Meadows. She had to ride side-saddle, out on the main road in broad daylight for all to see, and would not ride Rattler so far in a side-saddle. Nat said it would do him no harm, and Clara knew this was true, but she liked riding Crocus. He didn't pull like Rattler. Rattler only went at racing pace, but Crocus kindly went as fast or as slow as he was asked. Rattler's nature was strong and bully-boy, but Crocus was kind and compliant. Crocus was a gentleman.

'You are a sweet boy, much too good for Nat,' Clara said to him, in no hurry once she was into the tree-shaded lane that went all the way to the Mayes' farm. The horse walked easily with his long stride and Clara loved moving through the rampant June countryside where even the untended fields were bright with flowers. Rich hay crops, almost ready to cut, spread on all sides, along with flourishing corn and roots. When Nat spoke of selling up, which he did quite often, Clara's insides shrunk with horror. She felt she could never move away from this earth, which she owned, to a smart, alien town-house amongst the smoke, the smells and the filth that abounded where too many people lived together. She could not go! Yet a wife was bound to obey her husband's wishes. These thoughts were always a cloud on her horizon.

But since she had heard of Mrs Mayes' summons to Prosper, another cloud of a different hue entirely had sailed into her consciousness. She wanted the story from the woman's own lips. Had she truly written to summon Prosper? Gabriel was vague: she was going to, he thought, but whether she had or not he didn't know. A letter would take some four months, and Prosper's return, if he answered the pleas, another four or five. Almost a year.

After three years of marriage, Clara had not forgotten Prosper. True, his image had faded and her heart no longer pounded at the mention of his name. But the memory of him was secure in her mind, her love for him unwavering. He had never written since her marriage. She had no idea if he even remembered her any more, but for herself she was utterly faithful in her love for him. Sometimes she wondered if her devotion was to a person who did not exist any more. People changed, especially when thrown at a malleable age into completely different circumstances. The Prosper she knew might come home as a disappointing person. How could she tell? But she was stalwart in her faith. It might be misguided but she held on to it, probably because her marriage to Nat was in trouble. Nat, having been so dominated by his father all his life, was like a rudderless ship without him.

'I miss him,' he admitted.

'Yes, we all do, for the better. You can be your own man now.'

But Nat did not know what he wanted. Like his father he basically held women in contempt and did not discuss with Clara the business of the farm. He had expected her to play a part like his mother, fussing in the kitchen, ordering servants, buying clothes. But Clara had sacked all the servants save the cook and housemaid, kept Jane for the children, bought no clothes and ran the stables like a man. Nat still had his manservant, a quiet, highly efficient and self-effacing elderly man called James, and his bailiff Gabriel, and lorded it over the motley workers that came from the village each day to labour. Clara was supposed to spend all her time running the house, but she spent most of it riding and breaking in young horses. She had simplified the house. She hated the pretty-pretty Regency fashions that Nat's mother had taken on and threw out the uncomfortable satin sofas on their little gilt legs and the gilded mirrors on all the walls and substituted old oak stuff still to be had in outdated country shops. She wished she could pull out the carved marble mantelpieces and go back to the huge old grates now covered up that lay behind, but she did not want to cause too much upheaval. Nat did not complain at her changes. He preferred her ways too, and found it far more comfortable to live with Clara, hefting his dirty boots onto her man-sized chairs without being chided.

'You're nice and easy to live with,' he admitted. 'And cheap too. My mother was always spending, spending. It drove Father mad.'

200

'I spend in the stables.'

'Yes, you're welcome to that. I like to have good horses.'

They had an easy enough relationship, but after the first few months they both found the other wanting. Nat found Clara too obstinate and determined on her own way, and Clara was shocked to find that Nat, like his father, expected to dominate by force. He could fly into frightening rages and had twice hit her. She had no redress against that. If she had ever been beguiled by his looks, it was an attraction that quickly died. But she never complained, for she knew that by comparison with most she was lucky.

To Clara, the Mayes' farm always looked like paradise, even when Prosper wasn't there. Or maybe her memories of riding over the hills and lying by the river with Prosper made her think of it like that. Crocus trotted up their long, well-tended drive, and in the stable yard a groom took the reins as Clara dismounted.

'I trust Mrs Mayes is in?'

'Yes, ma'am. She doesn't get out much any more.'

Mrs Mayes' face lit up when Clara appeared at the door. She was in the kitchen, putting bread in the oven, and Clara was shocked by how ill she looked. Always a tall, gaunt woman, she now was thin and haggard, her cheeks sunk in and all the gloss gone from her dark hair.

'Oh, ma'am, you don't look well!' Clara could not help herself. 'Let me do that.'

She hurried forward and Mrs Mayes made no objection, but sank into a chair at the head of the table. Clara arranged the pans in the huge bread-oven that took up most of the end wall of the kitchen and carefully closed the door.

'You should have someone to help you!'

'Oh, I do, but they have their days off, and the men keep on eating. The loaves they get through! There is no end to feeding them.'

'You make them too comfortable! I'm not surprised they won't leave home.'

'Only Prosper's gone. And Gabriel lives in your bailiff's cottage. The others are all here, and my husband – that's six men. And how they eat!'

'But your farm is so fine, all those workers.'

'True, we are a model farm. How can I complain?' She gave a bleak smile. 'If only my daughters had lived, it might have been easier.'

'Or your boys find wives.' What was she saying? The colour rose in her cheeks. Had Prosper found a wife?

'They spend enough time courting. But when it comes to setting up a home of their own – once a girl gets serious they get cold feet. Even though we've cottages to spare. My husband is too easy with them. But of course he likes their labour. It's better than hired labour.'

She spoke as if she were breathless, and sat holding her side as if in pain.

'You're not well, are you?'

'No. I'm not. I don't think I shall be here for very

much longer. I want to hang on until Prosper comes, and then I think I will be to the churchyard.'

'Oh no! Have you seen a doctor?'

'No. He cannot tell me anything I don't know. I can't face their bleeding and their physics. I'll die in peace.'

'No.' Clara remembered how Nicholas had suffered. 'Doctors drag it out. They haven't a cure for everything. I think I would feel the same. But maybe, if you rested – and seeing Prosper again . . .'

'Perhaps. He's on his way now. His ship was due in Cape Town a month ago, so he should not be long.'

Clara turned away, trying to hide her ecstatic flood of excitement at this news, but she could not help colouring up again, and Mrs Mayes actually laughed, and said, 'I think you still have a soft spot for my Prosper?'

It was impossible to deny it. Clara didn't know what to say. 'I'm married now,' she stammered.

'I know why you married. Perhaps if you had had a choice it might have been different. Prosper always enquires after you in his letters.'

'He's never written to me since I married.'

'No, well, he's a tactful boy. Perhaps he couldn't say what he feels in a letter. I know he hasn't forgotten you.'

'I have never forgotten him.'

Perhaps she shouldn't have said it but it seemed stupid to deny the truth.

'No, I saw what there was between you. But it's a long time ago – you were only children then. He might have changed. We might not know him now.'

It had never felt like children's love to Clara. She had never thought of Prosper as a child. She had been sixteen, he a year older. Life was short. Mrs Mayes was worn out with work and child-bearing, yet was still in her forties.

'I would love to see him again. Would you be able to come over one evening to dinner, you and Mr Mayes and Prosper?'

'Perhaps. If not, you must come here. I will send word with Gabriel when Prosper comes.'

A fortnight later Gabriel told Clara that Prosper was home.

17

'What shall I wear?' Clara groaned.

Jane laughed. 'I told you ages ago you ought to go to Norwich and spend some money on lovely dresses. But Prosper likes you in your farm clothes so why bother?'

'I've got to look beautiful for him, after all those rich English ladies out there that he's used to. They go to dinner parties all the time, all dolled up in spite of being in such a sweat. Charlotte told me. She has a cousin out there. All they do is look for eligible husbands.'

'I thought he was planting tea and chasing big game.'

'Yes, but there's lots of social life. It's not like farming here. We've never had a dinner party before, have we? Nat thinks I've gone mad, inviting them.'

'Well, you have a bit, haven't you? At the mention of Prosper Mayes—'

'I asked Anne. She said it would be very proper, and I ought to have dinner parties, a person in my position. But who would I ask? Charlotte and her father, but her mother wouldn't come, so that would be embarrassing. You're my best friend but you're a servant, I couldn't ask you.'

'Well, I could sit at table, then when the course is finished jump up and clear the dishes, bring the next course in and sit down again.'

They got the giggles.

'Gabriel could do the same. Sit down to eat and do the washing up afterwards . . . I'm not very good at servants.'

'Well, they don't leave after a fortnight which they always did with your mother-in-law. You've still got dear old Mrs Pymm and Molly.'

'Mrs Pymm's a great cook. Her eyes lit up when I told her there would be nine for dinner on Thursday. My parents and Jack are coming, Mr and Mrs Mayes and Prosper and Gabriel. "Oh how wonderful!" she said. Can you believe?'

Clara hated cooking.

'Molly can serve but I'll have to see she's got a clean uniform.'

'Let's look at your dresses then, see what's best. You did buy something nice when you got married, I remember. A red silk thing. I've never seen you wear it.'

'No, I never have. I change for dinner at night, but only into a clean skirt and blouse. Nat would faint if I put that dress on. He doesn't bother, after all.'

'No, but he always dresses well. Or haven't you noticed? He's got some very nice clothes and looks fantastic when he bothers.'

Clara knew Jane fancied her husband. Gabriel was trying to court Jane, not very successfully, and Molly the housemaid was in love with Peter the young groom. And I am in love with Prosper, Clara thought. They were all of an age and full of desires. Only Charlotte professed to love nobody. 'I'm saving it,' she said. 'I shall know when I meet him.'

'But maybe you never will,' Clara warned her.

'Then I will be my own self.'

Clara hadn't invited Charlotte, pretending the party was strictly family. But in her heart she was afraid Prosper might fall in love with her. Charlotte was so beautiful and everything Clara knew she wasn't: free, witty, educated, open and generous. Clara thought herself old already, with two children, and her hands not white and smooth like a lady's, her hair dusty with the stables and cobbled roughly into a bundle.

'I will do your hair,' Jane said. 'I will dress you. You will look a million times better than all those ladies in India.'

And she did. She was as good a lady's maid as she was nursery maid, and Clara, seeing herself in the long mirror in her dressing-room, said humbly, 'I should pay you more, Jane. I shall tell Nat. You are fantastic.'

'I am paid enough working here, after the miller's wife. I don't want more.'

'You want Nat,' Clara said. She didn't know what prompted the words, save that Jane's preparing her to meet Prosper seemed to have strengthened the confidence between them. Jane knew all her secrets as it was; she might just as well acknowledge her own. But she covered this one with a laugh.

'Yes, if I didn't know him too well!'

Clara hoped it wasn't too obvious to Nat that she

wanted to please Prosper. He was surprised when he saw her, she could tell by his expression, although he made no comment. But James, his valet, had likewise made an effort with him, and he looked very impressive in his close-fitting white breeches and expensive black boots, high white cravat and black cutaway coat. He had not grown thick and heavy like many farmers, but retained his fine figure and the arrogant upright carriage that set it off.

He smiled and said, 'We have forgotten how smart we can be! My mother was always wanting parties but Father only invited his farmer friends, and their wives were terrible – oh, how boring, talking of turnips all night.'

'Mr Mayes will probably talk of turnips.'

'Young Prosper might have some stories. Gabriel tells me he's been hunting tigers and suchlike. A far cry from a few tame pheasants.'

'I've got his mare still. I expect he's only come to fetch her back.'

She tried to be casual, but her pulses were racing. She doubted whether Prosper was as excited.

Her parents and Jack arrived and then came the sound of carriage wheels and hooves in the drive and Nat and Clara went to the door. Peter had been primed to take the horses. Clara knew Prosper and his father would have preferred to ride over, but Mrs Mayes looked a frail enough figure after the carriage ride, coming to the door on her husband's arm. Prosper walked behind.

Clara looked at him and he returned her glance

and in that moment she knew he felt exactly as she felt. It was strange, the unspoken message, the assurance. Possibly they could not have found words. She greeted his parents and then, to Prosper, held out her hand.

'It's lovely to have you back.' Her words were so prim, yet her eyes were shouting at him: come back to *me*! Come back and never go again! I love you! I want you! He wasn't changed at all, the greeny-gold eyes so caressing, the soft brown hair tied carelessly back, the figure so lithe and slender. He wasn't plumped out with good living or red-faced with drink or loud with self-confidence. Just her own quiet, understanding Prosper back.

'Clara, he whispered and kissed her hand briefly. If he did not look into her eyes then, she knew she dared not look either.

'Prosper!'

Jack homed in and thumped Prosper round the shoulders and Clara was never so glad at her brother's impetuosity. Whisked apart, sitting at opposite sides of the table for dinner, Clara was able to settle her racing blood, cool down, take stock, yet she still felt as if she trembled. She was afraid it might show. She could not address him, but had to let the others ask questions, draw him out on India and his life there. Nat, having had plenty of practice in his youth at social gatherings, was a perfect host and Clara's silence was overlooked in the general conversation. She wanted so desperately to be alone with him. But if she were . . . whatever would happen? She was in no position, married, with children, to look at another man. She scarcely heard his stories, aware only of her overwhelming joy that he had acknowledged her as he had, scarcely able – like herself – to find words. She had no doubt of his feelings. Jack was already asking him straight if he found the English girls out there to his liking, but he shook his head and said, 'No. They only look at young officers in their smart uniforms. I can't compete.'

Clara caught his eye across the table and he smiled and flushed up like a boy. At no time during the evening did she put herself in a position to speak with him, yet she was constantly aware of his every word, his every movement. To her great relief they did not sit talking all night, for they had a long journey home and it was obvious that the visit had taken a toll on Mrs Mayes. She put a bright face on the evening, but it was obvious she was in pain and very tired. Her husband watched her anxiously and soon suggested the time to break up. Nat sent for their carriage.

As they bade their farewells on the doorstep, Prosper said softly to Clara, 'Shall I come for my mare in the morning? Will it be convenient?'

'Yes, oh yes! I will have her ready.'

'Very well.'

And he smiled and departed, leaving Clara alight with joy. In the morning! Scarcely any time at all! And she had been wondering how on earth to contrive further visits without anyone becoming curious. She knew now that Prosper would find a way.

The family all came back into the house for further drinks round the fire. Gabriel was invited to stay, rather than retire to the bailiff's cottage and Nat got out more of his father's best port and sent for fresh glasses.

'Perhaps we should do this more often,' he said to Clara, and she forebore to mention that he did it nearly every night with his cronies in town, and smiled in agreement.

'Save we haven't many friends to ask. The Mayes came twenty miles after all.'

'No. They're all peasants round here.'

Clara saw her parents exchange amused glances. Nat had only ever contrived a passing acquaintance with her family and had never suggested they dine with him and Clara on any regular basis. Anne was in and out with the children, but Sam and Jack rarely came, only on farming matters.

'Your mother doesn't look long for this world,' Sam remarked to Gabriel. 'Is that why Prosper is home?'

'Aye. She's pined for him, her favourite.'

'The youngest,' Anne said. 'It's often the way. Like Ellen, perhaps.'

'Ellen could have written. She knew her letters. She was clever enough,' Sam said.

The fact that Ellen had never written weighed heavily with Sam. Other transportees were known to send word home, saying how well or how badly they were doing, and letters were quite often published in the newspapers giving information about the new communities springing up in Australia. Clara knew that a letter from Ellen would have put a new spring in her father's step. Without word, they could only think the worst, that life was so bad there was no point in writing. Or perhaps she was dead. Three years without word was long enough.

'She is seventeen now, coming eighteen. She must be a lovely lass.'

'Maybe she will come home after her seven years. We could always find the fare for her,' Anne said. 'We won't give up hope.'

'A lot prefer to stay, so I've heard,' Nat said. 'It's a fair country and they give you land. Think of that – give it you!'

'Yes, and it fair kills you making it productive,' Jack said.

'It fair kills you here, making it pay.'

'I think the horses make more money than the land. I'd like to see Linnet matched before she gets in foal again.'

'I'd like to see her against Rattler.'

'Or Crocus.'

'Linnet's in foal again but a match wouldn't hurt her,' Clara said. 'We could match all three.'

'A match is for two.'

'Let's have Rattler and Linnet then. We should have done it when she first came. But Linnet needs getting fit.'

'That's your job,' said Jack to Clara. 'You've been neglecting your duties.'

'I've been breeding too, you forget. Having babies doesn't go with getting trotters fit.'

'Get Linnet fit then, and we'll have a match.'

'It's stupid when we own them both. How can we have a bet?' Sam grumbled.

'Other people can.'

'Only if they trust us. They'll think we know which will win.'

'We don't know. That's the point of having a match.'

'Rattler will win,' Clara said.

With too much to drink, the conversation was deteriorating fast and Sam and Jack, prompted by Anne, shortly took their leave. Anne kissed Clara and hissed, 'Be careful, my dear. I've eyes in my head.'

'I hope Nat hasn't,' Clara whispered back, and laughed. But she saw Anne was anxious. Perhaps she should be too.

Clara announced her plans at the breakfast table.

'Prosper is coming for Cobweb this morning. I may ride back with him a little way on Linnet. Start getting her fit, what we were saying last night. Her foal can come along.'

'Only slow. You don't want her to go off milk.'

'I'm not stupid! But she could be fit soon after the foal's weaned. It's so big it can come off her shortly.'

'It's a good one though. Give it best, match or no match.' Nat paused and then said, 'And you can start breeding again, Clara. A brother for Robert. You breed as good as Linnet. I'm proud of you and my children and we've riches enough here for plenty.'

Clara did not reply to this. Not if she could help it, was her instinctive answer, yet she knew it was inevitable. She was as fertile as the raw-boned bay mare from Chignall's.

'Be careful,' Nat said. 'She's a funny ride.'

'Yes. I know.'

Somewhere along the way, either at Chignall's or before, the mare had been badly ill-treated, for she was still nervous and difficult to handle, especially round the head. Young Peter was good with her, and Billy, the little one-armed protégé of the Garlands, now eleven, who came over to be with Clara, had a way with horses. He had 'magicked' her, to use Peter's phrase. Billy was grooming Cobweb 'to get her nice for Mr Mayes'. Peter had delegated the job.

'I'm going to ride back some of the way with Mr Mayes on Linnet,' Clara told Peter. 'So get her in and clean her up ready.'

She had become used to giving orders. All this work she had once done herself and the men respected her for her knowledge in the stables. Peter was a good groom, although still young, and an older man called Ralph worked with him. Sometimes old Sim from Small Gains came up and cleaned tack, sitting in the harness-room dismantling all the parts that Peter couldn't be bothered with and muttering about youngsters today not knowing their job. He was too old and crock now to do heavy work but paid his way with light tasks. Susannah and Robert loved him and would listen to his stories by the hour. Clara knew that he was even more knowledgeable about horses than either herself or her father and she was glad Peter and Ralph did not resent his presence. Most horse problems were sorted by Sim and he had a great array of amazing cures for nearly every horse ailment that existed, all mixed and pounded meticulously by himself. The horsemaster himself in the work-horse stables often came to Sim. The farm supported eighteen cart-horses, but their yard was separate from the home yard. The home yard held Crocus, Rattler, Linnet and her foal; Linnet's first produce by Rattler, a two-year colt; Nat's driving trotter, a very smart grey gelding called Snowstorm, and the two matched chestnut carriage horses, Punch and Judy. And Prosper's mare Cobweb. Nat did not bother any more with orders in his stables, leaving it to Clara, and the men were much happier under her command. He generally took Crocus out every morning round his fields, supervizing work, and Clara saw little of him till evening. The freedom suited her, and would suit her all the more if Prosper stayed for a while.

It was hard for her to stay calm, waiting for Prosper. She lurked out of the way in the harness-room, wondering if she were mad. Where would it lead her, loving Prosper? But she could not resist her feelings, stronger than the will that tried to tell her it was dangerous. Reason lost to instinct. She felt giddy with anticipation.

Soon she heard his horse's hooves coming up the gravel drive. She went out to greet him. He was riding one of his father's hunters. Peter came up to take the horse as he slipped out of the saddle.

'Good morning, sir.'

Prosper nodded to him. 'It is indeed.'

215

There was a whinny from the stable, shrill and excited. Prosper laughed at Clara. 'That's my mare! She heard my voice.'

Cobweb's nostrils were quivering with delight as they went in to see her. She nuzzled Prosper deliriously as he stroked her neck.

'My sweet girl, you haven't forgotten me. There's devotion, Clara.' He looked at her quizzically.

'Come in for an ale after your ride,' Clara said quickly. 'The boys will get her saddled and I will ride back with you a little way.'

'Fine. How well she looks.' But his eyes were on Clara, bright-cheeked with pleasure.

As they scampered out of the yard towards the house, he said, 'And your devotion too, Clara – how is that?'

'Just like Cobweb's!'

'And mine too. I have never stopped thinking of you.'

'And me – I've tried! Married, with two children – oh Prosper! It doesn't make any difference to how I feel for you.'

'We're in a fine pickle then.' But he was laughing. 'Let's enjoy now. To see you again is heaven. Let's not spoil anything.'

It was as she remembered it. Being with Prosper was just being herself reflected in him, as if they were twins. No explanations were needed, no barriers existed. No other human being had ever had this effect on her. And yet she was aware that she did not know him very well, if time was the criterium. They had had only a week together in the past, and then the visit to say goodbye, and then no more for three years. She was amazed that he felt the same after all this time. She had always put her enduring love down to some want in her life, her dissatisfaction with her marriage. It was like a story she told herself for comfort, a child at bedtime wanting its reassurance, her fairytale prince. She had never dared to think that her fairytale would come true, but now it had.

'How long will you stay?'

'It depends on my mother. She tells me she is not going to get better. I don't know if that is true but my father said she is fading fast, and she certainly looks bad to me. So I shall stay, and decide later. I came home because they all sent word for me. What could I do? But I don't mind, as it made a good excuse for seeing you again. That's all I thought about . . .'

'Truly?'

'Well, my mother too. But that was bad thoughts. Thinking of you being at the end of the journey was the prize, the bonus, the solace. It made everything all right. To see you again.'

'But I'm not free.'

'You're free in how you think. No one else can command you.'

'Not in what I do.'

'No. It's the thinking that matters. I don't think you love Nat?'

'No, I don't. I wouldn't have married him if I'd had the choice.'

'No. I know the story. Everyone knows. You had no choice, if you loved your father.'

'I've loved you all the time. But I never thought you . . . You never wrote to me.'

'I couldn't say what I thought in a letter, so what was the point? I could imagine Nat reading it when the mail was delivered.'

'Yes, he reads all the mail first. We are always waiting for a letter from Ellen but it never comes. And from you . . . only sometimes a message by Gabriel. Oh Prosper, how I have longed to see you again!'

They could not wait to be together, alone, out of the sight of the farm, and when their horses were ready trotted away briskly down the drive. Prosper rode Cobweb, his grey Arab mare, leading the hunter he had come on, and Clara rode Linnet with her foal gambolling excitedly behind.

'The sooner we get into the lane the better,' Clara said, laughing at the foal. 'If the mail comes early, we'll have no chance keeping the foal in order. And Linnet will take fright, I'm sure. She's very spooky.'

She had not ridden the mare since the first year of her marriage, before Linnet became heavy in foal, and had forgotten how uncertain she felt beneath her compared with Rattler, nervous and flighty like a thoroughbred.

'You shouldn't ride her if she's not safe!'

But Prosper was laughing. Being safe was not an item with either of them. Clara loved the challenge of the mare, coaxing the long, fast trot out of her that she needed to practise, while Prosper cantered at her side. He rode so easily, elegantly, as if he were born to it. Clara could not take her eyes off him. He had filled out in the three years he had been away, but was still a slender figure and very graceful in the saddle. Not like Nat who was a good rider but harsh. Prosper compelled obedience by an innate sympathy, Nat through fear.

Linnet threw out a couple of jolting bucks and Clara pulled her back, but she bucked again and took a stronger hold of her bit.

Clara shouted, still laughing, 'Goodbye Prosper! I don't think I can hold her!'

A bolting horse is best circled, Clara knew from experience, and pulled her out into an adjoining hay-field to give herself more room. The mare went into a gallop and put her head down. Clara hadn't the brute strength to compete and her laughing turned to dismay as the bucks came again, big enough to dislodge her in spite of the side-saddle's embrace. She bounced painfully once or twice on the pommel and then went flying through the air to land with a crash amongst the haystalks. Linnet went careering off with her foal in pursuit and Prosper came galloping over to her aid. He flung himself off Cobweb and dropped down beside her.

'Clara! Clara! Are you all right?'

Clara was moaning more with dismay than pain, aware that this was no way to spend time with Prosper. The ride was to have been a happy dalliance down the leafy lanes, not a wild horse display. She turned her groan into a laugh.

'Yes! Not dead!'

Not dead, but something was hurting badly. She wasn't sure what. Prosper put his arms round her and lay close. 'Clara, don't be hurt! I love you! I love you!'

'Oh Prosper!'

It was so lovely to have him beside her, the hurts didn't matter. His mouth came down on hers in a gentle, then fiercer kiss. She responded but as she moved into his embrace pain flooded her shoulder and she cried out. He moved away, his face crumpled with anxiety.

'What is it? Where does it hurt?'

He helped her into a sitting position. She wanted him to go on kissing her but saw that it was hardly the right moment for it, with whatever injury it was she had suffered making her catch her breath and four loose horses wandering over the farmer's hayfield.

'It's my shoulder.'

'Your collar-bone, I daresay.'

He unbuttoned her habit and undid her stock. She couldn't move her left arm and couldn't help herself, but thrilled to feel his warm hand on her bare skin.

'I can feel it. It's broken. What a curse! I'll tie your arm up with your stock and make it firm. I've done this twice – it takes a month to get better.'

'Nat will be furious!'

'He'll blame me. That mare's a pig.'

'It was his present to me when we were married, so we can blame him.'

In spite of the pain, Clara loved sitting in the sweet

warm grass with Prosper binding her together with her stock. His curling hair tickled her face. She kissed him, licking the salty sweat on his lips. They got the giggles, in spite of the disaster. The bound arm felt better and when it was done they sat together, resting.

'Are you all right to ride back, or shall I go for a carriage?'

'Oh, no, I can ride. Not Linnet though.'

'My dear Cobweb will look after you. I'll change the saddles.'

'You've got to catch them first.'

Reins trailing, their horses were grazing happily across the field. Prosper went after them one at a time and brought them back to Clara who sat in the grass holding them with her good arm. There was something so ludicrous about the situation she had to smile. If it had been Nat with her, he would have been furious. But Prosper was so gentle and amused. He did not even upbraid Linnet, but brought her back calmly. He changed the saddles.

Clara got to her feet. She did feel very wobbly and faint but was determined not to show it to Prosper. He lifted her on to Cobweb's back and kissed her again as he did so.

'Just relax and sit there. She will be as good as gold. I will ride Father's hunter and lead Linnet. She seems to have forgotten her fireworks.'

'I was a bit stupid. She hasn't been ridden for ages. It was my own fault.'

'With hindsight, easy to say.'

So they made their way back to Grover's in gentle

procession and, in spite of the accident, Clara would not have changed places with anyone, riding at Prosper's side in the shade of the great elms that edged the lane. He came close and put his arm round her.

'I will look after you. You need me! I can come every day to enquire after your health.'

'Yes, do. I won't be able to ride out. Nat won't see you. He hardly ever comes in during the day, not now haymaking is starting.'

'I can help out in the fields, ingratiate myself. Then he might ask me to stay to supper. I could make myself invaluable, so that I can stay here all the time like Gabriel.'

'Nat hasn't got a jealous nature. He only married me to get sons. He sort of loved me at first, but now he'd rather drink with his friends than stay in with me at night.'

'I drank with the men at night in India and it was very boring. I thought of you when I got bored, sitting on the verandah in the moonlight. I used to think the same moon was shining on you, and what were you doing? But when I heard you'd married Nat, I pre-ferred not to think what you were doing when the moon was shining.'

Clara laughed. Now that Prosper was telling her that nothing had changed between them, he had not forgotten her, her whole world seemed to be spinning, as if the sky had turned upside down. Or perhaps it was the pain that throbbed in her shoulder making her dizzy . . . was it her battered brain that was making her laugh when her whole body craved a soft bed to rest on?

When they got home, she slid out of the saddle into his arms. The grooms came running. Prosper told Peter to go for the doctor and took her into the house, calling for Jane. Clara was bound up and dosed and put to bed, and Prosper took his leave once more.

Clara lay in bed bathed in the afternoon sunshine, dizzy with happiness.

18

Mrs Mayes sank fast during the summer. Clara rode over three times a week to sit with her, and if she missed her time Mrs Mayes asked for her. Anne questioned that she didn't have friends closer to home to comfort her, but she knew Clara had other reasons for being at Great Meadows so often.

'You're playing with fire,' she said to Clara. 'The sooner Prosper goes back to India the better.'

'I would have waited for Prosper if I had not had to marry Nat.'

Anne had no answer to that. She knew she wasn't the only one who could see what was going on between Clara and Prosper for, circumspect though they were, they found it hard to hide their love for each other. When they were together there was an unspoken intimacy, a joy in shared feelings, that needed no words to convey. Anne recognized true love when she saw it and knew that her cautionary words fell on stony ground. Once she had loved in the same way and she could scarcely disapprove, but she was afraid for the children and of Nat finding out.

'Does Nat suspect?'

'He scarcely notices me. Why should he? He's out on the farm all day and drinking at night. We rarely meet.'

'I don't think he was cut out to be a farmer. He likes company and he seeks it, but with the wrong people. He never wants to talk work with Sam or Jack or consult them about anything. It's strange. Jack would be friends but Nat always stands off.'

'He's gambling at night. I think he's quite deep in. He's not happy, I can tell, but he gets angry if I enquire about it.'

'Where will it all lead? You've the children to think of, after all.'

'Thanks to you and Jane, the children are very happy.'

Anne laughed at that. 'Aye, I'm a good grand-mama. I could not bear to be parted from them if ever Nat changes his plans. We none of us are in charge of events, after all.'

'Prosper will go back to India. And then it will be over.'

Clara knew that Prosper's mother had only a few weeks to live. Clara had never discussed the future with Prosper but found the courage to say to Anne what she found hard to admit to herself.

'We never talk about it,' she added. 'Anything could happen.'

But as Mrs Mayes sank weaker and weaker on her pillows, Clara saw her happiness running away like sand through an hour-glass. It was a summer of bliss with Prosper, riding backwards and forwards through the flowery lanes, training the horses, getting Linnet fit for the match the men were proposing after the harvest. When Nat was away in the evening to his gambling den, Clara would get into her breeches and ride Linnet astride down the road to the turnpike, teaching her not to break, to lengthen her stride, to get into a racing rhythm, and Prosper would gallop beside her on his mare, hard put to keep up, and they would laugh all the way. The dust on the road was damped by the evening dew and all the smells of the hedgerows hung in the autumn air, and as the stars started to shine faintly in the darkening sky, Clara felt that she was living in a dream, that this much delight was unreal. To have Prosper beside her on his ghostly mare . . . she wanted the road to go on for ever and the night never end.

Charlotte came to Grovers to enquire after Mrs Mayes.

'She's dying. Every day she's weaker. She'll be gone by harvest time.'

'What a muddle – they need her so! All those men, and never one married. Poor lady.'

'There, Charlotte – your chance! A choice of seven and a beautiful home for the running!'

'Seven? I thought one was occupied with you, Clara?'

'I was counting Mr Mayes in. Yes, one is occupied with me and it seems everyone knows but my husband. Oh Charlotte, the muddle is with us. I dare not think of the future. After his mother dies, Prosper will go back to India.'

'Sometimes what is forbidden is more attractive than what is there for the asking. Perhaps that is how it is with you, Clara.'

'Perhaps. But we can't help how we are. It's impossible.'

'I envy you, loving like that. Even if brings grief.' Charlotte smiled sadly.

'Prosper won't go until the harvest is in, and we're matching Rattler and Linnet soon after so he'll stay for that. We've still time. I try not to think about it. Just think today, tomorrow. No more.'

Mrs Mayes died just as the harvest was starting. Clara and Prosper sat with her at the end, through a long, hot afternoon. From the open windows they could see the reapers starting work with their scythes, advancing in a line over the waving corn as neat as soldiers, leaving the silver stubble at their heels, setting the hares running and the dogs barking.

'An inconvenient time to die,' Prosper's mother whispered.

'No, Ma. Any time is as bad for us. You need your peace now. Shall I fetch Father?'

'Yes. If he won't be angry.'

Prosper went out and Clara sat in the chair by the bedhead. She realized how well-practised she was at seeing out the dead: her mother, Margaret, Nicholas, now Prosper's mother. It had not made it any easier, the practice, nor did she know any more, even being so close, as to how death was.

'Is Prosper gone?'

'Yes, to fetch your husband.'

'Take your happiness with Prosper, Clara. I shouldn't say it – but – I can see – how it is with you. Take it. So rare . . . the chance of happiness . . .'

Clara could scarcely hear her. Mrs Mayes, whose life had been one long devotion to duty, was telling her to damn duty.

'I would love so . . . for you – to be my daughter.'

Those were the last words she spoke to Clara. When Prosper came back with his father, dusty and sweating from the reaping, she slipped away. She walked down to the lovely river where she had first lain with Prosper. They had never made love wholly, not then nor since, even with lying together in the summer fields. They never spoke of it. It was there, to be taken, but they did not take it. Perhaps if they had, their affair would have gone differently, she could not tell. But she regretted nothing. Even if he went away, without, she would still be bound to him. Until he married someone else, then she would be left with her summer of memories and – perhaps – a consuming regret. How could she tell? Theirs had not been a summer of lies and scheming and hiding and deceit and shame, which it would have been if they had consummated their love. It had been on another plane altogether, in a way that she could not have believed possible if someone had told her of it about another couple. The more she thought of it, the more strange it seemed. Impossible. Yet that was how it was.

And then she wept, lying amongst the reeds: for Mrs Mayes dying, for Prosper's grief, for her failure to be happy with Nat, for Ellen, for her future without Prosper. For Prosper. For Prosper.

Sam uttered what no one else dared say. 'Damned inconvenient of her! A whole day off for the funeral just when we can least afford it.'

'And a damper on the horkey. The Mayes owe it to their workers, but it won't be much fun,' Jack said.

'Fine ones you are!' Anne exclaimed. 'That woman worked herself into the grave for that farm and you grudge her one day off!'

'We've had too many funerals round here,' Sam growled.

So they dressed in their hot, black best and Nat drove them in the carriage over to Great Meadows. Jack rode Rattler. The coffin was taken to the village church on one of their wagons pulled by two gleaming Suffolk Punches, their brasses gleaming, their ribbons all black and white. The men of the family walked behind and the farm workers and villagers trailed in from miles around and stood silently round the church when the inside was full. Thinking back to Ebenezer's funeral, Clara saw how different it was for someone much loved, instead of hated.

'The boys will all go off and get married now, you see,' Clara heard one old lady say (which proved true, within the year, for five of them).

Standing beside Nat singing the last hymn, Clara was aware of women's eyes sneaking towards him and knew that he was the most handsome man in the church. Yet she had no feelings for him beyond a sisterly acknowledgement, sharing a breakfast table and a supper table with him most days, usually in silence, reminding him of duties he might forget, appointments, making sure Robert was clean when he decided to notice him. If she was a really boring wife, it was how he had made her. Like her having Prosper, he could easily be keeping another woman and she would not know, or scarcely care. Even with the horses, it was Gabriel and Jack she discussed them with more than Nat. He was not interested in riding in matches any more. It was a terrible truth to acknowledge, but she saw him slipping gradually more and more into the habits of his dreadful father.

In the pew in front of her sat Prosper. She could have touched him if she had put out her hand. His hair was loose, curling over the high collar of his best black jacket, his brown cheeks freshly-shaved, his fingernails clean: spruced for his mother as she would have wished. She had always sighed over his careless dress and appearance. A tear rolled down his cheek and it was all Clara could manage not to lean forward and comfort him by laying her face against his. But he had to put his arm round his father who sobbed uncontrollably. The six eldest brothers carried the coffin out of the church to the open grave outside, and in the blazing August sunshine with the birds singing a chorus all around her, Mrs Mayes was laid in the dark earth and covered over to rot.

'And that's that,' Clara thought, sick as though the earth was covering her.

And in that moment, the worst moment of all, she thought of the woman telling her to take her chance of happiness. Her voice so soft and broken, perhaps she had said something different. Had she not taken her chance of happiness? Perhaps that was what she had said. Now Clara wasn't sure.

Anne put her arm round and said, 'Come away, Clara. She deserves her rest. It was a good enough life, after all. She never wanted for anything.'

Clara wasn't sure. 'She lost her little girls.'

'So did your father, save for you. But he's happy now.'

'That's thanks to you,' Clara said, taking Anne's arm. It was true. Anne was a rock in their fragile family.

There was a spread of food and drink laid out back at the farm, but all the men were anxious to get back into their fields while the weather held so fine. Sam and Nat would not stay but Prosper asked for Clara to stay to help.

'I will bring her back later,' he said to Anne. 'All the way. My mother would have wished her here.'

He smiled his lovely smile at Anne and she could find no words of protest, although the look she gave Clara was plain enough.

'I'll tell Nat.'

'I'll come if he wants me to,' Clara said.

But they all knew he would say nothing. Nat had gone to the stable yard to fetch their carriage; Clara went off with Prosper into the house to play hostess.

'She's part of the family here,' Anne said to Sam. 'I don't know what Nat is thinking of, allowing it.'

'He likes his freedom too,' Sam said.

'The sooner Prosper is off again the better, although it will break her heart.'

'Hearts are often broken in our family. We're used to it.'

'Sam – so bitter! Yours is in one piece now, surely?'

'I cannot forget Ellen. That she has never written! When that coffin went into the earth, I was thinking it could have been Ellen, for all we know. As good as. Her disappearing is worse than having news of her death.'

'Yes, not knowing is worse, I agree. But she never wrote easily – she was too impatient, always on the move.'

'Well, I don't think of her any more. But today, it came back to me. I saw her in that coffin. Don't ask me why. Along with her mother and Margaret, all gone.'

Anne thought that the sooner Sam got back to his harvest fields the better.

'Come on, cheer up. Here's Nat. This funeral wasn't to do with us, after all. We're only here as neighbours.'

Nat pulled up the pair of chestnuts to halt beside them. He was a fine whip and enjoyed driving, better than riding, but Clara was not interested in being driven and did not care to go out with him. She always thought the way he drove Snowstorm to his curricle was highly dangerous, although so far he hadn't turned it over.

'Clara's staying to help with the guests,' Anne said to him. 'Prosper will bring her home later.'

Nat, although he said nothing, scowled ominously and shrugged.

Anne continued, 'There's no women in this family. She's needed. I would stay too if the men didn't need their dinner tonight.' She did her best.

Nat whipped up the horses and they drove home in silence.

It was dusk when Clara left Great Meadows with Prosper. Prosper drove her in his father's gig, pulled by a sturdy cob. She was tired and sad and Prosper too was silent, haunted by his mother's death. In the darkening fields, reapers were putting up their scythes with the fall of the dew and gangs of women who had tied the cut into sheaves trailed wearily away to their scattered cottages. They called goodnight and Prosper answered and one or two who knew what the day had brought to Prosper added a blessing or consolation. The Mayes were much liked in their neighbourhood. Clara could not conceive of the same happening to Nat in a similar situation. Now that Mrs Mayes had died there was no more point in Prosper's staying, but the outlook was too bleak to discuss.

It was dark when the cob pulled up outside the kitchen door at Grovers.

'Is Nat in, or is he away at the gambling tables?'

'See if Crocus is in his box. If he is, Nat's at home.'

Crocus answered them by sticking his head over his door and whinnying to the visitor.

'Will he be angry with you?' Prosper asked.

'No. He'll be snoring. He drinks too much. I wonder Crocus gets him home half the time.'

'I'll see you in if you wish.'

'No. Don't worry.'

But Nat was in his study, drinking alone. When Clara went in, he called out to her.

'Who brought you home?'

'Prosper.'

'I don't know why I bothered to ask. Was he kissing you along the way?'

'What, so soon after laying his mother in her grave? Are you mad? I stayed to help with the guests. Mrs Mayes would have wished it. It was a very sober drive home.'

'I'm pleased to hear it. You don't think I'm truly so stupid not to have noticed what's going on?'

'No. And don't think I'm truly so stupid not to have noticed you gambling and drinking away your inheritance. We've neither of us made much of a go of this marriage.'

Her ascerbic reply stopped his argument. He fetched another glass from the cupboard and poured her a glass of port. She did not want it, but when he pushed it roughly towards her she sat in the chair opposite him and took some sips.

'We don't meet often,' he said. 'Not as often as you meet Prosper.'

'Prosper is going back to India now his mother has died. And I've never been unfaithful to you, whatever you might think.'

'Is that true?'

'Yes.'

'You surprise me. I thought you a whore.'

'Thank you.'

'You are nowhere near the beauty your sister was – and Ellen too, when she was grown – but there's something about you, Clara, a spirit, a fire, that entangles a man. But you resist, you are hard, you ride like a man, you do not pander to a man, you slip through my fingers, I cannot relate to you. You are always aloof and so damned clever. If you were to run this farm, it would make more money. If you were to support me and love me, I would be twice the man.'

This speech silenced Clara completely. A drunken diatribe, yet it touched her deeply, made her ashamed. Her cheeks burned. She drank her glass of port to the bottom.

'I hate this farm. I hate what I do. My gambling debts are awful. My family has cut me off. The only thing I have that I value is my son Robert. My son Robert is my treasure, my one reason for regretting what I have become. I want to be worthy of him.'

'There's Susannah too.'

'I don't know if Susannah is mine.'

'She is yours. There is nothing at all of Martin in her. She has your eyes.' She nearly added 'your temper too', but forebore.

'My children then. I set great store by them. If you are to leave me, you will not have the children.'

'Why are you saying all this? Because you're

drunk? I cannot make you happy, it is out of my hands. Our marriage was a bargain. I have been faithful to you. What more do you ask? I have not spoken of leaving.'

'You will not be happy when Prosper goes.'

'No. But that is the bed I have made. I will lie on it. You must do the same.'

Nat let out an oath, almost a snort of rage, and crashed his glass down on the table so that the stem broke off.

'You sanctimonious prig! Is that all you can say? Have you no heart? If you have I've yet to see it! Your horses know you better than I do!'

'What am I to say?' Clara shouted at him. 'Do you want cuddling like a child? Do you want your mother back? She fell over herself to give you everything you wanted – perhaps you should run back to her and tell her all your troubles! That would please her! I don't know where we go from here, Nat, any more than you do. But we have a good living, a fine home, the children – surely you can rise above your miseries? They are all of your own making.'

'Oh you're right! You're right! You're always right!'

Clara left him and stumbled up to bed, feeling sick and tired to death. But when she lay unsleeping beside the heavily snoring hummock of her husband, she could not get out of her head poor Mrs Mayes' words: 'Take your happiness . . . so rare, the chance of happiness.' They went round and round in her head, yet she could not see a way to it, not without destroying the happiness of so many people around her which, sanctimonious prig that she was, she could not contemplate.

19

The harvest was taken in and the harvest parties, or horkeys, were held on all the farms, with the workers being supplied with as much as they could eat and drink, and dancing and falling into ditches all the rest of the night. This was the country pattern, totally familiar to Clara. She helped at her parents' horkey, and supervised and presided over their own. The atmosphere at the two events was quite different. At her parents' the workers were well-paid and loyal, mostly the more highly-regarded workers in the village, and their partying was joyful and fun. But at Grovers' where the workers were the motley pickings of Ramsey the gang-master, underpaid, overworked and unregarded, the behaviour was crude and greedy and the drinking excessive. Nat sat at the head of the table but did not mix with his men, talking only to Gabriel and his horsemaster and professional horsemen, not with the poor toilers at all. Clara tried to mix with the women she knew, but she felt like a fish out of water. Jane was far more easy with them than she was. It brought home to her how her marriage to Nat had set her up the social scale; older women who had played and laughed with her as a child now bobbed a knee to her and called her ma'am. At least they showed her their friendship, which was not extended to Nat. Nobody made a move to speak with him, save a man who was drunk enough to try and demand a new roof on his cottage, which belonged to the farm. He got short shrift. Clara noted how Nat's attitude was just the same as his father's had been. She followed the man and spoke to him herself, and he was pathetically grateful.

'If you could put a word in with the bailiff . . . the little ones are sleeping in a room where all the rain comes in and they're coughing all the winter.'

But when others saw that Clara was taking an interest, she was prevailed upon again and again, until she was forced to withdraw. She thought, 'This is no way to run a farm.' Good work rarely came from unhappy workers. If Nat was not gambling it all away, the farm made enough money to support its properties and their tenants. It made a lot more than her father's, the acres so extensive.

But a happier application was from those who were demanding a new match between the horses, now the harvest was in. It had been promised.

'Do you know which is the better, ma'am?' an old man asked. 'You ride 'em both, I know.'

'The match will be to find out, that's the point. I've been concentrating on the mare and she's fit and knows the job, but between the two of them . . . I've no more idea than you have. We've never matched them secretly, as I've heard some suggest. I wouldn't lay a bet myself.'

In her heart she thought Rattler would trounce Linnet, but Linnet's nervous disposition made her hard to fathom. Clara loved them both equally. But to show them off successfully would increase their value. She wanted to give her father the filly bred between the two of them, to replace old Tilly. When she was ready to break, Jack could have the training of her. Save – the old truth – the produce of two great horses was rarely as good as either. Rattler's parents were just nags, the sire unknown, a straying gypsy colt.

'I'll make sure we give you a date very soon. While the weather's still good.'

'Aye, it makes for a good break from the rut.'

When the horkey was over, Clara wanted to point out to Nat that he would get better workers if he treated them like human beings, but since the conversation that had taken place after Mrs Mayes' funeral she did not feel capable of speaking to him at all. She had not seen Prosper since the day of the funeral, as he had been drawn in to the harvest at Great Meadows, working all hours. She had no idea when he was departing, or how long it took to arrange a passage. She did not dare ride over now she no longer had the excuse of visiting Mrs Mayes, and time suddenly hung heavily, flooded with the misery of being parted from Prosper. This is what it will be like when he is gone, she thought, what it will be like for ever.

It was a still, cloudless late September morning. She had ridden out (in the opposite direction from Great Meadows) and then turned Linnet out into her field, wandered out into the garden and sat on the seat under the rose-arch. After the vigorous riding her body was now pleased to relax, but her mind as always turned to its aching void, her longing for Prosper. Grief now overwhelmed her and tears started to pour down her cheeks. The force of it took her unawares. It was as if she was unleashing a veritable dam of sorrow, held back all the summer. For now there was no future for her, not only with Prosper, but not anywhere that she could see. She was barely twenty-one, and a failure on all counts, as a wife, as a mother, as a home-maker and comfort to the poor like Anne and Charlotte, a failure at everything she could think of save as a rider and trainer of trotting horses. And how paltry that was in the scheme of things! Her shoulders shook. She put her head in her hands and wept.

'Mama.'

Through the storm in her head she heard the little voice.

'Why are you crying?'

She lifted her head and wiped her eyes, ashamed. Susannah stood in front of her in her pretty muslin dress and white pinafore, staring at her with Nat's dark gypsy eyes full of sympathetic tears.

'Susannah! Oh, Susannah, my darling! Don't!'

She put out her arms and lifted the child up into her lap and buried her dripping nose in the soft curly hair.

'My little one, it's all right. I'm not crying!'

Across the lawn she could see Robert too toddling in her direction, arms outstretched, shouting, 'Mama, Mama!'

At the front door Jane watched, and then turned away inside.

'Robert! Bobby boy! Come to Mama!'

For once in her life Clara realized she was only too grateful for the children's chubby arms round her neck, their bouncing and pushing and sweet baby smell. Did Nat really think she would abandon them? She hugged them ferociously, until Robert wriggled free.

'Do you love Mama?' she asked.

'I love Jane,' said Susannah.

'I love Jane too.'

'And Mama. Love Mama too.'

Robert was holding out a broken-off stem of one of the gardener's prized carnations. 'Mama, flower.'

He was so sweet, the image of Nat, that Clara started crying again to think that he was going to grow up as crass and cruel as his father. So she picked up Robert and hugged him again and swore he would never go the way of his father. Not if she could help it.

'My darling boy! Are you Mama's boy?'

'Yes,' he said.

'He's Papa's boy,' Susannah said. 'Papa says so.'

'Papa's boy,' repeated Robert.

So Clara had to laugh, and Susannah's face lit up. 'Mama not crying any more.'

'You've cheered me up, my little pet. If I have you, I am happy.'

What a lie! Without Prosper she would never be happy. If they had been Prosper's . . . oh, if only! But at least they had stemmed her stupid tears. She had to

242

laugh at their earnest desire to stop her crying. They were so sweet.

'Horses,' said Susannah.

'On the road, darling. Not ours.'

She turned to crane over the hedge and saw two well-bred post-chaise horses trotting along from the direction of the village. To her surprise they were pulled up outside their gate, still for a moment, then they turned and started trotting up the drive.

'Why, we've visitors! Whoever can it be?'

She hastily blew her nose and mopped up her face, somewhat dismayed at being caught unawares. She took the children's hands and walked at Robert's pace up the lawn to the sweep of gravel in front of the house. The chaise was just pulling up. A couple got out and the groom unloaded a large trunk from the back of the chaise.

'Whatever—?'

Clara swung Robert into her arms and hurried forward.

A man turned to greet her. He was in his late twenties, tall and authoritative-looking, dressed in a very fine dark-blue uniform with much gold braid, and snow-white breeches. He looked to Clara like a naval officer of high rank. The tricorn hat he pulled off to greet her revealed a head of shining blond hair.

'Madam.' He made a formal bow. 'I am Philip Grover. Your servant, ma'am.'

Clara gasped. Her gaze turned to the woman he was with. Incredulous, she found no words. The blood drained from her tear-smirched face and she reeled as she stood.

'Why, Clara, I thought you were always the strong one!'

And her sister Ellen caught her as she fainted in her arms.

20

Fat Hams Annie was an ex-convict who had done her time and married another ex-convict, Fat Hams' Johnny, a mild rather dopey man who had been jailed for debt. In his case the appellation of Fat Hams was in the possessive: he was the property of Fat Hams Annie.

Fat Hams Annie was a tyrant, a huge, hulking, swearing bestial woman who stank of sweat and rum, but who worked non-stop. Her slaves (Barney, Millie and myself, Ellen) were expected to work as hard as she did on a quarter of her rations and at a fraction of her weight and strength. Her former slaves had either died or disappeared, we never found out which, although there were two stringy older men who hung in there, building barns, drinking her rum and living in her house. Her husband didn't seem to do anything at all, but we gathered later that he had been freed and given a large portion of land, for which she had married him. Everyone was given land when they were freed, more or less as much as they wanted, but lots of them, like Johnny, had no idea how to work it. Annie went to work for him on assignment and when her time was up, more or less took over. We were on assignment, that is: farmed out to ex-convicts for labour. We still belonged to the government and had certain rights, although what they were we never discovered. I think we could have complained, but Annie was clever enough to leave no weals on us, even when she flogged us. She had a padded stick but the strength of her fat hams made it as lethal as a cat-o'-nine-tails. The bruises looked like a dark storm at night. We often got a crack of her arm across our heads which made our brains rattle, or no supper, which was more a relief than a punishment given what she provided for us to eat. Fried dog, Barney reckoned, or kangaroo guts. It was worse than what we got on the ship, but we made up for it by snitching her figs in the field and apples off her trees.

For the farm we worked on, set on a slight hillock that looked down on the harbour and the settlement, was in fact a paradise compared with our place at home. Annie had not had the opportunity to go farther out over the mountains and raise sheep, which is where the real money was made, but she was astute enough to see there was a trade in supplying vegetables and chicken to the settlement below and a future fortune in owning land so close to the harbour. So her land was a patchwork of vegetable fields and orchards, chicken runs and pigsties. She had no horses so everything on the land had to be done by hand – or hands, ours. At least Barney and I knew how to work on the land, but Millie had scarcely ever seen soil or grass in her life and could not believe what was being required of her. Seeing me milk a cow nearly made her faint. Her home had been the London docks from which she had never wandered until making her one and only amazing journey to the far side of the world. I thought I didn't know much but, compared with Millie, I was a fount of knowledge.

Annie gave us a hut to live in. We weren't allowed in the house. The hut was about ten feet square and had three bunks one above the other, a table and three chairs. That's all. There was a tap outside. There was nowhere to put our things, for we had no things. I put Robbie's gold ring, my only possession, on a string in my drawers, for I didn't want the other two to see it now that I wore no stockings and went barefoot. I had the remains of the clothes I had set out in which I used for a pillow, and Annie gave us working dungarees of coarse blue cloth which kept us decent. At least, with the tap, we could keep clean, even if there was no privacy. Millie and I didn't count Barney. He was too young, although I know he considered he had priority over me. He cared for me and helped me when I was down and brought me any titbit he could find, even once a piece of fudge he stole from a pan in the kitchen window.

Once he said, 'I love you, Ellen.'

I laughed.

Of course, all we dreamed of was escaping to better things, preferably a ship back to England. I know Robbie had told me that boarding one and getting away with it was impossible, but from what I saw the searches weren't all that thorough and I had an idea that a few backhanders went a long way towards succeeding. Of course the people who smoothed the way neither knew nor cared what happened when the fugitive came out of hiding on the high seas. Stories were rife that they got thrown overboard. But that didn't stop poor devils trying. I thought maybe Robbie would come back one day and smuggle me a berth. I was always on the lookout.

Getting a kinder boss might have helped, but no convict had life easy, except the ones who had served their time and got lucky, and some – in the chain gangs – had it worse, with terrible floggings if they didn't work like beasts.

Annie was more like an animal than a woman. When the combined strength of the three of us couldn't move a huge cart of dung or lift some rafters onto a roof, she would come along berating us and taking on the task herself, like some legendary colossus, her great red arms bulging with muscle. In a way, one had to admire her. At least she didn't lie in a chair giving orders; she worked as hard as her slaves. The difference was she fed like a king and drank like a trooper and had a great flocky bed to sink into at night, and time off when it suited her. We had no time off, working from first light till last every day without fail.

In the summer, heat fatigue would overcome us and even Annie's wrath could not get us to our feet when we were near fainting with exhaustion. Her cure was to throw a bucket of water over us and leave us with a kick.

'Useless kids! Not worth my time o' day!'

The heat was terrible to us used to bleak Norfolk winds, but I suppose it was better than being frozen to death, and there were days, especially at dawn or in the cool of the evening, when the beauty and peace of this strange place seemed to enter the heart. They said if you went up on to the new road which the chain gangs were building over the hills to Bathurst, you could see forever over plains of grass. They said it made you feel queer, just to look at such space, the horizon seeming farther away than the eye could see. But for myself I wanted no more space than that between me and the harbour, and the shorter that might become, the better. I loved going down there pulling our vegetables in a cart behind Annie, to sell to the shops and barracks and prisons, and to walk along the quay when she went to buy fish and see the new ships come in. I was forbidden to speak to anyone but took care from the way I walked and used my eyes that the sailors noticed me. At fifteen, sixteen, I knew I was a beauty.

'I love you, Ellen,' Barney would whisper.

'You keep your hands to yourself!'

I would shove him off me angrily. Millie would laugh. And cough. She was so thin that every rib stood out on her bare, breastless chest like the structure of a ship in the building. Annie called her a useless cow, but could see that her hectoring stood no chance, for Millie scarcely had the strength to lift a box of apples.

'I want to go home before I die,' she said to me one night after a bout of coughing.

'Some hope!'

'I know you're scheming to get on a ship some-how. You wouldn't go without us, would you?'

'Three of us! You're joking.'

'Three of us could help each other. I would give you my money.'

Surprisingly, Millie had a stash of money under a loose floorboard in the hut. She used her erstwhile skills as a pickpocket when she went down into town with Annie and had even taken an opportunity or two to lighten Annie's own purse. Even Barney had some wealth in a gold watch he had found on the road. That was also hidden in the floor. In fact, apart from my gold ring, I was the only one without any treasure. Millie was adding to hers all the time, little by little.

The thought of seven years in this situation used to cripple my brain. Seven years would take me to twenty-one, an old maid. My best years, my flowering years, to be spent digging and weeding and shovelling manure, mucking out pigs, drawing the guts out of hens for the table . . . and I used to complain about my life back at home because I had to milk two cows and run a few errands! I know there were many convicts like Annie who had made a go of it and had no desire to return home, but I was not one of those. I hadn't even liked what I had thought of as hard work back home. I used to read about great parties in London and Bath and Brighton where the king feasted all the lords and ladies and they ate and danced all night in their fantastic clothes with servants bowing and scraping before them: that was the life I used to dream about. Now I was as far down the pile as it was possible to go, beaten and fed scraps like a dog. I lay in my bunk and vowed I would leave this place and make good if I died in the attempt.

But the years dragged by and nothing was any different. Barney was fifteen and Annie took him out of our hut and lodged him in the house with the two men, but he was still drawn back to us when he had the chance. He was hopelessly in love with me, but I gave him short shrift.

'When our time's up, Ellen, we could set up together and get married and have children. They would give us what land we liked. We would get rich and employ our own government men. Think of it – our own place and our own house! It would be paradise. I would do anything for you, Ellen, you know I would.'

Poor Barney!

'I'm not wasting myself on you, Barney.'

He was so stupid! Though it was true he was a good worker and knew the land, unlike many of the idiots who did their time and were given land and did not even know how to grow a potato, let along keep a flock of sheep.

'I'm going home when my time's up,' Millie said.

She already had the fare and more besides under the floorboard. How she did it I'm not sure but I know she stole out of the hut at night and presumed she was back at her old profession. I never asked. I slept too heavily. How she even managed to keep alive was beyond me, slat thin and with her hawking cough. But she had spirit. Spirit kept her alive. Until her time ran out and she could go home.

I watched all the ships that came into the harbour. Mostly they were old merchant ships trading from Holland and France and from nearer islands; sometimes British ships with yet more miserable convicts, and occasionally smart British naval ships came in for water. Then the habourside was thronged with British sailors. You could keep the tars – my eyes were for the officers in their gorgeous uniforms and I made sure, if I got a chance to get near the harbour, that they all noticed me. I walked along with my head up and my hair loose and I knew they fancied me, being at sea for so long without any women. But it dawned on me as I grew older, cleverer and more desperate, that the ones most likely to be bribed into getting me aboard were the dishonest, slit-eyed lower orders. Not the scum, but the ones who ordered things, like the bo'sun, the carpenter, or the man in charge of sails. They were on my level – or what had been my level before I became a government slave. But bribed with what? I had no money, and I would not use my body on anyone beneath me.

One day a ship of the line came into port, very smart, with sailors to match. Its captain and officers were invited to dine at Government House with Sir Ralph the governor, and Fat Hams Annie muscled in to sell her produce straight to the cook. She hustled down to get her orders, and on her return we had to set to and kill, pluck and draw enough chickens to feed some seventy diners. Meat kept for no time in the heat, so the same day when they were all laid out clean and ready in the handcart and covered with muslin to keep the flies off, it was my job to haul the cart over to Government House. Annie marched in front as usual, chatting to all and sundry. I felt like a dog. Millie was too weak and Barney too strong for the job: Barney had been set to mending a hole in the barn roof.

'Going looking for lovely officers?' he mocked me as I got ready to set off.

This because I had combed my hair out of its braid and put on a clean shirt.

I didn't answer him. He was getting malicious since I had declined his offer of setting up house together on our release. As if that was what I wanted! Millie adored him but he wouldn't look at her.

'I don't want all her diseases,' he said.

Well, I didn't blame him for that. Poor Millie.

As I heaved the handcart up the driveway to Government House, the governor's carriage came down and we had to scuttle out of the way. Sitting with Sir Ralph were a couple of laughing officers, all done up in their gorgeous uniforms covered with gold braid despite of the heat, and so handsome I stood and gaped. And soon to be sailing home to England. Oh, how my heart turned over with longing! Take me with you! I will take up no room, ask nothing, only a crust a day, and I will do all your chores, your laundry, your polishing, lick your boots . . . tears trickled down my cheeks with longing, all mixed with sweat. Annie gave me a rough shove.

'The dinner's tonight, stupid, not next week.'

We delivered the chickens and she stood talking to the cook.

'Get back home,' she barked at me. 'Don't waste time here. Get on with your jobs.'

I stumbled out into the blaring afternoon sun and, ignoring the cart, hurried back towards the harbour. The great ship swung at anchor in the bay, putting to shame the polyglot merchant ships that lay by the quay. She was leaving the day after tomorrow, they said, back to England via Cape Horn. A crowd of her sailors were getting drunk in the bars along the quayside. I walked slowly, ignoring their whistles, but with my eyes wide open for any likely person. A man I knew who worked in a carpentry shop was throwing out off-cuts for cooking fuel and I took courage to approach him.

'Thrown off the old cow?' He smiled.

'She's still gossiping in Government House. I had to drag a load of chickens up there for the dinner tonight.'

'I saw you.'

I nodded towards the ship. 'I want a berth! If only I had the chance – I would do anything to get on board.'

'Money's the only thing as'll get you on board the *Prometheus*. If you found the right man to bribe.'

'I've no money. And where's the right man?'

He laughed. 'You find the money and I'll find the man.'

'You're joking?'

'No. All I know it's a humane ship. The captain – Grover – he don't put stowaways overboard or strand 'em on an island. They speak kindly of him. There's some ships where stowing aboard is just another way of committing suicide.'

'What did you say the captain was called?'

'Grover.'

I was stunned by hearing this name. Was it possible that this was Philip Grover, whose father I had murdered? The runaway son was said to have joined the Navy. It couldn't be . . . And yet the coincidence seemed extraordinary. Surely this ship was meant for me!

'You wouldn't pay someone for me, and I send you the money back from England? I know my parents would send it, I promise you!'

'Even if I had it, I wouldn't trust you that far, my darling. I'm not daft.'

Oh, but what a chance, I thought, staring at the ship. Might it be Philip Grover's ship? It seemed meant, almost as if he had put in here to Sydney on purpose to pick me up. God meant it. I determined to set eyes on the captain. He would be at the dinner tonight. If I got up and came down to the harbour late I might see the officers leaving Government House. They surely wouldn't leave before the small hours? We often saw the lights and heard the drunken departures and singing from where we lived. I had no prospect of speaking with him, but to see the officers go aboard, see how the land lay, might put an idea into my head.

The following night would be the time to go, if I could think of a plan. The ship was to sail at dawn the day after, on the tide.

My mind was whirling with these thoughts so that I felt almost faint. I staggered home up the hill, hurrying to get there ahead of Annie and save myself a beating. I made it just in time, but she hit me anyway for leaving the cart. My head sang. I went into our hut and vowed, if it killed me, to sail on that ship.

We generally went to bed early, exhausted. Millie did not go out at night much any more, and this time I was relieved that she went to sleep quickly and I was able to slip out by midnight. I hurried down to the quay which was awash with sailors, and sought out my carpenter friend again. I had had a few ideas since seeing him last. He was at the door of his house, drinking, but not too drunk to take in what I wanted to say.

'If I promise you the money, and I come here tomorrow night, will you get me on board?'

'How much money?'

I mentioned the sum that I knew Millie had hidden under the floorboards. 'And a gold watch too, if that's not enough.'

He was surprised. 'That much should persuade someone, yes. It would be unwise, I suppose, to ask how you are coming by it?'

'Yes, it would.'

'If you hang around, I'll see what I can do.'

'I'm going over to Government House to spy on the officers. I want to see them come out. I'll call on you on my way back.'

'Take care, child. There's a lot of men about with too much rum in 'em tonight. You should be tucked up in bed.'

I was perfectly well aware of the danger, but put a sack over my head and shuffled along bent over, with a limp, like an idiot, of which there were several around. I had been in Sydney long enough to know the rules of survival. I took to the tracks behind the harbourside houses where I knew how to evade the guards and soldiers, and made my way through bushes and cow-pasture into the gardens of Government House.

I suppose the dinner parties there were the nearest I was ever going to come to seeing 'high life' in this God-forsaken country. It was amazing how the governor and his officials and their ladies made such a stab at imitating English manners. Their dinner table could have been in a smart house in London itself, with its candelabras and silver dishes of fruit and wine bottles and sparkling glass, and servants (convicts, no doubt) all standing to wait on the guests. Glimpsing all this through the windows, hanging around in the bushes and then watching the departures as the night wore on, kept me in a feverish mood, especially when the naval officers eventually took their leave. If one of them was Grover, I did not know enough about uniforms to tell which was the captain. Leaving for England in just over twenty-four hours! No wonder they were laughing and joking. They were tall and handsome and well-fed, full of spirits, not like the creepy officers in Sydney whose life

257

was spent dehumanizing others and whose faces were mean and cruel. I hated this place! For all its bounty and sunshine, the cloudless sky, the sparkling beauty of the harbour . . . I was tired of scratching its stony soil, herding its stinking animals, being beaten and shouted at, having nobody to care for me . . . I was only seventeen and I might have been seventy for the way I felt and for any future I possessed. The prize that dangled before me in the next twenty-four hours seemed so stupendous, I would do anything to snatch it for myself.

Even steal Millie's money.

'I will bring it with me,' I promised my chippy friend when I returned to the harbour.

'If you have it in your hand tomorrow night, there will be a man here taking new sails back to the ship, and you can go in a sailbag and be dumped on board. It will be very uncomfortable and you might get hurt or discovered, but that's the risk you take. He'll put you in the sail locker and you stay there until the ship is well out at sea. After that, it's out of his hands. That's the deal.'

'Yes, yes! What time shall I come?'

'Say, midnight. Come here.'

'Very well.' I was in such a fever of excitement as I made my way home I did not know how I would get through the following day. Or how I dare steal Millie's money. But she would never need it, so what did it matter? Nothing mattered save making my escape. I was totally possessed by not being thwarted in this escapade: I could not contemplate failure.

I slept heavily almost till dawn, and was wakened rudely by Fat Hams dragging me out of bed onto the floor and kicking me in the backside.

'Can't you hear the cows bellowing to be milked? What's wrong with you? Are you sickening for something? Get to your feet, you lazy . . .' Etc, etc, all very nasty words. The last time, I thought. This is the last time I will have her haranguing me with her foul tongue. The last time the bile of my hatred would rise in my throat to choke me. If my plan to escape did not succeed, I would never come back here. I would run away and take my chance in the bush. But it would succeed – I was utterly determined.

I thought the day would never end. I had to show no excitement, no nervousness. Yet I was sweating with fear and wondering all the time if I would get the chance to take the money. I wanted to get it out from under the floorboards before we went to bed, as I was terrified that Millie would wake and see me if I left it till when I was departing. We had to work together lifting potatoes all day, but my chance came when she decided to use the privy behind our hut. We always took a long time in there, to take a rest; it had become a habit. Fat Hams Annie was haranguing Barney down by the stream well out of the way, so I nipped into the hut, lifted the floorboard and picked up the money which was in a linen bag. It was heavy! I groped around for the gold watch too, snatched it up and ran outside and dropped it over the wall of one of the pigsties, covering it with straw. The pigs were all out just now, none of them farrowing, so it wasn't likely to be disturbed. By the time Millie came out of the privy I was back at the potatoes, and no one had seen me. After that I kept wishing I had put the money farther away, in case Millie stayed awake and watched me depart. I fretted and sweated with nerves till I thought I would go mad and by the time the sun started to go down and we went to collect the gunge that passed for our dinner, I was so tired I could hardly stand. Millie asked me if I felt all right.

I snapped at her and Barney told me to be civil.

'You're getting more like Fat Hams every day.' He was always getting at me, ever since I had told him I wasn't going to throw myself away on him. It was all I could do not to hit him. But so much was at stake, I had to keep my temper.

'I've got a headache,' I said, passing it off.

We had to pluck chickens after dinner. When I finished, I swilled myself off under the tap and said I was going to bed. Millie came too. She had the bottom bunk because she had no spare strength to climb up further. I settled myself and lay listening to her hawking and coughing, as she tried to get comfortable on the awful straw paliasses that we used for mattresses. It was well before midnight, but I was fretting to go. I thought she would never sleep. If she saw me go out, I would say I could not sleep for my headache and wanted to walk in the moonlight. It was not unknown. I often could not sleep even if I was tired to death. My brain was always thinking up plots to escape. But now, tonight, it had a plot to work on, and it was spinning at such a rate I found it almost impossible to lie still and quiet. I tried to make out I was sleeping by breathing long and slow, but my breath trembled and my limbs twitched. I was terrified Millie would suspect something because both she and Barney knew as well as I did that the naval ship, the *Prometheus*, was leaving at dawn for England.

At last, as I lay there, the snuffling and coughing from below petered out and the night was silent save for the eternal distant animal noises from the bush. I gave it ten more minutes, then swung my legs down from my bunk. I gathered up the spare clothes that made my pillow and slipped outside in my night-shift. I waited outside, trembling. But Millie made no sound. I went to the pigsty and scooped under the wall for the linen bag. My fingers closed on it immediately. I lifted it gently and clasped it to me to keep its sweet jingling quiet. I shrugged my clothes on over my night-shift and set out for the harbour. Barefoot, I travelled as silently as a native, the excitement in my throat choking me. The hardest bit was surely over? I trusted my chippy friend to see me right now I had the money.

There was a lot of toing and froing in rowing boats back and forth from the ship as the men made back from their last sally ashore for many weeks. The harbourside was busy, lights flaring from every door-way. I had no trouble finding my friend. He was sitting drinking in his shop with three men to whom he gestured. 'Your friends tonight.'

'We don't want no introductions,' one of them said. 'She don't know us and we don't know 'er.'

'Remember that,' Chippy said to me.

'Yes.'

'Show us the money.'

I tipped the contents of the linen bag out on the table and placed the gold watch beside the pile. The men were obviously surprised.

'Not come by honestly, I'll be bound.'

I didn't answer.

'Aye. But if we're caught, you're on your own, remember. It don't pay for loyalty.'

There was some altercation as to how much to give Chippy 'for the introduction'.

'You're not putting yourself on the line, mate. No flogging for you if you're found out.'

They argued. I did not listen. I could not believe I was safe yet, and would not feel so until the sea rolled beneath me. Perhaps the hardest part was still to come. I could not stop my limbs from trembling with fear.

It seemed the men had some new sails to collect from the sail shop nearby. They would carry them back to their tender, and on the way add me to the collection. A tattered sailbag lay on the floor.

'Get in that and scrunch your knees up to your chin, make a ball like. You'll be dragged and thrown and maybe get hurt. But we'll do our best.'

They wrapped an old tattered sail round me to 'soften your corners' and then lifted me into the sail-bag and pulled the cord round the neck. It was suffocating and I was terrified. I could hear them laughing in a muffled way, and then I was dragged out into the street and left. I knew I mustn't move even a fraction, and the cramps started to bite, but I told myself this was a small price to pay for my freedom. I don't know how long I waited, but it seemed an eternity. I could hear boots tramping past and voices and a dog peed on me, and I suddenly thought they had tricked me: taken my money and that was it. The thought was terrifying. I started to quietly sob, beside myself with fear. But Chippy would not let that happen!

And while I was getting hysterical in my suffocating parcel, there was a sudden jerk and I was swung up in the air onto a man's back. I was so relieved I now had to stop myself from shouting with joy. Oh the bliss of that short ride! Then the swing down and the fairly gentle drop on to the bottom boards of the boat. At last I felt the swell of the sea underneath me. Cramped agonizingly as I was, I was almost delirious with the success of my plan. Surely the worst part was over? I was at sea, on my way to England.

I gathered I was part of quite a large bundle of sailbags. Some seemed to be large and extremely heavy, judging by the grunts and swearing of the men heaving them on to the ship. Our tender knocked softly again the side of the great *Prometheus* as the disgorging went on. Then, suddenly, I was swung wildly upwards and dropped violently onto a hard deck, so hard that I was almost knocked unconscious. I bit my tongue so as not to cry out, for I was now aching in every cramped limb and almost beside myself with pain, not daring to relieve my joints by the slightest movement. How long was this going to last? I was almost weeping with self-pity. My bag was jerked out of the way and another sailbag landed on top of me. I whimpered beneath its all concealing largesse, hidden now, and probably forgotten.

But no. Shortly afterwards I was dragged a long way along the deck and dropped heavily into a hold, then dragged again and, at last, lifted over what I supposed was a bulwark and thrown into a corner. A hand undid the cord round the neck of the bag and a voice rasped, 'You're on your own now, matey. This is the sail locker. How long you stay down here is up to you.'

I could move at last! I wriggled myself upwards so that my head came out of the bag and my cramped knees could straighten out. It was pitch black and I could see nothing. I reached my hands free and felt around, and realized I was lying amongst mountains of flax sails. I straightened my body and then pulled the flax over me so that I was hidden. If the government men came on board to search, at least they would not use their bayonets amongst the sails, and after a while I had wriggled myself down so far that I didn't think I would ever find a way out, let alone be found.

At last I could relax, for I was now out of danger. I suppose I dozed, for the next I remember was the noise of the anchor being got, the windlass somewhere above me grinding inexorably and a thudding of feet as the men pushed it round. Somewhere up ahead of me the great chain links clanked into the locker. Then shouting. Feet running, the noise of sheets flogging, the creaking of blocks. The ship all round me came to life like a great lion stretching from its lair. I felt the sea take it, at first in the harbour still soft and sheltered and then, as I lay rejoicing, the sea off the harbour mouth came long and smooth, lifting and dipping, and I could hear the rustle of water folding back off the bows . . . on our way to England! I lay and wept for joy. I was delirious. There would be no putting back. I was going home!

21

Clara was in the kitchen, ordering lunch for the un-expected guests. Jane was at her side, as shattered as Clara.

Clara said, 'You'd better go across and tell my parents. Tell them to come up. They'll probably pass out, like me.'

'I've shown them to the guestrooms and put out towels and things. A bedroom each, though the way Ellen's behaving it's like they're married.'

'I can't believe it! Has Philip come to take this farm? Poor Nat!'

'He's in the Navy still, why should he?'

'The Navy's decommissioning ships fast now the war's well over. Maybe he wants to settle down. And Ellen – oh my God! What a shock! I can't think straight any more.'

'Sit down, Clara. I'll send young Peter down to your parents and take a stiff drink to your master. He's in the study waiting for Philip to come down.'

'Yes.' Clara felt incapable of ordering anything.

The motherly old cook, Mrs Pymm, said, 'Yes, ma'am, stop worrying. I'll make you a drink of summat that'll bring your brains back, just wait a mo'.'

Clara gave in and sank into a chair, her legs still trembling, and Susannah climbed into her lap.

'Pretty man,' she said, 'With gold tassels.'

'Yes, pretty man.'

The legendary Philip Grover, in the flesh, in his immaculate uniform and tricorn hat, bowing graciously to her in the garden, accompanied by her convict sister Ellen, was – not unnaturally – a shock to the system that Clara could not overcome easily. How it had come about that the two of them should arrive together was totally beyond her powers of imagination. She sipped the steaming brew Mrs Pymm brought her, so strong it almost made her gasp. She had no idea what it was but it did seem to clear her head. She knew Nat had always worried about Philip returning but she had always told him he worried about nothing. So much for her intelligence. Now his worst fears were realized. For God's sake he might take up business in a city somewhere and expect her to follow him! But surely her fears were running ahead . . .

She got up and went out to Nat's study.

But Philip was already there with Nat, out of uniform now, in a loose cravat and tobacco-brown jacket but still with the uniform white breeches and silk stockings. He was powerfully built and as blond as Nat was dark, with the bright blue eyes of his other siblings, and for all his undoubted air of authority he had a kindly air. He jumped to his feet as soon as Clara entered, in the manner of a true gentleman, and this time embraced her kindly.

'I am sorry to have given you such a shock. It wasn't meant. Ellen misled me, I'm afraid. I expected to visit her parents first but she said turn left at the gate when it should have been right. I do apologize.'

'Now I have recovered, I am delighted to meet you, sir. I scarce remember your leaving, I was only small.'

'Fifteen years since. Why should you remember?'

'You won't find much changed here, after all your journeying. It must seem strange to set eyes here again. And Nat—'

'Nat was ten when I last saw him.'

Nat at that moment looked about fifty, as obviously shocked as Clara and knocking back a large glass of brandy. It struck Clara that his brother was a true gentleman, and Nat had become more of a country clod even during the time she had known him. The company he kept was doing him no favours. The contrast between the two of them was marked.

'I never thought to see you again,' Nat said bluntly. 'No word all these years. It wasn't kind to our mother.'

'No. I regret that. I shall make amends.'

'Nat has never seen her since our marriage,' Clara put in, nettled by Nat's tone. 'She did not take kindly to me as a daughter-in-law.'

'Her mistake, I'm sure.' Philip laughed, easing away discord.

'Well, it's common enough. No doubt Ellen has told you all the complications between our two families?'

'Yes. She stowed away on my ship in Sydney harbour. When I found out who she was I could hardly put her in irons as she deserved. She told me her history. I found it quite astonishing, as you can imagine.'

'I hope it was the truth she told you.'

'Embroidered perhaps. I shall find out, no doubt.'

'She killed our father,' Nat said bluntly.

'He near killed me, the reason for my leaving. I would not hold it against her.'

It was to Clara's great relief that at this ascerbic turn in the conversation, Ellen appeared in the doorway. This time Nat got to his feet, his eyes widening in admiration. At seventeen, Ellen had blossomed into the beauty that Nat remembered in her sister Margaret, with the same bright golden hair, pink cheeks and blue eyes. She had the laughing, come-hither demeanour that attracted men, and her childish happiness was like the sun breaking into the gloomy study. Clara was suddenly aware of her own unprepared dress and the dishevellment left from her stupid weeping in the garden. She knew she had never had the looks of her two sisters and until now it had never unduly worried her. But, seeing Nat's face, it struck her angrily, bitterly. She saw at once that Ellen was going to revel in the regard of the two brothers. What was her relationship with Philip, she wondered? Surely he was too steady to fall for the likes of Ellen? From being a stowaway convict, she was certainly now a very well-dressed young woman, presumably due to Philip's generosity.

'I must go and look for our parents. They've been sent for,' Clara said abruptly, and left the room. Her sudden jealous feelings dismayed her. There was something about Ellen's triumphant confidence that disgusted her. But why? Of course Ellen was overjoyed to be home. Why should it be otherwise?

When her parents arrived and set eyes on Ellen, there was shock and amazement all round, with Anne pale and faint like Clara had been and poor old Sam with tears pouring down his cheeks, and Jack – at least – laughing his head off. There was such confusion amongst all the introductions and garbled stories that the lunch was not brought out for another hour. Clara's head was going round like a top. Susannah kept shouting, 'Auntie Ellen! Auntie Ellen!' at the top of her voice and even little Robert was taken gingerly on Philip's white knee and told his uncle sailed a big ship at sea. Robert had never seen the sea but he had a model ship in the horse-trough. 'Sip. Sip,' he nodded gravely.

But Clara noticed that Ellen was far more interested in the two brothers than in the little children, and even her parents were less interesting to her than they. Sam and Anne, after the first excitement, were quietly taking it all in, eyeing their estranged daughter, as well – no doubt – wondering as to what happened next over the ownership of Grover's farm.

After lunch, Nat elected to take Philip round their acres. Anne and Sam went back home and

Ellen promised to follow them down after she had 'settled her things'. Her trunk of luggage was as big as Philip's.

Clara went upstairs with her and sat on the bed while Ellen shook out several dresses, all of them smarter than Clara's best.

'He's been good to you, our Philip,' she remarked.

'Oh yes, a darling. He's such a dream, been at sea all these years and he's scarcely ever set eyes on a woman. He's like a child. I love him dearly.'

'Does he love you?'

'Of course he does. When we settle down here, I'm sure he'll marry me.'

Clara had to steady herself before she dare speak again. She could feel her heart thudding with rage against her rib-cage.

'What do you mean, settle down here?'

'Well, it's his, isn't it? The eldest son. He's retiring from the Navy. Didn't he tell you?'

'What about Nat and all the work he's put into the farm all these years? Does he get the sack?'

'Well, I daresay they'll arrange something between them. Don't be silly, Clara. It's not that difficult. I thought you'd be thrilled to see us, such a surprise. I never thought you'd faint though. Not tough Clara.'

'You must be tough, Ellen, after being a convict all those years. You never wrote, that was the worst. The worst for our parents, that you never sent word. Why didn't you?'

'To get hold of pen and paper? You must be joking!'

She then told Clara all about her life with Fat Hams Annie and Millie and Barney. She had drunk a good deal of wine over the lunch and it all spilled out, even the admission of taking Millie's treasure hoard to pay for her escape.

'You took it, just like that?'

'She was never going to use it, Clara. What did it matter?'

Her callous disregard for the ethics of what she had done shook Clara. This older Ellen had a hard edge that the child had never had. Already Clara was finding her difficult company. And had she come to stay? As she chattered on, mostly about the naval officers on the voyage home, annoying Clara more with every word, Clara decided suddenly that she was still mistress of Grovers.

'I'll get a groom and a cart to take your trunk home,' she said. 'Our parents will be expecting you.'

'But can't I stay here?'

'No, of course not. Your place is with our parents, surely?'

'But—'

'They've been pining for you for three years now. You can't possibly snub them by electing to stay here.'

'I want to stay with Philip.'

'Philip will want to talk with Nat. He's only brought you home out of kindness, I think. After all he's done for you, I don't think you should presume on him any further.'

Ellen was furious at Clara's words.

'You've no idea how it is between us! It's more

than kindness, how he is with me. Why do you think—'

'Ellen, your duty is at home. Philip will be less than a quarter of a mile away. If he wants to be with you he only has to walk for five minutes. Don't be so ridiculous. We will all be together a great deal in the near future, it's quite obvious. And there is no place for you here.'

'There will be, you see,' Ellen hissed.

Clara had to stop herself from slapping Ellen's face. She could not believe that Philip had spoken of taking over the farm and making Ellen its mistress. It must be Ellen's own idea of the future.

Clara left the room and sent for Peter.

'Knock at her door and say you've come for her trunk. Bring it, whether she protests or not.'

Peter grinned. Word had gone round the farm like wildfire, Clara knew, that Philip Grover had turned up out of the blue with Ellen Garland the convict. No doubt the whole village knew by now. Clara could almost sense the smoke rising, the hubbub. Her head ached violently with all the assaults on her brain.

But Peter got the trunk and Ellen departed with it. Then Clara felt sorry for Anne and Sam, so soon to find out just what sort of a person their long-lost daughter had turned out to be. Then she thought perhaps she herself had misjudged her, being so on edge with all the happenings of the day. She did not know what she thought. But when Philip and Nat returned and Jane brought out a tray of tea into the garden, she was comforted by the accord that seemed to be flowing between the two brothers. Nat was now all smiles and Philip was relaxed and smiling too. Philip's company was everything that Ellen wasn't: intelligent, kindly and tranquil.

'Ellen has gone home. She didn't want to, but I made her. It's her place, to be with her parents just now.'

'You told her what to do? That was brave of you.' Philip smiled.

'She's changed a lot in three years. Although that's not surprising.'

'She's a survivor, your Ellen.'

Thank goodness it was 'your Ellen' and not 'mine', Clara thought, and changed the subject.

It did not take Clara long to realize that Philip was the one Grover who made up for all the failings of the rest of the family. His years of command at sea had given him a formidable presence. One would not easily cross him. Yet his authority was of a quiet character, not sharp. He spoke reflectively and let others lead the conversation, but managed to draw them out into more interesting directions. He obviously knew more of world affairs and politics than was ever dreamed of in Gridstone, where the only news was of fluctuations in the price of corn. He had sailed around the world several times, met governors of high office, faced death and disaster, honour and humiliation, yet remained without conceit or bombast – or so it seemed to Clara in her first assessment of the man. After the excitements of the day she felt calmed at last, sitting in the garden with this new relation who was like a rock compared with his volatile, discontented brother. The autumn sun sunk low over the shaved fields and the scent of the late roses in the bower where she had so recently been weeping hung in the still air. Philip's property was showing itself off in the best possible light, and Clara could see that it charmed him. What the outcome of his arrival would be she could not see, but it pleased her to see Nat so transformed, not giving a thought to going out as he usually did to drink and gamble. He seemed fascinated by Philip's experiences at sea – not unnaturally, as none of them had ever had the chance to hear about such things at first hand. But Philip was not anxious to talk about himself. After a while, Clara left to help Jane put the children to bed.

'What a day! Whoever would have thought – guessed – at the way things happen!'

'What a lovely gentleman he is,' Jane said. 'For a Grover – what a miracle!'

'But whatever is going to happen? Ellen says he's leaving the Navy. Does that mean he wants our farm? Whatever shall we do?'

'Don't fret. He's not the kind of man to throw you in the street. I'm sure he'll set the master up in some-thing else and see you right. If he decides to stay, that is.'

'And Ellen – oh, my poor parents! She's a harridan!'

'Clara did well for herself, marrying Nat,' Ellen declared.

'She did not do it out of her own heart. She did it

to get Jack back. You knew all this before you went away. I told you.'

'Well, he's very fine, and the house so grand. It was a good deal.'

Ellen was sitting down to dinner in her old home. The old men, Soldier Bob and Sim eyed her nervously from the end of the table and Jack, opposite, was finding it hard to work out how his naughty little sister had turned into this rather amazing, beautiful woman. She was toying with her plate of mutton stew and potatoes and pushing the meat aside.

'The meals we had on the ship – you wouldn't believe! I ate with the officers every night, out of Philip's kindness, and they had great roast joints and wine and sweets, just like in a great house at home.'

This was not strictly true. She had sat with the officers on occasions but mainly she had eaten alone in her own cramped little cabin. Philip had had great difficulty in protecting her from the attention which she attracted by her ways and her looks. She had been under lock and key most of the time and only allowed on deck escorted by the dourest of midshipmen. But from her telling, the journey home sounded like that provided to rich passengers on a fast packet.

'I bet it wasn't like that on the way out,' Jack said. 'What became of poor old Barney? He was really brave, sticking up for you in court.'

'Oh, he's all right. He wanted me to stay and marry him when our time was up, but I wouldn't.'

'He was a sweet lad at heart,' Anne said.

'Nothing much has changed here.'

'What did you expect? This place never changes. We've extended the house – you can see – so there's a bedroom for Jack. Your bedroom – Clara's bedroom – is empty. I've made it up for you. You will be comfortable there.'

'I thought I might stay at Clara's.'

'But this is your home, surely? They've their own life up there. We don't visit much, hardly at all.'

'We can do with you here too,' Jack said, to needle her. 'There's more cows to milk than there used to be and the pigs to feed. You'll be good at all that after your practice in Australia. From what you said over lunch, farming's your trade now.'

'Yes, and I don't ever want to do it again!'

'Oh come, Jack, she's only just set foot back here. Give her time. She's got to settle down and make her life anew.'

But Anne was already realizing, with sinking heart, that Ellen's longed-for return was not going to be without its difficulties. For all its anguish, her departure to prison had made home life at Small Gains much easier. Anne had never dared admit it. She had also noticed Ellen's proprietorial air over Philip which she found distasteful.

'She'll get back into the way of things,' Sam said. 'We've the match between the two horses next week and there's to be a fair of sorts, so she'll meet all her old friends. Show off your pretty new dresses, Ellen.'

'I suppose Philip set you up when you got ashore?' Anne asked.

'Yes. I only had rags, and he let me spend what I liked in Portsmouth. He's been so kind.'

'He could've thrown you overboard,' Jack said with a certain relish. 'I've heard they do, some of 'em. Although generally near some island of sorts. There, you might be running around in a grass skirt now with a load of cannibals.'

Ellen wasn't amused. 'I'd forgotten how beastly you are, Jack.'

'Yes, and I'd forgotten how discontented you were when—'

'Jack! That's enough! Squabbling like children again and Ellen only just set foot in the door.'

Only Sam, smiling indulgently, was taking Ellen to his silly old heart. Anne groaned inwardly at the prospect before her. Maybe Clara would take her back to Grover's.

But the next day, Clara said she wouldn't.

'I can't bear to see her setting herself up before Philip. He is so sweet, he won't rebuff her. He calls her his kitten, with claws. She seems to think he will marry her, but she's out of her mind.'

'She's very attractive! Even quite intelligent men away from women for so long can fall for a minx like Ellen,' Anne said.

'No. Let's not give her the chance. And she will butt in between Philip and Nat who are truly long-lost brothers. They talk all day. Nat can't have enough of Philip's stories about the sea, and Philip loves riding round the farm and just looking at the countryside. So long from home, he says. He sniffs it all in. Neither of them talk about the future at all, and yet it's clear that Philip is here to stay. If he throws us out, whatever shall we do for money?'

'Your horses, Clara! You will be showing them off on Saturday. Linnet has a colt and a filly already and one in her belly. If they do well you won't starve.'

'Is Jack fit to ride? He's not done a lot of practice. I suppose because it's just in the family he's not taking it too seriously.'

'Oh don't worry. He's very keen. He wants to ride Rattler.'

'Good. Linnet needs more handling, and Gabriel is more used to her ways than Jack. He's very sensitive with her. I don't want her spoilt. She's still young and has lots of matches ahead of her.'

'Well, sensitive is one word that doesn't suit Jack, I'd say,' Anne said.

They laughed. The match was a good antidote to their Ellen worries, and Clara was praying that it would be her opportunity to meet Prosper again. She was desperate to know how soon he would be departing. She was sure he would come, as half the county was coming and everyone from far and wide was agog to set eyes on Philip Grover. Word had it that he was very rich from all the prizes he had taken from French and Spanish ships, but he had never spoken of it (unless to Nat?) and Clara had no idea where the stories came from. He had – in spite of speaking of it – made no move so far to visit the rest of his family, not even his mother. 'After this horse match,' he now said, but it was obviously through duty more than inclination.

Clara had arranged a dinner party for the evening of the match, and invited the squire and his wife (she was bound to come this time, with the lure of the famous sea-captain) and Charlotte, and Lord Fairhall and sweet Edmund. With the gentlemanly Philip to hand and Nat now behaving less like a country clod under his influence, she saw that it was expected of her to make a formal introduction of Philip to the surrounding gentry. She asked her own family too, but Anne and Sam preferred not to come. 'It's not really our place, Clara,' Anne said in her calm, staid way. But Ellen insisted on coming. There was no denying her. She was already trying on which dress she would wear.

'I don't want her there,' Clara said to Anne.

'I'll give her a good talking to first,' Anne promised. 'And, let's face it, she's of interest to the nobs. None of them has ever met a convict yet.'

'No. But she mustn't butt in. After all, Philip and the squire have everything in common, the squire being an old navy man. I don't want her swanking about her doings in front of the gentry. Tell her she's only to speak when spoken to. Or she can entertain Lady Alderbrook. Two termagents together. They will get on.'

'Clara!'

'Do you think I dare ask Prosper? Prosper and his father together? That would be seemly, surely?'

'You'll have a very uneven table, nearly all men. Lady Alderbrook will be shocked. It's not done in society.'

'I can tell her I'm still learning! Women: her

Ladyship, Charlotte, me and Ellen. Men: Philip, Nat, the squire, Lord Fairhall and Edmund. That's already one too many men. With Prosper and his father – and surely Gabriel and Jack must come, after the match – that's five too many men.'

'How lovely!' Anne said, laughing.

'What shall I do?'

'It's only Lady Alderbrook who will tut-tut. Does it matter? I'm not sure about Prosper though, Clara. His father, yes, being so new widowed. He needs a party.'

'But Prosper will have to bring him. Or else Prosper can come as Charlotte's escort. They are good friends, after all, and that makes it proper, if Nat asks.'

'I think you make your own rules!'

'I can always make an excuse by saying I'm not yet well-versed in the ways of the gentry. That will go down well with Lady Alderbrook. The highest gentry of the lot, dear old Lord Fairhall, he won't notice anything amiss, whatever we do. He'll be too busy searching the salad for biological specimens.'

In the end everyone was invited, including the frail vicar, Nicholas' father, and then Clara persuaded her parents to come too.

'And we'll give Lady Alderbrook the guest list and if she doesn't like it, she needn't come. And we'll all be better off. That's settled.'

The invitations were dispatched by the grooms in all directions and Clara found she was more wanted in the kitchen than in the stables. But there were plenty of men to turn out the horses. Rattler and Linnet had never looked better, well-matched in size if not temperament. Clara herself could not predict who would be the winner, Linnet still an unknown quantity. Still she had not set eyes on Prosper, and she longed for the day of the match to see him again.

She went into the stables the evening before to say goodnight to the horses. Nat and Philip were jawing away as usual over the port after dinner. The weather seemed set fair for the match, the night clear and starry and cold, and with luck the sun would shine tomorrow. The course was their usual twenty miles, out from the Queen's Head to the turnpike inn and back, twice. The horses knew it well although they had never been asked to race together. Linnet had a good reputation from three years back with her old master, before she had had two foals for Clara, but she was match-rusty now. Most of the money would go on Rattler. Yet only Clara knew how well-trained Linnet was, for no one saw her riding astride across the cart-tracks and down the lanes early before the sun was up and late after it had gone down. No one knew the hours Clara had put in. Only Sam knew he had bred in Clara a horsewoman after his own heart, as dedicated as he had been in his prime when he had matched his old mare Tilly and beat allcomers. Tilly was thirty now and cosseted in the Garland orchard in her old age. Sam's heart was in the trotting horses and always had been, and so was his daughter's.

'My old sweetie Linnet.' Clara caressed the mare's flitching ears, talking softly to her. She was a nervous, high-strung mare. Her eyes saw spooks everywhere. Rattler was brash and bold and nothing frightened him. If Gabriel kept brave Rattler in Linnet's sight most of the way she would follow, reassured. Then, if Gabriel had the chance, he could pounce and pass Rattler on the post. Clara would instruct him in the morning.

'Plans, plans, Linnet, but how do we know they will work? Little goes according to plan these days.'

Clara laid her cheek on Linnet's neck. The mare's winter coat was just starting, soft and furry. She was a fine bright bay. Rattler was dark, nearly black. Her two darlings. She had to say goodnight to Rattler too, restlessly awaiting her in the next stall. It was like tucking up the children, kissing their sweet noses, just the same. But she preferred looking after horses to looking after children. How lucky she had the loyal Jane. She hoped that Jane would marry Jack eventually. They had an erratic, laughing relationship that could well be a basis for love. But nothing like hers for Prosper. She could not think of anyone she knew who loved as passionately, as hopelessly, as her stupid self.

'I will see him tomorrow, Rattler. My dearest darling Prosper. I love him even better than you, so you know how much that must be.'

Nat had not demurred about Prosper coming to dinner with his father. He had merely said, 'Why not? The more the merrier.' In such a mood, he might well have invited his mother and uncles, Clara thought anxiously, but thank goodness he didn't.

22

It seemed, with a good harvest safely in, the sun shining brightly and the long-lost Grover sea commander on public show, that the Saturday for the match was attended by half the county. It would have pleased people more if the match had been less friendly – they liked a bit of animosity when it came to matching horses. But the Garland woman's word that she did not know herself which horse was the better was taken in good faith. The Garlands had a reputation for fair dealing. And the sight of Linnet looking twice the mare she had when owned by Chignall was impressive. She rolled her eyes, showing white rims; her nostrils were wide with nervousness at the crowds and slivers of froth floated from her lips. Clara led her to the starting post. Jack rode behind her on Rattler, and her father and little Billy were at her side. Gabriel stood waiting to mount.

'Well, we don't mind which one wins. We win whatever,' Sam laughed.

'We don't want either of them thrashed,' Clara said to Jack. 'Remember.' It was a long time since Jack had ridden in a match.

'I'm not that daft,' he said, and grinned at Gabriel.

'Play fair, you two!' someone shouted. 'No cooking up the result as you ride along!'

There was lot of jocularity and taunting. The Queen's Head had already sold a great deal of ale and the green was covered with riders who liked to follow the race on their motley collection of animals, including donkeys and cart-horses. The stewards shooed them all out of the way as the two competitors waited at the post that was both the start and finish. Rattler started to go up on his hind-legs with excitement.

'Let them away!' Clara called to the starter, and he dropped his flag.

Both horses plunged as one, straight into the long trot that Clara had taught them, no canter strides, no disobedience. There was a loud cheer and as the ragged crowd set off in pursuit, Clara relaxed at last. Her job was finished.

Nat had gone off on Crocus, and Philip had met the squire and was in deep conversation. Ellen was telling tales to a group of her erstwhile school-friends, obviously loving her notoriety, Jane had the children up on the green with Anne, playing and chatting. Sam went into the ale-house and Clara at last had time to look for Prosper. He was waiting for her on his mare, Cobweb. He slipped from the saddle and came over to her.

'Oh Clara, I've missed you so!'

'And I you!'

But it was no place to let their feelings show. They walked casually together as if they were talking farming.

'Are you going back to India soon?'

'Yes, very soon. My father wants me to stay but I can't. I can't live here and not have you, Clara. Not any more. Flesh and blood won't stand it.'

His face was anguished. She had never seen him like this before. But she had nothing to say. There were no answers. A friend of Prosper's came up, laughing, and the moment passed. The two men went off together and Clara went blindly to find Anne and the children.

Anne was looking angry. 'Look at that,' she said, nodding her head in Philip's direction.

Clara saw that Ellen had joined the conversation between Philip and the squire and was commanding their attention. Clara was shocked at her presumption.

'She's no manners at all! How dare she?'

'I've done my best to keep her away from your place and Philip, but she talks as if she thinks he's in love with her. Do you think he is?'

'He suffers her, I must say, far more than I feel able to. And look at her – she's so pretty! They don't seem at all put out at the interruption. I'll make sure she doesn't sit near them at dinner tonight! I can't believe Philip would fall for her silly wiles.'

'Well, it does happen. He's obviously a man not used to women and now ready to take an interest. And Ellen's always made sure she gets what she wants, by fair means or foul, I'm afraid – long before she fell from grace with the law.'

But Clara thought there wasn't much she could do about other people's entanglements. Her own were occupying her completely. She went to seek out the old vicar at the rectory gate, remembering how he used to invite them up the church tower to get a good view of the finish. She loved him for being dear Nicholas's father, her own father-in-law, whose name Susannah bore. Nat resented Susannah's name being Bywater, although he must know that he was her true father. The old Rev's rheumy eyes blinked with pleasure at seeing her.

'You are coming to dine with us tonight?' she reminded him. 'I will send transport, so it will be easy for you.'

'Yes, my dear. I'm looking forward to it.' He was shrunken to a sparrow, so frail as if a breath would blow him away. 'Do take your friends up the tower. It's like the old days, this match. How Nicholas used to love it, do you remember?'

'Yes, of course I do. I think he's here in spirit.'

They could both see his grave just inside the churchyard gate with the flowers on it that she and Susannah brought every week. Seeing it, Mrs Mayes's last words came into her mind unbidden: 'Take your happiness with Prosper . . . so rare the chance of happiness.' Why did she suddenly have to remember this? She always had the unreal instinct that Nicholas was still living in Prosper, as if he whispered in Prosper's ear with his jokes and his way of thinking about things, his philosophy and his spirit. They both of them were quite unlike all the other men she knew, the Nats and Jacks of the farming world. It was uncanny, this stubborn intuition that raised its head whenever she remembered Nicholas. She often thought he was speaking to her, laughing at her, from heaven.

'Oh, you are stupid!' she said to herself as she climbed the tower steps.

The two horses came to the turning point with scarcely fifty yards between them, as she had guessed they would. Rattler was in front. But Linnet looked good, not tired at all. They both thought they were finished and had to be urged back out onto the road again, but were quickly away, with great cheers following them. Another thirty-five minutes would see them home. Good horses could do eighteen miles in the hour. Hers were good. If they both came home in ten minutes over the hour they would be feted; if only five minutes over, famous. Their stock would be sought after and fetch big prices. All this was common knowledge to the people on the green, who always flocked to see the good horses, just as if it were Newmarket. Here in the country you could keep your skinny, overheated thoroughbreds; it was the trotters who were admired, as fast at the trot as the thoroughbred at the gallop.

'To own two such, you are a lucky woman,' an old farmer said to Clara as she came back to the green.

So now, as the last minutes ticked past, Clara put everything out of her mind but her horses, and went down to wait at the post to see them in. Would Linnet have the strength left to make her final effort? Clara knew – had proved – that Rattler had the fighting spirit, not to be passed. Just like old Tilly. She still knew nothing about Linnet in that respect. But the boys would be racing now, both intent to win. Some big farms were already promising to take on the winner with a horse of their own.

Distant shouts and cheering heralded the approach of the competing horses. It was just four minutes past the hour by the squire's gold watch. Clara was thrilled.

'That's a good time! They've done brilliantly!'

They came in sight, neck and neck. Everyone started shouting and Clara felt the excitement pulsing in her bloodstream, to find out how they compared. Horses rarely finished so close. Both Gabriel and Jack were crouched, giving it their all, but neither using the whip for the horses too could do no more. Clara saw then that Linnet had the same big heart as Rattler and, although she could already see that Rattler was going to win, she swelled with pride for the mare, so brave and strong even in defeat. Rattler beat her by a length, but it had taken all his courage and he pulled up gratefully, Jack leaning over his neck exhausted, but pulling the horse's ear in gratitude.

'What a match! But that mare's a good 'un, to go so close!'

The crowd enveloped them. Clara fought her way to Linnet's head. She was sweating, unlike Rattler, and very nervous at the crowd, her white-rimmed eyes rolling anxiously.

'Give her some room,' Clara commanded.

Gabriel jumped down and bent to loosen her girth. He was sweating as much as Linnet, exhausted but laughing.

'We may be beat, but no disgrace, eh?'

'No, Rattler had his work cut out! Well done, Gabriel, to go so close. And she's not harmed, I'm sure.'

Once Clara would have had all the work of cooling off the horses, leading them home, seeing to them in the stable, but now the grooms came for them, and all she had to do was praise them for their big hearts and see them off for their stables. And then think about her dinner party.

There was no sign of Prosper, which was all for the best. Clara walked home with Anne and the children, her head whirling once more.

'They were great, Clara, your horses,' Anne said. 'Sam is like a young man again, so excited. He's so proud of you! It makes me so happy to see him like this again, after all his grief. First Jack going, and then Ellen, I thought it would break him. And now—' She laughed. She, like Sam, looked as if several years had dropped off her.

'All your problems are over, you think? You've still got Ellen, remember.' Clara was laughing too.

'Oh, we'll manage her between us. Your good influence, Clara, and mine—'

Anne came home to help her with the dinner party. Never having attempted anything so grand before, and knowing that some of the guests were used to the highest standards, it was a scary business.

'And the seating order – I've made some plans but I'm not sure about it—'

Clara wanted to be next to Prosper, that's all she

knew. Ellen must be stranded away from Philip, but to wish her on the poor Rev . . .

'Oh no, he doesn't deserve that!'

'I think you should put Charlotte by Philip, and Ellen down the table with Edmund and her father.'

'And I will have the Rev on my other side,' Clara said.

'I'll take on Lady Alderbrook, put her by me,' Anne said bravely. 'And Lord Fairhall on her other side. If protocol is anything to go by, he's at the top, so then she can't be offended by lowly me.'

They got the giggles and Clara began to feel better about everything. Soon she would have Prosper at her side, that was all she could think of now. The dinner was going splendidly in the kitchen, with old Mrs Ponder and her niece helping Mrs Pymm, and Nat's valet James dressed in his butler's gear ready to receive the guests, and Jane and him to serve. All was excitement. Clara withdrew to get herself dressed. Jane came up with her to help.

'My hair! My hair!' Clara groaned.

How could she compete with Ellen's cloud of blonde curls and Charlotte's exquisite, professionally-coiffed head, up at the back and sweet curls escaping round her ears? Such artless dishevelment took hours to achieve.

'Oh, I can do that, don't worry,' said Jane, combing out the thick, pinned-up braid that had sufficed for a sporting day.

'You're brilliant! What should I do without you?' Clara breathed. And, out of the blue, the words came unbidden to her lips: 'You should marry Jack and be one of the family!'

'He's only to ask,' Jane said, smiling.

'Is he so slow?'

'Not very, but he's not got that far yet, no.'

'Shall I prompt him?'

'No. Let him take his time. I know where I am with him.'

Clara laughed. If only she knew where she was with anyone . . . 'Lucky you!' They would make a perfect pair.

By the time Jane had finished with her, Clara had to admit that she looked as good as she was ever likely to: not spectacular like Ellen, but the dark red silk dress – although seen out more than a few times – suited her and gave her a rather noble air. No frills, but a stately dress whose colour brought out the hints of auburn in her thick brown hair. Jane was good with hair. With hot tongs she manufactured the obligatory escaping ringlets round the ears in a very becoming fashion.

'Prosper won't recognize me,' Clara whispered.

'He loves you even when you're covered in horse dung,' Jane said stolidly. 'That's truly what matters in love.'

'Oh, Jane, if only—'

'No tears! You'll spoil it all. It will come right, somehow.' She gave Clara a quick hug. 'Maybe he won't go.'

But his words echoed in Clara's ears. She knew he would.

She went downstairs to join Nat in the hall. With James to attend him, he looked as elegant as any of the nobility and was far the most handsome man in the gathering. They greeted their guests somewhat nervously, but with Philip joining them the atmosphere eased and was quickly convivial, everyone familiar with each other and happy after the day's events. Even Lady Alderbrook was all smiles as she took in Philip in his full dress naval uniform. She presented her daughter Charlotte to him and Clara, standing alongside, saw Charlotte's eyes widen with delight as Philip took her hand. Clara glanced up and saw the look on Philip's face, and she suddenly wanted to laugh out loud. In one moment she could see that they were both completely taken with each other. They neither of them made any effort to hide their sudden delight looking into each other's faces. Clara could not understand how she had not foreseen this reaction. It was so obvious: they were made for each other, love at first sight!

The room filled and Clara had to concentrate on her guests. The only people not there yet were Prosper and his father. Clara's eye was on the door all the time, although James had given up receiving people and was now offering a tray of claret. Clara saw the old Rev to a chair and fetched him a drink and then dear Edmund came to talk with him and Clara was free to go to the door once more, looking for Prosper and his father. Perhaps they had had an accident? Her pulse beat heavily in her throat with nervousness. She saw Ellen standing by the naval men, trying to enter into the conversation, but they were not heeding her. She had taken in Charlotte at Philip's side and her reaction sat harshly on her young face. Clara realized that three years of being a convict had done her sister no favours. Perhaps she herself was lacking in compassion to have taken such an active dislike to her. Ellen had survived, and it took guts to do that. She went forward to speak to her. Ellen turned angrily and said, 'Don't sit me next to any of those old codgers, Clara, or I shall go mad. I want to sit next to Philip.'

Clara's sympathy faded abruptly. 'You'll take your place where you're told. You're the youngest and least important person here.'

She needn't have added the last but wasn't upset to see the flare of annoyance in Ellen's face.

At this moment, James, having left the drinks, announced Mr John Mayes and Mr Prosper Mayes. Clara did not know how she could hide her feelings from the rest of the company as she went to greet them. She felt that 'I love you, Prosper!' was written starkly in great letters across her hot forehead. Jane's silly little curls stuck to her damp cheeks.

'I'm sorry we're behind time,' Prosper said, 'Our horse picked up a stone and we had a devil of a job to dislodge it. And now of course he's sore, so we had to come slowly.'

'But all's well,' said Mr Mayes. 'I've really looked forward to this little outing, takes me out of myself. Nothing's the same at home any more.'

'No. It's only been a little while, after all.'

The old man had aged suddenly, Clara saw. His girth had receded since his wife's illness and he was beginning to get bent over with the rheumatics like nearly all old farmers.

'You wouldn't believe, all my boys are off looking for wives since their mother died. All save this one here and he's only eyes for you, my dear, we all know that. Oh, if only you could take my dear wife's place at home with Prosper at your side, how happy we would all be!'

'Father!'

The old man had not wasted any time in putting Clara's desires in a nutshell. No beating about the bush. Clara actually had to laugh at his outspokenness.

Prosper then covered it by saying, 'Perhaps you should look for a new bride yourself, Father. You're not so far gone. But make sure she's a good cook.'

Prosper looked so lovely in his dinner clothes – his soft curling hair tied back over the high cravat, a greeny-gold waistcoat matching his greeny-gold eyes – that Clara had to tear her gaze away to attend to seeing her guests to the table. She noticed Ellen eyeing Prosper and hurried to see her ensconced safely between Jack and Gabriel. Gabriel had more sense than to fall for Ellen. The two naval men, Nat, Lord Fairhall, Lady Alderbrook, Anne and Charlotte were safely at the top end of the table, Charlotte directly opposite Philip so that they could take in each other's attractions to their heart's content, and she was at the other end with Prosper and the Rev, with Prosper's father sitting next to her own so that they could talk farming, neither having any other conversation. Sitting down at last and having the food served by James and Jane, the claret flowing, Clara felt grateful that her social anxieties were allayed for the time being. The company was very convivial and even the dreaded Lady Alderbrook was all smiles. (Clara guessed because she had suddenly seen a great catch for Charlotte, right under her nose.)

'So I hear you are going back to India shortly?' the Rev said to Prosper.

'Yes, my ship sails on Tuesday, from King's Lynn,' Prosper said.

Tuesday! Clara had to stifle her shock. It was Saturday, so that was in three days' time.

'So soon!' she could not help blurting out.

'I told you the reason, why so soon,' Prosper murmured to her.

The Rev mumbled on about his days in India and Prosper made civilized conversation in his entirely agreeable way, while Clara tried to make herself bright and interested instead of giving way to screaming out loud. Tuesday! Her life was going to come apart with a vengeance. Without the joy of meeting Prosper in her timetable, she did not see that there would be any point in living, any point in getting out of bed in the morning. For what? The dark days were closing in and her life seemed to have come to an end. There was no future for her with Nat.

But the rest of the table were laughing and chatting and even Nat himself seemed to have fire in his eyes as if his future was as bright as hers was grim.

Jack and Gabriel were discussing their race across Ellen who was well and truly contained between the two of them. Anne was actually making Lady Alderbrook laugh. Her dinner party, so dreaded, was quite obviously a roaring success.

She had forgotten the stupid ritual of all the women rising and leaving the room at the end, while the men stayed drinking port. It was Prosper who whispered to her that she should initiate the women's departure, when James set the port decanter at Nat's elbow.

'I will see you before you leave?' she hissed.

'Of course, don't worry. We join you presently.'

He moved up the table to join the other men after the ladies left, and Clara's last backwards glance saw him chatting to Jack. But he had taken the Rev under his wing first and seated him tenderly next to Lord Fairhall, his friend. His kind and considerate manners were so different from Nat's! Nat had pushed back his chair and, well away on the drink, was laughing loudly with Philip. Even so, it was good to see him so happy. Philip had made a difference to their household.

'Oh, he's so lovely, your Philip, Clara!' Charlotte whispered as they crossed the hall to the drawing room. 'Why didn't you introduce me sooner?'

'I'm so sorry! But he talks all day with Nat and they ride out together. I've scarcely spoken long with him myself. But certainly you must see more of him. I'll arrange it, don't worry.'

'Even my mother approves, can you believe?'

'You are lucky, Charlotte! Prosper tells me he is leaving on Tuesday.'

'Oh Clara, how awful for you! I thought maybe he would stay – he is his father's favourite, just as he was his mother's.'

'And mine.'

'Yes, and yours.'

They settled themselves around the drawing room. Clara wondered what on earth they were supposed to do, and asked Charlotte in a whisper, and Charlotte said, 'You play the piano to us and sing, and we do our embroidery and gossip.'

She gave a mischievous smile and at the same time Lady Alderbrook said, 'Do you play, Clara – amongst all your other talents?' and nodded towards the piano that Clara had never noticed they possessed.

'Oh, gracious me, no!'

But to her amazement her step mother stood up and said, 'Life's not all horses, Clara,' and whipped off the cloth that covered it. A cloud of dust went up. Charlotte sneezed and then had to cough into her handkerchief to hide her laughter, but Anne opened the lid, and started to play.

'It badly needs tuning, Clara. You must ask Edmund.'

Clara remembered that Anne had played with enthusiasm on the school piano when she had been a teacher, and she filled what might have been an embarrassing silence between the five of them. Charlotte sang a few songs with her in a practised manner while Ellen sat glowering, and then when they had finished she asked Ellen about her experiences in Australia.

'What's it like, this wild continent? Lots of reports come back that it's very beautiful and most people want to stay out there.'

'It's beautiful without the people there. All the people are vile.'

Clara realized they were on dangerous territory, drawing Ellen out on her experiences, but Lady Alderbrook was all ears and Anne was on the alert to change the subject if Ellen started her bragging and lying. But Ellen made little effort to shine in female company. No doubt she had noticed the quick liaison between Philip and Charlotte and was harbouring evil thoughts. She was abrupt with Charlotte, especially when she enquired after Barney.

'Oh, Barney fits in with the types over there. He'll make his way all right.'

'I suppose, unlike you, he has no one here to come back to, poor lad. I hope he does thrive when he's set free.'

Lady Alderbrook then said, 'But are you still not at risk, Ellen, if the authorities find out you are here? I understand that escaped prisoners are sent back to complete their sentences if they are apprehended again.'

'Oh, that won't happen. Philip will get me off, I'm sure.'

Her cocksure voice was unappealing. Clara had not thought of the possibility of her being sent back, but no doubt Lady Alderbrook was right. Her husband was a magistrate; she would know the score.

At this point, to her relief, the men straggled in to

join them. Clara was desperate to see Prosper alone before he left and fortunately he declared that his father was tired and they were ready to leave, having a long journey ahead of them. Clara said she would see them out.

'If your horse is lame, you may borrow one of ours,' Nat said.

'That's kind of you, but I think he'll be fine after his rest.'

They said their farewells, and Clara went out with them. They went through the kitchen by force of habit, where all was now clean and tidy, and Prosper said to his father, 'I just want a word with Clara, Father, before we go. I'll be out in a moment.'

Mr Mayes smiled and went on down the passage to the back door. As soon as it clicked shut, Prosper turned to Clara and they fell into each other's arms. Prosper covered her face and throat with kisses.

'Oh, Prosper, don't go! Don't go! I can't bear it!'

They had never been so wild before in their embraces, because it was the last, the ending. Clara sobbed.

'I can't bear it! Oh Prosper, don't go!'

'Can't you see, I have to! This is why I have to, because it's impossible! Let it be over, it's unbearable!' He thrust her away. His voice was thick and angry. 'If you find a way – somehow – I will be there for you. You can send for me. But now – there is no way we can be together. You can see that!'

'I can leave Nat! He doesn't love me—'

'You can't leave your children. And they are his

300

children, you can't take them away from him. You know it's not possible. Don't think I haven't thought – every way – I've tried. I've got to go, it's the only way.'

Clara clung to him, but he pushed her away from him. Now he too was crying. He almost threw her to the ground and ran. The door crashed to behind him and Clara was left shaking. She sank into a chair at the table and lay her head in her arms and wept convulsively.

'Prosper, oh, Prosper!' she moaned.

'Heavens, what a fuss you make at saying goodbye.'

Clara scarcely heard the voice at first, and then when its sense penetrated, she lifted her head and saw Ellen standing watching her. She tried to stem her hiccupping sobs, dashing the tears away with a tea-cloth that lay on the chair arm.

'I wonder what Nat would make of it? What if I were to tell him?'

Clara found words impossible. She fought to steady herself, beating down the desire to scream and bang her head against the wall. She hated Ellen then with as much passion as she loved Prosper, her emotions rocketing violently.

'So, what if you were to tell him?' she ground out.

'I can hold it over you, Clara, what I saw just then. Arrange for me to live back here, and then I won't tell Nat what I saw.'

Clara let out a bark of a laugh. 'Tell him, stupid child! Tell him what he already knows! Much he will thank you for it.'

Ellen scowled. 'He knows? Gracious, you're all at it here. I saw him kissing Jane yesterday.'

'Oh, did you? You certainly keep your eyes open, don't you?'

Ellen's words gave Clara a jolt, but did not hurt. What on earth did it matter if Nat kissed Jane? Jane had always fancied Nat, who didn't? Only his wife.

God, her head was reeling and she had her guests to see to. She heaved herself to her feet and brushed her damp curls back from her face. She must not stand under the candles whatever she did. She could make excuses by seeing the Rev to their carriage and sending him on his way.

But the squire said they would deliver the Rev home and Clara had to stay talking till gone midnight. Luckily the conversation was so lively that she did not have to take much part. Gradually the party broke up and the carriages were called. Philip escorted Charlotte outside to where her father's pair of beautiful white carriage horses were waiting and Clara heard Charlotte invite him to call for tea the following day.

'I shall be delighted,' Philip's voice purred.

'And bring Clara too, and Nat if he can spare the time.'

'Of course.'

The carriages trotted away down the drive, their lanterns bobbing in the soft autumn night, and Jack laughed and said, 'Call our carriage, Clara, or have we got to walk?'

'We could've come with old Tilly in the wagon,' Sam laughed. 'Aye, but you're in with the toffs now, Clara. They fair enjoyed themselves, didn't they?'

Then he saw Philip smiling and added, 'Begging

your pardon, sir, but this is the first party our young pair have given, in your honour, I daresay. We're not used to dining the gentry, you see. But very pleasant it was.'

The drink had loosened his tongue but Philip took it in good part.

'Clara is an excellent hostess. It was a splendid evening,' he agreed.

Ellen pushed in to make sure he said goodbye to her, and he kissed her hand and said, 'Goodnight, my little kitten. Sleep well.'

The little kitten, Clara noticed, had scarcely sheathed claws, having held up her face to be kissed on the lips. She scowled at the rebuff and Anne hurried her away, covering up with a fulsome farewell.

Clara stood on the doorstep watching them go, trying to calm her wild spirits in the peace of the night. All she wanted was to saddle Rattler and chase after Prosper, and if he had been alone she knew that nothing would have stopped her. She could not believe that that wild clawing in the kitchen was their last goodbye, so brief and cruel. There was no sweet memory there to last the years. But she had known the end was coming, and how could it have been otherwise?

The only comfort was in knowing that his love for her was as passionate as hers for him.

23

The next day it rained. Clara went for a long ride in the opposite direction from Prosper's home and her spirits stayed with the weather, at rock bottom. Even lovely Rattler's gaiety could not lift them. She prepared for the tea party at the Hall without any sense of anticipation, although at any other time she would have been excited by the invitation, never having been inside the Hall before. Lady Alderbrook had turned out much better than she had feared the night before, charmed by Philip and his possibilities as a son-in-law no doubt. But what a good match, Philip and Charlotte, Clara thought, and how strange that she herself had not foreseen it.

Nat wanted to drive the horses himself in spite of the rain, so Clara sat in the carriage with Philip.

Philip said to her, 'Has he spoken to you about his plans?'

'Plans? No.'

She was startled that Nat might have plans. Certainly she could see that he was a changed man since Philip's arrival. He made no move any longer to join his nefarious friends at night; instead there had been much conversation after supper between the two of them, after she had retired to bed.

Philip said, 'I'm surprised. I won't speak of it then.'

'I'm afraid we don't confide in each other much. He hasn't told me whether you are going to take the farm over or not. I know it's yours, after all.'

'Yes, I'm leaving the Navy. But Nat must tell you himself – maybe this afternoon. He was speaking of it to the squire last night.'

Clara was chastened by her ignorance and ashamed by her lack of interest. 'I haven't been a very good wife to him, I'm afraid. He doesn't speak with me much.'

'I know how your marriage came about. It's been hard for you and I admire you for what you've done. You've a fine household and two lovely children. Nat has no room for complaint.'

Clara was scared at Philip's confidence, dreading that Nat wanted to move into business in the town. He had spoken of it often enough. She could not live in a town! Her greatest joy was to ride out and take in the day-by-day change of every hedgerow, every verge, every field of crops and copse of trees all under the great arc of the Norfolk sky where the clouds rolled in cold from the North Sea or warm and soft from the west. How could she live in a town house with only a street to look down on and roofs blocking out the sky, and the only birds to be seen caught in cages hanging on walls, singing their sorrows to the stinking air? She would pine and die like the captured thrush.

Philip wisely changed the conversation. 'Your

friend Charlotte is a very attractive young woman. Tell me, is she spoken for? I find it hard to believe she is still unmarried.'

Clara laughed. 'No, she swears she has never found anyone worth her while up to now, although her mother is always finding her suitors. She's very independent.'

'I admire that. I'm hoping she might look twice at me.'

'Oh yes! I hope so! She's my dearest friend and you would be perfect for her. Everyone loves her.'

'I'm not very good at party manners. Some of my young officers – oh, they can charm the birds off the trees with their sweet talk, I can only stand and be amazed. I've had very little practice in that department, I'm afraid. It's always been the ship for me.'

Clara laughed. 'That will go down well with Charlotte. She hates being shown off at balls and having to make silly conversation. She is very down-to-earth. But her mother appeared to take very kindly to you, I thought, and so did she.'

'You think so? I hope that's true. We'll see.'

Clara found his self-deprecation touching. She thought he was made for Charlotte and could not see that he had anything to worry about. Not nearly as much as she did.

At least the company took her mind off her grief for the time being, for she had to be on her best behaviour, slightly out of her depth with the gentry. Philip's presence had shot them up the social scale. The squire had never entertained the Grover family in the past. The carriage moved smoothly up the long winding drive through the squire's park, whose gates gave on to the village green by the church. Clara spared a glance for dear Nicholas's grave. How he would be laughing now at her anxieties! He too had been in love with Charlotte, and Clara had met Charlotte many times at Nicholas's sick-bed.

The squire's head groom and under groom received them and Nat jumped down from the box as they took the reins. He was laughing, shaking the rain from his driving cape, and looking eager and excited as Clara remembered him when he had been courting her sister Margaret. What a pity she did not love him! He was so handsome and spirited when in the mood. Clara, gazing around at the beautiful acres of the squire's grassland, sighed at the thought of going into tea instead of taking a horse and going for a gallop. Charlotte would agree with her there – unless she was agog to meet Philip again.

And she was. Clara could tell by the trouble she had taken to look her best and by the animation in her face. They made their civilized greetings (Clara having to stop herself from the habit of bobbing a curtsey, which was very hard to get out of) and passed through an elegant hall and into a very fine drawing room with long windows looking out over the park. Tea was brought by well-trained maids whom Clara recognized as village girls – Lady Alderbrook was said to be a hard task-master and Charlotte said none of them stayed long. At least Clara with her lack-a-daisical ways had no trouble keeping staff, but then her china was not so sparkling, her cloths not so starched and her servants so servile. She noted all this with interest, to keep her teeming mind from breaking into altogether more anguished territory.

At least after the tea the men did not dismiss the women to linger over the port decanter, but followed Lady Alderbrook to some comfortable sofas in the long windows and took the cigars the squire offered. There was some talk again of matching horses, of politics (very little), and the weather for ploughing, and then the squire turned to Nat and said, jovially, 'And are you sure of your plans for the future, now that your brother is throwing you off your land?'

'You know I am only too pleased to be thrown off my land. Did I ever say that I liked farming? I hate it and can't wait to go.'

'Go where?' Clara asked faintly.

'You don't know?' said the squire, obviously surprised.

'As long as she's got her horses, she won't mind what I do,' Nat said, softening the truth with a charming smile.

He turned to her and said, 'I've decided to join the Navy. Philip is taking me down to London tomorrow to visit the Admiralty, where he swears he can get me a place on a ship going to the Caribbean. He can pull strings, my big brother. I'm off to see the world!'

Clara thought she would fall off the sofa. The shock was like a physical blow, robbing her of breath and speech. Charlotte jumped to her side and put her arm round her in comfort.

'Really, Nat, how can you spring such a surprise as that in company? You've cooked all this up between you without a word to Clara? Shame on you!'

Philip looked abashed and said, 'Yes Nat, this is a cruel way to go about it. What a shock for her, so sudden!'

'She will not mind,' Nat said tersely. 'To be free of me will not distress her. Will it, Clara?'

'Come now, Nat, we don't want a domestic fracas in public,' said Lady Alderbrook sharply. 'I thought we all knew what you were planning . . . to have left poor Clara out of it is rather thoughtless, to say the least.'

'Yes, I'm sorry if I've embarrassed you. I do apologize, it's not good manners. Perhaps I thought it would be easier to break the news to her when we were not alone, but that was selfish of me. I'm sorry.'

'She won't have to leave home, after all,' Philip said. 'I'm not going to put you on the street, Clara. I wouldn't dream of it. Nothing will change for you. Come, Clara, perhaps Nat was cut out to be a sea-captain right from the start, and he will make you riches that the farm – according to him – will never make. I am content to learn this new trade – change places with him, and your bailiff Gabriel will teach me the ropes.'

'No, Clara, nothing will change for you. Come and take a turn with me, while it sinks in,' Charlotte said.

She held out her hands, and Clara got up from the sofa and went out with her into the hall. Charlotte led the way into a pretty little writing room and sat her down at the desk.

'There. Gather yourself together. I can't believe you didn't know! We all did.'

'It's my fault. We scarcely ever discuss anything. And he's been so closeted with Philip lately – no wonder . . .'

'But if it's what he wants, Clara . . . he will be so much happier. And you will be free. They are away for years when they get a ship. Look at Philip. Think about it, Clara. You will be happier too, I think.'

'I am thinking!'

So hard, she thought her head would split. To be free, rid of Nat, was like turning into a piece of thistledown and blowing down the wind. But the thoughts too spun like thistledown. Nothing made sense.

'I can't take it in.'

'No. It is wicked of him not to have told you until the last minute.'

'I expect he was afraid. I can be a harridan . . .'

It was later in the evening that Nat came to talk to Clara alone.

He said, 'You won't be much distressed, will you, when I go? I don't think I am breaking your heart by leaving.'

'No.'

'You lead your own life so completely, I saw no point in forewarning you. It will make so little change. I would not come back, either, were it not for Robert and Susannah. Whatever you do, Clara, I don't mind, but the boy is all I have, and I trust you utterly to see that he is happy. I know I can trust you on that, or I would not go.'

'Yes, of course. They mean as much to me too.'

'I forbid you to take them to India, should you choose to follow Prosper. I forbid you. And you must never leave them.'

'Nat! I will never leave them, I promise you.'

She was surprised by his vehemence. Now with a purpose in his life he seemed suddenly like a stranger, and a much more likeable person. As if he saw her puzzlement, he tried to explain: 'I realize now I should have left this place and made a new life for myself as soon as my father died, not tried to follow him. He soured me for ever from this land, this house. I have known nothing else all my life and it was Philip who opened my eyes. If only I had had the courage to go earlier, like Philip! But it has taken me so long to get out of the shadow of my father. I should never have married you, Clara.'

No, and she would have been free to marry Prosper. But now it was too late.

'It's not been all bad, Nat. We've the children, after all, and we've been happy enough in our way. I think you are right to make a fresh start.'

'Well, I knew you wouldn't wail and have hysterics when I told you, like most women would. You're tough, Clara. And we've had our loving moments, after all. I shan't forget you.'

So they parted friends, and the next morning, Clara and the children waved them off in the carriage, with Nat's trunk safely stowed. He did not want to come back. Philip said he would have to stay in London until a post as midshipman was found for him, hopefully on a ship sailing at once. Clara could see that he was as excited as a child. She had never seen him so happy. Even his parting from Robert was a laughing romp and from herself a brief, brotherly embrace.

Philip kissed Clara and whispered, 'Put in a good word for me with your friend Charlotte, Clara. I shall be back as soon as I've seen Nat right.'

So Clara stood with the children and Jane and waved the carriage away and realized that her whole life had changed in the last twelve hours, completely without warning.

Jane said, 'Extraordinary! I can't believe it!'

Clara remembered what Ellen had said about seeing Nat kissing Jane and smiled. 'You will miss him more than me perhaps?'

Jane coloured up. 'Yes, I shall miss him.'

But they knew each other too well to prevaricate. Clara wanted to be alone, to think, and Jane took the excited children off for a walk. All Clara could think of now was Prosper: if he had not left home yet, perhaps she could catch him to take a happier farewell, even persuade him not to go. Was it possible? She doubted it but the idea, once taken hold, would not be put away. At least, she thought, a good fast ride to Great Meadows would put her brain to rights, whatever the outcome. And astride too, damn convention. There was no one to tell her what to do.

She ordered Rattler to be saddled and went indoors to change. She bundled her hair up underneath one of Nat's caps and pulled on her old riding-in-the-dark jacket and worn breeches and boots. To feel herself her own master was strange and exciting. It was not only Nat who was embarking on a new life. If only she might be in time to catch Prosper!

She rode Rattler down the drive and was just turning into the road when Ellen came running down the drive from the farm.

'Clara! Clara!'

'What is it?' Clara held Rattler in impatiently.

'Have they gone? Philip and Nat?'

'Yes, they've gone to Portsmouth. What's it to you?'

'What's it to me! Why didn't Philip say goodbye? Why didn't he take me to the squire's yesterday? What have you been saying to him?'

Her face was screwed up with rage. For all her beauty, Clara thought she had never seen a girl so unattractive as Ellen at that moment. Any shred of sympathy she had felt for her dissolved.

'You weren't invited to the squire's, that's why Philip didn't take you! And he's gone to Portsmouth on business with Nat. It's nothing to do with you. Why should he take you?'

'Because he cares for me! And he knows how I love going to town. It's as bad as Sydney this place, for all that's going on! I shall go mad without him!'

Clara laughed. 'Go mad then. For he's no interest

in you, Ellen, get that straight. He's fallen in love with Charlotte. He told me so, and can't wait to get back to her. And when he comes back I forbid you to come up to my house badgering him. He was kind to you because you were in trouble. That's all there was to it. So stop pretending it's a great romance between you because it's nothing of the kind and you are just a stupid little girl making trouble everywhere you go.'

Ellen screamed at her, 'It's not true! I hate you, Clara! You're just as stuck-up as you always were! So righteous! Don't I deserve my happiness now after all I've suffered? What do you know about suffering and hardship? Philip was kind to me, he loved me! How can that have changed?'

'Oh Ellen, come on! How could he do otherwise than treat you kindly considering how it was? It doesn't mean he fell in love with you. See sense, for goodness' sake. You've got everything ahead of you now and a kind and loving home. What more do you want?'

'I shall go mad in this dreary place! It's as bad as Sydney here – even worse! Everyone so stupid and stuck in the mud. I can't stay without Philip! I shall go away on my own, no one will stop me. I shall go to London!'

She burst into great hiccupping tears and Clara, about to ride on, was compelled to rein in Rattler again.

'Ellen, stop it! You mustn't break Father's heart again. If you go to London, go with Father's blessing. He knows people – he will find someone to help you.

But stop behaving like a spoilt child. No one will love you the way you are. Be grateful for what you have, for heaven's sake, for being free!'

Wasting precious minutes haranguing Ellen irked Clara, holding on to Rattler's impatience. But Ellen's desperate figure, clutching her shawl round her in the autumn nip, her tear-wracked face held up in despair, touched her heart in spite of the animosity she felt towards her.

'I will help you when I come back, if you stop being so stupid about Philip and stop making life hell for everyone. Jack and I will sort it out, I promise. But don't hurt Father – *don't*, Ellen!'

She could wait no longer. Her wild promise blew away on the breeze as she let Rattler go. The problem of Ellen must wait for later. Underneath the convict layer of villainy she thought the old Ellen must still be there somewhere. Perhaps it was her optimism alone that made her think that, but one clutched at straws. It was a straw she was clutching at now, to hope that she might catch Prosper before he sailed.

Tearing down the main road, she felt as if fetters had dropped off her. Nat had let her live her own life, yet his presence had always dictated her actions. What did she want in this life after all, that she didn't have? And the answer was Prosper. *Prosper!* She shouted his name out loud, half laughing, half crying. She must catch him before he went, to tell him how much she loved him. She wanted him so badly. She coaxed Rattler into his racing trot. He flung out his forelegs and tossed his head with excitement and she crouched over his back talking rubbish to him, to herself. Her spirits veered so wildly she thought she was going mad.

She covered the twenty miles to Great Meadows in fifteen minutes over the hour, and slowed as she approached the house. All was quiet and no one came to take Rattler, so she slipped off and led him to the kitchen door. It was open.

'Mr Mayes,' she called. 'Are you there?'

A maid came out and said she would fetch him and in a few minutes he appeared, his face lighting up when he saw who it was.

'Has Prosper gone?' She could not wait for niceties.

'Why yes, my dear. He's a long time gone. I drove him out myself to catch the stage to King's Lynn. It arrives in time to catch the ship.'

Clara strove not to scream her dismay. She was too late. Whatever stupidity had made her think she could arrive and nicely kiss him goodbye? She realized now that she had wanted to stop him, to make him stay. But her freedom had come too late.

'I – I wanted to say goodbye. My husband has gone to join the Navy. I—'

She didn't know what to say.

The old man said, 'There, my dear, I'll get the horse put away and you come in and have a drink. I heard them talking about Mister Nat joining the Navy at your dinner but I didn't take it in properly. I thought they were joking. My hearing isn't all it was.'

Clara let Rattler be taken away and went into the

familiar kitchen. It seemed bleak and empty without Mrs Mayes working away at the big table.

'I thought I would be in time to catch him before he went. He said the ship sailed tomorrow.'

'No. I think it's tonight. He needed to be there by ten.'

'Maybe they want them on board early. Perhaps it sails in the morning.'

'It'll be on the outgoing tide, whatever time that is.'

'If I went, do you think I might catch him, to say goodbye properly? He doesn't know about Nat going away.'

'But there's no coach until tomorrow.'

'No, on Rattler. I shall ride.'

'All that way? It's sixty miles or more.'

'That's no trouble to Rattler. He's very fit.'

'But you, my dear, alone? It will be dark before you get there and there's rogues on that road at night. It's not safe alone even for a man.'

'No one can catch me on Rattler, you know that. And do I look like a rich lady? Anyone seeing me will let me pass, I'm sure. I shall frighten them more than they me.'

The old man laughed. 'Well, you've a spirit, I like it. I won't stop you, although one of my boys could go with you if you wish.'

'No. That would slow me down. You haven't a horse to keep up with mine.'

'No, that's true.'

But he insisted that she ate and drank before she

317

went, although now the idea was fixed in her head she was fretting with impatience. Mr Mayes sent to get Rattler back and came to the gate with her.

'I miss you coming here. Be careful now, and pray God you won't be disappointed.'

He gave her a leg up on the horse and she bent and kissed him. Then Rattler was away with a racing start and her heart leaped up with his as he flew up the rise out of the valley. Stupidly, she realized she had not asked the time. But what matter if she didn't know when the boat sailed? She knew the way at least, for after Thetford it was turnpike all the way, and with luck she would be through the forest before dark.

But the winding lanes that led them out on to the Thetford road were tedious and she did get lost twice, having to shout to a labourer on each occasion for directions. These came slowly, the men amazed at her appearance and expecting a man's voice. One of them told her wrong, another twenty minutes lost. By the time she was through Thetford, it was already dark. Several men had gazed after her curiously. Could she no longer pass for a boy? After bearing two children she supposed it was unlikely. And perhaps it was the horse they were admiring, for not many came as proud and fast as Rattler, who did not let the traffic impede his imperious progress. He was as quick and agile dodging carts and people as a cat. His hooves spun sparks from the cobbles. Pray to God he doesn't lose a shoe, Clara thought, for he was due for the farrier. She could not have prepared for this. The events of the last two days had come upon her like a hurricane, blowing all before it, scattering reason. She didn't know what she was asking of Prosper, whether she would see him or not. Just to say goodbye, to have his arms around her again? Or to stop him going? She only knew she wanted to set eyes on him again, even if it was for the last time. And if the ship was gone when she reached the quay, she thought she would die of a broken heart. But did people die of broken hearts? Don't be so stupid, she said out loud. But she was beyond making sense of her impulsive action. She *was* stupid.

At least the road was dry and sandy, not deep mud which it had might have been, and Rattler could make a good speed. She judged the pace for him to last out, for it would be near on ninety miles for him in a day, what with her losing the way and coming out of her way for Great Meadows. He had a steady cruising speed, below racing speed, which she asked him for now the way was plain. No more stopping and starting and dodging traffic. Just steady, saving him.

The road was empty save for the odd farmer making for home and a few late travellers in private gigs without lanterns, and mostly drunk. It started to rain and the forest closed in, the dark pines heaving uneasily above her in a wind she could not feel. She did not like the feeling of being hemmed in, used to her own wide wide skies, and Rattler too seemed to be seeing ghosts, spooking every now and then at things she could not see. The rogues, it seemed, were staying at home for she had no frights. Only, as the miles rolled by and the rain came down steadily, she began to lose her early enthusiasm. All this and the ship was bound to have departed, she began to think. The saddle was wet beneath her and her clothes could not keep out the rain. It trickled down inside her collar and seeped through her hat to make a soggy, uncomfortable mat of her hair. She was getting tired and began to sit down to the stride instead of posting, but in a while this became more tiring so she changed back. Perhaps it gave Rattler a little variety; she guessed he was beginning to wonder where his next meal was waiting.

At a crossroads she did not know which road to take, for no signs said King's Lynn, only Swaffham and Downham Market. There was nobody to ask, only the eternal dogs barking. A few windows were lit but she was disinclined to knock and disturb people, looking as she did (even worse, no doubt, now she was wet through). She pulled up, chewing her lip anxiously, and Rattler put his head down and shook himself like a big dog coming out of a river. He ran with water, and steamed gently all round her.

'Poor boy, we're not there yet. But which way?'

She turned down the Swaffham road and saw a man coming out of a stable carrying a lantern.

'Is this the road for King's Lynn?'

He gaped at her and mumbled something indecipherable.

'King's Lynn?' she bawled impatiently.

'Aye, aye.' He backed away and disappeared down an alleyway.

'Thanks for nothing,' Clara muttered.

The stars showed momentarily, coming and going between the rain-showers, and a lucky glimpse of the Plough showed her the north, which was the way the road went. King's Lynn was north. So she set off again at the trot, but she was disheartened now and beginning to feel tired. Being soaked through did not help. But she would die for Prosper, that much she knew, and if she failed to catch him, at least she would have the satisfaction of knowing that she had tried.

The road to Swaffham was good and plain and she was unlikely to get lost again, although she guessed there were short cuts through the lanes, did she but know them. The rain still came down but after a while she came out of the forest and a full moon behind the clouds gave a fair light. There was nothing along the road save a poor unlighted cottage here and there. She felt she was in a foreign land now, so far from home, and was relieved after ten miles or so to see the outskirts of Swaffham. It was as dead as the unpeopled road she had just ridden with scarcely a light showing, and as she rode into the big market square Rattler's hooves echoed off the blank-faced buildings.

'Now where?' she wondered. Only lanes and alleys led out of the square. Surely there must be a big turn-pike road to King's Lynn somewhere, even if she was out of her way?

She came to it. A sign at a crossroads, the left turn marked 'King's Lynn, 15 miles.'

Thank God, she was on the right road and nearly there. Her leap of faith communicated itself to Rattler and he set off again, his trot as jaunty as ever. What a horse, she thought! He was as brilliant as Tilly had been and – whatever happened in her life ahead – she knew she had a pearl of great price in her beloved horse.

'I love you, Rattler!' she shouted into the night, more to keep her spirits up than for any good reason. 'I love Rattler! I love Prosper!' And she pressed him on.

The last miles rolled past and the unfamiliar smell of the sea came on the water-laden breeze. She had no idea of the time. She was tired to death, all her limbs aching, her body soaked with sweat and rain. But at last the outskirts of a big town reached out into the sodden fields. A few signs of life: a horse pulling a laden cart, a boy skipping along with a jug of ale in his hand.

She shouted to the carter: 'Where's the quay?'

He waved his hand to her left and she pressed on, feverish now. What if she missed the ship by minutes? She would die!

The sea smell came hard, and down an opening she saw a mast against the sky. Lights shone down there, and the sound of wagon wheels over the cobbles . . . Rattler tossed his mane, spraying water, and turned to her heel. Fast down the road, sparks flying . . . there was the quay. Fishing boats bobbed on the tide, large and small, tethered to bollards and a larger brig lay down-stream, deep with coal. Clara hurried Rattler along towards where she could see higher masts and yards against the dark sky. Thank goodness there was just enough light to make these things out. The boats lay on a quay along a wide river and lights flared to illuminate what looked like the imminent departure of the largest ship, a three-masted packet. It swarmed with sailors and passengers and the gangway was still down, while a dockhand stood ready at bollards fore and aft waiting to cast off.

Clara skidded Rattler to a halt by the aft bollard and slithered off, almost falling in a heap. She clung to the saddle as her legs threatened to give way.

'What ship is this? Where is she bound?'

'It's the *Andromeda*, bound for Antwerp, and then Bombay.'

'Is there time—? I have a message for someone on board! Is it possible – oh, I must find him before it goes! Can you—' She could not speak for an excruciating stitch in her side.

The man regarded her gasping, extraordinary appearance with some concern.

'I'd say it's a bit late, dearie. But maybe we can send a boy up the gangplank before it's taken in.'

'Oh please! For Prosper Mayes. Just shout for Prosper Mayes.'

The obliging dockhand called to a little boy who was watching the proceedings.

'You hear that, lad? Run up the gangplank quick sharp and call for Prosper Mayes. There's a lass here with a message for him. You can do it if you're quick.'

The boy looked frightened. 'I might get stuck on board!'

'Don't be stupid. Run up, quick sharp, and deliver the message. They'll hold it for you. What's the message then, miss?'

The boy waited. Clara wailed, 'I love him! I'm here! Tell him I'm here. I want him!'

The man burst out laughing. Clara burst out crying. The boy looked from one to the other.

'You heard, mate,' the man said to him. 'Run quick sharp.' He was still laughing.

The boy sped off like a rabbit. The gangplank was just about to be hauled up but the boy shouted, 'Wait a minute!' He jumped on it and ran to the top and bawled at the top of his treble voice. 'Prosper Mayes! Prosper Mayes! She wants you!'

A member of the crew came along to apprehend him, but the boy gabbled away at him and turned and pointed to Clara down on the quay.

'Come down, lad,' the sailors on the plank shouted, 'or you'll be at sea in a minute.'

The crew member gave him a shove and he half-ran, half-tumbled down the plank.

'Are we waiting?' shouted the sailor at the bottom.

'No, no! Haul away!'

But he turned and shouted down a companion-way, and then up to the passengers on the deck watching the departure. 'Prosper Mayes! Are you here? Prosper Mayes, a message from a lady.'

Another voice of command from the poop: 'Cast off aft! Cast off, for'ard!'

And against the dark sky the white sails were loosened from their lashings and blossomed like clouds against the rain. Clara held up her face, the tears running down her cheeks, hot against the cold rain. The man beside her said, 'Sorry, lady,' and cast the great rope hawser from the bollard. It fell into the water with a splash and a sailor on board started to pull it in.

'Oh, Prosper!' Clara wept.

But out of the light in a companionway, a figure suddenly made an appearance and ran to the rail. It was Prosper. Clara dropped Rattler's reins and ran blindly to where the water was widening between the ship and the quayside. She looked up into Prosper's mesmerized face.

'Nat has left me! He's gone! Oh, Prosper, come back, please come back!'

She did not know what she was saying, standing there like a madwoman with her arms waving. Whatever was she asking, now that the loosened sails were billowing out with a fair wind in them? The ship was moving away fast.

The figure at the rail looked down, laughed – laughed! – and in one quick movement swung his legs over the rail. He kicked off his shoes, flung off his coat and, standing on the bulwarks he jumped out into the water. With a great splash he went under, disappeared, and shortly surfaced opposite the quay where Clara was standing.

'Clara!' He was still laughing. 'He's *left* you?'

'Yes, he's joined the Navy. Gone away!'

'How did you get here? I don't believe it!'

'On Rattler. I rode.' As if holding a conversation with a man drifting in a fast-flowing tide was all in a day's work, Clara hurried to keep alongside him.

'Please, Prosper, don't drown!'

He struck out then with a strong stroke right below her and came to the wall where she stood. There was no grip on the wall and when she got down and held out her hands, she could not grasp his. But suddenly her dockside friend appeared at her side and leaned down beside her. Prosper could reach him, and with a beefy heave the man landed Prosper in a heap on the quayside.

'Are you sure this was what you wanted?' he asked curiously.

'Yes,' said Prosper.

He got to his feet and turned to Clara and held out his arms and embraced her ecstatically. They squelched together, salty seawater in the kisses that Prosper devoured her with, rain on her lips, hot tears in their eyes. The ship, *Andromeda*, making all sail, was already disappearing into the darkness.

The dockhand turned away and went to catch Rattler who was grazing on some tussocks of grass he had discovered.

'That's some funny owner you've got there, mate,' the man said, and stood waiting, the reins in his hands, until the horse might be decently returned to its rider.

the
end